QUEEN
OF THE
WEST

QUEEN OF THE WEST

JR ZINK

Copyright © 2022 JR Zink
All rights reserved.
Cover design by PixelStudio
Cover Photo: Winder, J. W. , Copyright Claimant. View of Cincinnati, Ohio. Photograph. Retrieved from the Library of Congress, https://www.loc.gov/item/2007662637/
ISBN (paperback): 979-8-9863053-0-1
ISBN (ebook): 979-8-9863053-1-8

CHAPTER 1

March 1855

Annie stood studying the large paddlewheel churning the Ohio River, propelling her toward her new life. She had escaped from her mother and siblings in their stateroom to the lower deck of the steamship Buckeye State. She watched the engineer as he shoveled coal into the boilers and efficiently responded to the bell that clanged incessantly, directing him to slow or speed the paddlewheels. The sweat-drenched man shouted across to the engineer working the opposite paddlewheel's mechanics. The sounds of the steam engine's hissing and paddlewheel's splashing filled the cramped, dim space.

The boat's whistle blared, and Annie jumped back. The crewman had told her that they blew the whistle to alert passengers of hazards in the river and a possible impact. She saw no signs of a crash but noticed a handsome young man looking at her. He stood almost six feet, with blonde hair, sharp facial features and a dimpled chin.

"What are you looking at?" Annie said.

"I'm sorry. I was watching you," Max said, smiling and speaking loudly over the noise. "You're interested in how it works?"

"Yes, it's fascinating machinery. I'd like to understand how the steam moves the paddlewheels, but I can't see much from here."

Max moved closer to her and pointed. "The coal heats the water in the boilers and creates the steam. The steam pushes a piston inside that metal housing, which moves the arm connected to the paddlewheel's crank."

She turned from where he pointed, toward him. "Is that cotton sticking out of your ears?" she asked.

"What? Oh, yes, it's to dampen the noise. It's so loud. It never stops." He removed the wads of cotton from his ears.

"You're a delicate one, then? Do you have a parasol for the sun, too?" A grin spread across her face.

His cheeks reddened. "No, it's just, I've spent so much time on these steamships up and down the Ohio and beyond. I like to read, and it's hard to concentrate with all the noise," he held up a book.

"I'm teasing you, but you look like an invalid with it sticking out of your ears," she said.

"Enough about my appearance. You should talk."

"What do you mean?"

She stood about five and a half feet, a smattering of freckles across her cheeks and soft curls of red hair pulled back in a bun.

"Your attire," he said.

"What about the way I'm dressed? Are you insulting me?"

His face flushed red again. "No, I'm sorry, I've never seen anything quite like your trousers on a lady. Let's move up here so we can talk without shouting," he said, guiding her to the front of the deck, away from the boat's machinery.

"They're bloomers," she said.

"You resemble a jester in them."

"Well, it seems you are intent on insulting me," she said.

"Now I'm teasing you. Please don't take offense." He smiled.

"They're very comfortable and practical for riding on boats in the wilderness with all the stairs and planks and the rough landings. You try wearing a corset and long dress traveling to the western frontier."

"You're going to the frontier? What is your destination?" he asked.

"Cincinnati."

He laughed. "That's hardly the frontier."

"Look around you, man," she said, raising her voice and pointing to the shoreline. "All I've seen since we passed Wheeling are trees and fields of grass."

"I can't argue with that; however, the frontier is well beyond Cincinnati. It's a city with plenty of civilized comforts. It's called the Queen City of the West."

"Yes, I've heard it called that, but I grew up in New York City. I've heard vast unsettled lands, and even Indians still surround Cincinnati."

"I've never met any Indians. You'd have to go farther west to worry about savages."

"Annie!" A young man called as he descended the staircase from the upper deck.

Annie groaned and turned away from him.

"Is he bothering you?" asked Max.

"No, he's my brother."

"Annie, Mother says you shouldn't be down here; it's no place for a lady. She wants you to come back to the room." Her brother bounded down the stairs and over to Annie. "Who is this?" he said, looking at Max.

"Just a clever young man that I'm passing the time with. I'm perfectly safe. Mother need not worry."

"Annie, come on," her brother said as he pulled on her arm.

"I'm Max Mueller," said Max reaching out to shake her brother's hand.

"I'm Anthony; pleased to meet you." He shook Max's hand.

Annie said, "Good afternoon, Max Mueller. I hope to see you again before our journey ends." As she walked to the steps, she stopped, shook Max's hand, and smiled at him. "Good day, sir."

He smiled at her. "Good day, Miss Annie. I enjoyed meeting the most interesting lady with the most interesting attire on the Buckeye State."

As they walked up the stairs, Anthony whispered to Annie, "Why were you talking to him? I don't think Mother would approve. He was eyeing you improperly."

"He was not. We were just passing the time. Don't mention Mr. Mueller to Mother. It will only upset her," said Annie.

#

After dinner, Annie returned to the lower deck, feeling claustrophobic as she walked along the tall stacks of cargo under the low ceiling. With the sun setting, the deck was darker and the shadows longer. She passed crates, barrels, bales and baskets. Her piano was down here somewhere. Men dressed in ragged clothes, some with dirty faces and hands, looked up from their groups on the floor as she walked by. One cluster of men and women sat in a circle, laughing and talking loudly. She walked purposefully, watching them out of the corner of her eye. She relaxed when she reached the open-air portion of the deck and found Max sitting on a bench facing the bow. He sat in front of a large crate away from the other deck passengers and boat noise. "Good evening," she said in a quiet voice.

He sat up straight. "Good evening, Miss Annie. This deck is no place for a lady in the evening. Let me accompany you upstairs."

"Thank you, but I'd like to sit in the quiet, too, if it's all the same to you. Unless you're planning to do me harm, I think I'm quite safe."

"All right. Weren't you afraid coming down here by yourself?"

"There are plenty of people on this boat and little privacy. It's similar to parts of New York City that I walk. I'm not easily scared."

"Bad things happen on the lower decks of these riverboats. There are scoundrels all around us. I advise you to stay on the upper deck, but since you're here, would you like to join me on this bench?"

"Thank you, that would be nice. You look much more inviting without the cotton sticking out of your ears," she said.

"And you look much more inviting without the bloomers."

She laughed. "Mother insisted I adhere to decorum for dinner, but this dress is a hazard on this boat. I'm not sure who I was dressing for; we've met an eclectic collection of frontiersmen, immigrants, farmers and merchants."

"It's very becoming on you."

"You made no mention of my attractiveness when I dressed in bloomers earlier today. Why, just because I have a dress on, do you suddenly feel at liberty to comment on my appearance?"

"I didn't mean to offend you. Please forgive me."

She saw a sincerity in his blue eyes that disarmed her. He had an inviting face and a sturdy frame. She had never courted a man but enjoyed bantering and flirting with the men she met at salons and lectures in New York. "What are you doing out here, all alone in the front of the boat?"

"Trying to find some quiet. I'm staying down here with the deckers where there are too many people. My employer doesn't pay for me to sleep in a stateroom, nor do I require it, but I need some quiet time each day to reflect and pray for my sanity."

"You sleep down here?" Annie asked.

"Yes."

"Where?" She scanned the crowded deck.

"I have a blanket. I find space. The cotton balls come in handy at night, too. Sleeping amongst a few dozen men can be noisy."

"Do you wake up refreshed?"

"Refreshed enough."

"Where do you eat?" she said.

"There's a stove for use by the passengers. I cook beans that I brought. I have pork and bread. Sometimes I share with another fellow."

"It doesn't sound very appetizing."

"I'm not eating for the pleasure, but rather nourishment for my body. It's only a three-day journey. What did they serve in the grand saloon for dinner?"

"It was chicken, beefsteaks, pork, potatoes, some vegetables and pastries for dessert," she said. "The staff does their best to make it fine dining, but it was nothing like New York restaurants."

"Well, a lady like you is accustomed to a certain standard of living. I'm sure the captain's staff does their best. I hear the new steamboats built in Cincinnati are even finer than this one—like floating hotels. You'll see them under construction in the boatyard just before we reach the landing in Cincinnati," he said. "Why are you traveling there?"

"I'm moving there. I don't want to, but I have no choice."

They sat quietly, the sound of the boilers and the paddlewheel's splash in the background. It was a warm spring evening, and the breeze from the slow-moving steamboat was refreshing. The sun was setting, and the hills surrounding the river seemed endless. The large trees cast shadows on the grasses along the riverbank.

The boat's whistle blew, and they heard shouting as the vessel slowed. The paddlewheels stopped, and the relative quiet was a relief. They moved around to the port side in time to see a rowboat lowered from the steamship onto the river. Two crewmen, a man and a woman holding a child, sat in the rowboat. Deck hands dropped several bundles and a trunk into it. One of the crewmen rowed them to the Kentucky shore. They saw a farmer walking from a log cabin toward the river. The crewmen helped the man, woman and child step on land, greeting the farmer. The woman stood clutching her child, watching as the men removed their possessions from the boat and placed them on the grass. The men returned to the boat and rowed back to the steamship.

"Why are they abandoning them here? What did they do?" asked Annie.

"They didn't *do* anything," said Max. "I met Mr. Johnson and his wife yesterday. They're from Philadelphia. They're answering an advertisement for land in eastern Kentucky."

"That poor woman," said Annie. "Where will she sleep tonight? How will they survive on their own?"

"They'll make their way. I think they'll find hospitality from their new neighbors. The family in that cabin will likely put them up for the night and direct them on their way. They were very optimistic about their future. He saved his money in Philadelphia for two years to buy land and establish a home here."

The whistle sounded again, the paddlewheels started, and the riverboat resumed its voyage. They stood and watched the couple and child grow smaller in the distance.

"Shall we return to our bench?" said Annie. They walked back to the bow and sat.

"Assure me Cincinnati is nothing like that place where that family got off the boat," said Annie.

"No, it's a city, full of people. You're worried about your move?" said Max. "Why are you moving there?"

"My mother has married a man from Cincinnati, and we're all going to live with him. I wished to stay and live in New York by myself, but my mother wouldn't entertain it. I'm eighteen, old enough to start my own life, but there are too many branches across the path for a woman. I'm leaving the only home I know and the city I love to go to a wild, uncultured place. And I'm leaving my circle of friends for no one."

"I've never been to New York. What's it like?" said Max.

"It's alive. Performance halls and all kinds of shops and factories. Numerous parks and so many people. Always a lecture or a theater performance to see. It varies from neighborhood to neighborhood. The shops of Broadway are most often talked about, but I loved to spend time near the Bowery. It offers a fine selection without the snobbery. New York has its problems; vagrants, the destitute, and the drunkards, but I wouldn't trade it for any city on earth.

"We lived in a three-story house on Fifth Avenue until Daddy died. He was a banker on Wall Street. The money ran out, and Mother, my sister, three brothers, and I moved into an apartment. Then Mother and Mr. Neltner married, and now we're moving to Cincinnati where he has his law practice."

"I'm sorry about your father. That must have been difficult. How did he die?" Max said.

"He died of cholera during the epidemic six years ago. I miss Daddy so much. He was like me, loved music and adventure. Mother became even more somber after he died."

"I'm sorry. My youngest sister Agnes died of cholera as well."

"I'm sorry to hear that. Listen to me, talking about myself. I'm all right. Tell me about you. What do you do besides ride up and down rivers on steamboats?"

"I am in the employment of Mr. Jonathan Niles and his brother James. I manage the accounting and business dealings for Niles & Company, an ironworks enterprise. I sell to customers, purchase materials from vendors and supervise the installation of iron fixtures. This week, I was in Pittsburgh buying some steel for a special project and am bringing it back to our shop. Someday I hope to be made a partner in the business and build my fortune."

"So, you live there, in Cincinnati. How long have you been there?" she said.

"All my life."

"Do you have a family there?"

"Yes. I was born in the German neighborhood north of the canal. My mother and father, three brothers and three sisters still live there. I rent a room with a family downtown."

"How do you find living in Cincinnati?"

"It's all I know. There are plenty of opportunities if you are willing to work and apply yourself. I am not hesitant to work to better my position. The city grows every year. It is now the country's fifth-largest city and is the launching place for people and goods heading west. Factories and markets with furniture, building materials, news, sundries and food continue to spring up like flowers in the spring. The landing is crowded with boats daily, loaded with the items to build lives in the west. Meanwhile, the city expands to accommodate the increasing population and commerce."

"You make it sound like an exciting place. Maybe I'll find something there for me?"

"Indeed. For any man willing to apply his brain and work hard, there is opportunity."

"That is the problem everywhere," she raised her voice and stood up.

"What is the problem?" he said.

"Any man. I'm not a man. For men, there is all this opportunity. I have the intelligence and ambition, but my sex limits me."

"Whoa, Nellie. Calm yourself."

"Why should I calm myself? The world is unjust. Am I to just accept it?"

"I hear your plight, but it does little good to work yourself into a frenzy."

"You don't understand. You have unfettered opportunity."

"I wouldn't go that far," he said. "I have great opportunities with my education, but we all must live within our circumstances. I was born into a family of meager means. Many treat me as a foreigner in my own country because my parents came from Germany. There are doors that the well-to-do keep shut from even the most ambitious."

Annie said, "I feel the same. I am an American but not given the same opportunities as a man. I have limited education and occupation options, and I am dependent on a man for my life. That is a form of enslavement."

"You are equating a woman's life to that of a slave? You, who has the means to sleep in a stateroom and eat in fine restaurants. You have plenty. I think there is a difference. Slavery is immoral."

"Yes, there is a difference in degree and overtness. Would you say women's place below men is moral? Men passed the laws of this nation, and I am subject to them with no way to alter them. I have limited property rights. If I marry, I relinquish my property to a husband, become his property, and vow to obey him. I am treated as a subjugate person."

They both sat silently for a while. The sun had set, the only light cast by the near-full moon and the thousands of stars in the sky. Max looked at Annie and saw tears on her cheeks. She wiped them away.

"I never considered what the world looks like from a woman's perspective. I've never met a woman who had such dreams for herself."

"Oh, you have, Max. They just don't share them with you because their confidence to express their dreams has been taken from them since they were little girls. I will not suppress my dreams and accept a life limited by the circumstances of my birth."

"In that way, you and I are alike; our refusal to accept a place set by others," said Max. "Why do you feel so strongly?"

"I've felt this way as long as I can remember. I never liked anyone telling me what to do. I'm sure I was a handful for my parents. My mother would constantly punish me and curtail my activities. 'Young ladies don't do that' and 'Don't be unreasonable' were two of her most common reprimands.

"When I was five or six, I had a playmate, a boy named Ansel. We were both the oldest in the family, and our mothers had us together all the time. I remember running in the park, racing him, playing games and chasing the ducks near the pond. At some point, my mother started restricting me from doing the things Ansel did. It was my first memory of being told boys were allowed to do one set of things, but girls were expected to behave differently. One day, she insisted I sit on a bench quietly with a doll and watch Ansel. It didn't make any sense to me, and I resisted her limits. I remember more than once being dragged from the park in a tantrum by my mother. I fought her all the way home, and only my father's rational, soft voice could calm me."

"You were a passionate child," said Max, smiling reassuringly.

"I was always inquisitive and prone to activity rather than docility. As I grew older, I encountered similar arguments about things even more important to me. Then, I was told what to wear, read, study, and even how to sit or laugh. My mother telling me that I couldn't pursue things that made me happy made no more sense to me than telling me I couldn't play with Ansel anymore because I was a girl. Her enforcement of society's expectations of women stamped the joy of life right out of me."

"It sounds as if you have been frustrated from a young age. Was your childhood only unhappiness?" said Max.

"My father was my only solace. He acknowledged the limits I encountered but encouraged me to push against them, to a point. He understood my frustration and accepted that I was a unique individual and not a bad girl because I didn't want to conform. He told me I could do great things with my passion, as great as a man, but I had to learn patience. I don't think I figured that out before he died.

"I've spoken in an unrestrained manner. I'm sorry. I trust I have not offended you," Annie said.

"No offense taken. I've never met a woman who speaks so openly against the ways of the world, but your reality is yours. Mine is mine," he said. "You are an extraordinary woman."

"And you are an unusual man—one with a receptive ear. I have enjoyed our conversation. I hope that your opportunities bring you good fortune." She stood up.

"Let me escort you to your deck. That won't subjugate you too much, will it?"

She laughed. "No, given the lack of light and the scoundrels who haunt the lower deck, it would be prudent."

Max held out his arm, but she refused it. He acknowledged her refusal with a smile. When they reached the stairs, he stopped. "It has been a pleasure, Miss Annie. I wish you success in your new life in Cincinnati."

"Thank you, Max. Goodbye," she said and turned and walked up the stairs. He watched her until she was out of sight.

CHAPTER 2

Annie stood with her mother, Sarah, sister Caroline and brothers Caleb, Anthony, and John outside their staterooms as the steamship approached Cincinnati. There were dozens of keelboats, steamboats and ferries moored or docked along the waterfront. Several others floated mid-river. Annie looked toward the city of buildings with church steeples rising above the rooftops. Smokestacks spewed black smoke that hung over the buildings. Houses dotted the green hills that rose above the city on three sides. The boat floated toward a wide public landing that sloped steeply from the river up to the town. People, horses and carriages moved about the landing.

They watched as the steamboat slowly moved into position between two other boats. Her brothers pointed. Sarah searched the landing for her husband, Stephen Neltner. As the paddlewheels stopped moving, men on the shore lowered large wooden ramps onto the craft. Another man tied down ropes to hold the boat in place. Annie steadied herself against the railing as the ship rocked. The family moved behind a line of others toward the ramp.

"Boys, assist your sisters," Sarah called.

Caleb, sixteen, took his mother's arm as they stepped onto the bank. John, thirteen, took his sister Caroline's arm as she struggled with her parasol and tried to lift her skirt above the muddy bank. Fourteen-year-old Anthony tried to take Annie's arm, but she pulled it away.

"I'm quite capable," she snipped.

He quickly stepped aside, letting her pass. At her mother's insistence, Annie was dressed in a long dress with petticoats and boots, which promptly became mud-covered as she sunk into the ground. They slowly filed up the steep bank from the public landing, looking for their new stepfather. Several large mud-covered pigs ran across their path, forcing them to wait until they passed.

"Look, Mother, the queens of the city have come to greet us," Annie mocked.

"Oh. What are they doing here?" shrieked Caroline. "They smell terrible."

"Enough, girls," said Sarah.

"Mrs. Neltner!" a young boy shouted Annie's mother's name. He ran toward them, waving his hat.

"Yes, good morning," said Sarah.

"Good morning, ma'am. I'm Tom. We sent for Mr. Neltner soon as we saw the steamboat coming. He should be here shortly. Right this way, we have a hired carriage. He's bringing his carriage for the rest of you. Tom pointed toward the shop-lined street, twenty yards away, where dozens of horse-drawn carriages awaited. Tom pushed aside people, including a dirty beggar, a boy selling newspapers, a man offering carriage rides. "Stand aside, out of the way, be gone," he confidently demanded as he led the group to a waiting carriage.

"Good morning, ma'am," said the driver as he opened the door for her.

"Annie, Caroline and John, you come with me. Anthony and Caleb, you wait and ride with Mr. Neltner in his carriage," said Sarah.

"What about our things? I want to ensure the piano is safely retrieved," said Annie.

"You have no business hanging about the waterfront and supervising the labor of hired men," her mother said in a frustrated tone to Annie.

"But my piano," Annie protested, thinking of her tenth birthday gift from her father.

"It will be in the hands of capable men," said her mother. "Tom—you'll see to it, won't you?" she said to the boy.

"Yes, ma'am. Mr. Neltner arranged horses and carts for all of your things," said Tom as he closed the carriage door.

The driver pulled away. Annie mumbled, "He's just a boy but has more liberties than I."

Sarah shook her head. "Our journey is almost complete. Just a little longer now."

The carriage moved along Water Street to the west and headed north along the city's edge on Western Row Road. They passed blocks of brick houses interspersed with shops, stables, coal yards and other businesses.

Annie looked out the window, tears streaming down her cheeks. She wiped them on her sleeve.

"Annie, no more tears," her mother said. "You've done enough crying. Leave New York behind. This is our home, now."

"My life is ruined. Why of all men in the world did you choose to take up with this one? All the men in New York City?" said Annie.

"Because Stephen is the man who asked me to marry him. It's not like I had a choice. Few would want to marry a widow with children. We are all fortunate that he is such a loving and charitable man."

"But why did you feel a need to marry again at all? We could have stayed in New York."

"We didn't have the means to stay in New York. A woman on her own with five children. We would have been destitute. That's no life for my children or me."

Annie said, "We could have found a way if you had wanted to. Women in New York have more opportunities than in a place like this. Why did you elect to subjugate yourself to a man when it came with the penalty of uprooting your life, our lives?" Annie raised her voice, and her younger brother scooted away from her.

"I didn't have a choice," said her mother.

"You did," said Annie.

"Not really. This is the way the world is. You may not like it, but you need to accept it."

"I won't accept it."

"Annie. Why do you make things so difficult for yourself? Your father indulged you, listening to your dreams. He has given you a sense of false hope that you can be something you can't. He's gone now, and the rest of the world doesn't care what you think you should be able to do. I'm sorry, Annie, but settle yourself. This is your new life. Be more like your sister. She's a year younger but has accepted the world as it is and will be much happier for it."

Her sister Caroline looked out the window, avoiding eye contact with her mother and sister.

Annie closed her eyes and took deep breaths, trying to calm herself. She remembered her father teaching her the technique when she suffered from tantrums as a child. She knew arguing further with her mother would do no good. Another battle lost.

After twelve blocks, the driver turned left onto Clark, a quiet cobblestone street of upscale residences. About halfway down the block, he stopped in front of a large red brick, three-story house. It sat back from the street with stone steps leading up to a covered doorway. A simply-dressed woman opened the door and came down the steps to meet them. The driver hopped down and opened the carriage door. As they emerged, the woman greeted them. "Welcome, Mrs. Neltner; I am Helen," said the woman with a German accent, bowing her head slightly.

"Hi Helen," said Sarah. "These are my daughters Annie and Caroline and my son, John."

"You all must be tired after your long journey. Please come inside. I will show you your new home."

Helen led them up the stairs and into an empty foyer. The newly completed house smelled of fresh lumber and paint.

"Let's take off our muddy boots," said Sarah. "No need to soil the new carpets." They moved into the parlor. Sarah looked around the room, which was sparsely furnished.

"Mr. Neltner waited to buy any new furnishings for the house. He moved some of his things from his old house but wanted you to choose the furniture and decorating," said Helen.

"Yes, I see," said Sarah. "I bought some things in New York and had them put on the steamboat with us. I'm anxious to see what Cincinnati furniture makers have to offer."

"Can I see my room?" asked Annie.

"Yes, let's see our rooms," said John.

"This way." Helen led them back to the foyer and up the staircase. On the second floor, she showed them the bedrooms, the parents' in front, the girls' in the rear and a third where Helen would stay. There was a large room on the third floor with angled ceilings in the back that the three boys would share. There were beds and a few pieces of furniture in each, but no draperies and little else.

"Girls, we'll have plenty to keep us busy this summer, furnishing and decorating the house," said Sarah.

"I can't wait to select the wallpaper and fabrics for our room," said Caroline.

They heard voices in the foyer. Sarah went to the top of the stairs. "Stephen, is that you?" she called down.

"Yes," Stephen called, and they heard his footsteps, followed by the boys moving up the stairs.

Stephen and Sarah embraced and held each other.

"Darling, I'm so happy to have you here, with me, finally. How was your journey?" said Stephen.

"It was an adventure. But we're here, now."

Stephen moved to Caroline and hugged her. "Caroline."

"Father," said Caroline.

He moved to Annie and took her hand.

"What did you think of the steamboat Annie?"

"Fascinating machinery. Too loud for comfort. It needs a way to contain the noise. Full of interesting characters, though. We met all kinds."

"Did you now? I'd like to hear more about that later," said Stephen. "John, did you enjoy the journey?"

"Yes, sir, but I'm glad to be off that boat. Nothing to do but watch the trees go by and read." John turned to his brothers. "Come on; I'll show you our room." They ran up the attic stairs.

"No running in the house," Sarah called after them.

"Mrs. Neltner, I'll put out some food in the dining room. You must be hungry."

"Yes, we are, thank you, Helen."

In the dining room, they sat at the large wooden table, covered with a white tablecloth. They shared more of the stories of their journey from New York to Pittsburgh by train and the steamboat to Cincinnati. Stephen explained the house's construction status, indicating that there were still painting and trim pieces to finish. The iron fence, stair railings and gate still needed to be installed in front. He had arranged appointments at some carpet, furniture and drapery stores for Sarah and the girls. Stephen had also planned visits to friends' homes over the next few weeks to introduce them. As they talked, the hired men brought in their trunks and belongings.

The boys went outside to explore the neighborhood. The furniture arrived on two horse-drawn carts. Four men lifted the crates and barrels from the drays onto the street in front of the house. They unpacked the crates and carried the pieces into the house at her mother's direction.

When they set the piano down in the parlor, Annie sat on the piano bench and slowly played a song that was her father's favorite. As she played, she thought about how her father made her feel secure when she would come home crying and frustrated because someone had told her she was bad-tempered or un-ladylike. Sitting and playing the piano for him helped her lose her agitation and feel more optimistic. She longed for him today.

Annie finished and closed the cover of the keyboard. She ran her finger along its smooth, wood surface. "Oh, no!" Annie said.

"What is it?" asked her mother.

"The piano leg is broken."

"Oh, dear. It's not surprising, given all the shuffling that the instrument endured over the last week. We'll get it repaired. Not to worry, I'm sure the piano tuner will know just the man to repair it, good as new," said her mother.

Annie sighed. "I'm tired. I think I'll go to my room, unpack and go to bed."

"Yes, dear, why don't you. Things always look brighter in the morning."

Her mother found Stephen in his library, reading some papers. She entered and closed the door. They kissed and embraced for several minutes, talking.

"I'm so sorry you had to make that journey without me," said Stephen. "Are you all right?"

"Yes, just very tired. The boys took care of me. We are all a little anxious about leaving New York. It's a shock, especially for Annie. She's usually up for an adventure, but she resists this one. She craves spontaneity and new experiences. More than the others, she had started to form her place within New York with her friends. She is mourning the loss of them. She has been having a bout of melancholy. She's prone to it. I'm not sure how long it will last this time or what it might take to relieve her of it."

"I've arranged for you and the girls to have lunch at the Pendleton's next week. George Pendleton is an attorney and a state senator. His wife, Alice, has invited several prominent ladies to tea. Maybe a social outing will help," said Stephen. "I know you have much unpacking and settling to do this week, but Annie should get outside to breathe some fresh air. It would do her some good."

"You dote on her too much. Paying attention to her feeds her belief that the world will change if she pouts enough. Her father fed her hunger for attention, resulting in her believing she could do more than girls can do. As you and I have discussed, this move is her chance for a fresh start."

"She is a free spirit, yes, but has such a creative and exploring mind," said Stephen. "Have you told her about the teaching position? They are looking forward to filling the job."

"I will talk to her about it tomorrow."

CHAPTER 3

On Sunday afternoon, Max walked from his rented room at the Carson's house on Fourth Street to his parents' house. He walked north through the city past the shops, most of them closed in observance of the Sabbath. He approached Canal Street, which ran along the Miami and Erie Canal. He crossed over the bridge and entered the neighborhood north of the canal, known as Over-the-Rhine. It was named such due to the concentration of Germans who emigrated from the Rhine River valley region in Germany. There were no canal boats loaded with goods on Sunday, but a group of boys with sticks and rocks played about the foul-smelling water.

As he stepped over the bridge into the German immigrant neighborhood, the mood changed. Families were on the streets, milling about, talking and laughing and spilling out of the dozens of saloons and coffee houses. He greeted many of them by name and nodded at others, frequently conversing in German. The men looked different north of the canal; more had beards and mustaches, and they wore soft caps instead of the stiff ones that most native-born Anglo-Americans wore.

He walked into the Eichen Garten saloon. The room was 25 feet wide by 100 feet deep, lit only by the windows in front and the series of whale oil lamps along both walls. A wooden bar ran half the room's length with a mirror behind it. Several tables filled the remainder of the room. Men stood at the bar elbow to elbow, smoking long pipes and drinking from steins of lager beer. A middle-aged woman was drawing beers from a wooden keg behind the bar. She glanced up and nodded at Max as he walked the length of the bar and then around behind it. He walked up to her, and she leaned toward him so he could give her a peck on the cheek.

"Mother." They spoke in German.

"My boy. We missed you at mass this morning."

"Mother, let's not start today."

"I am happy for you, becoming a successful American businessman, but you can't forget where you come from."

"I attended mass at Saint Xavier downtown this morning. I am here now to spend the afternoon with my family and friends and relive stories and songs of the Motherland. How could I ever forget?"

She nodded her head and pointed to the beers on the bar. "Take these to the Weber's table."

"Where's Papa?" he asked.

"At his usual table. He's already relaxed with drink."

Max picked up the beers and walked through the back door into a shaded courtyard filled with families. The Webers lived just around the corner from the saloon. Like most in the bar, they came every Sunday after church and spent the afternoon socializing with their neighbors. Max knew almost everyone by name, and they greeted him as he moved through the crowd. He set the beers down, and they toasted him.

"Max, you wear such fine clothes. Are you running the shop yet?" asked Olga, one of the Weber daughters who was about his age.

"No, I'm still learning the business."

"I hear Niles is making locomotives now. Are you working on those big beasts?" asked Mr. Weber.

"Not me. We have a separate group of men who work on the heavy machinery. I work on the ironworks projects—decorative fixtures and items."

"You're doing well for yourself, then?" said Mr. Weber. "Your father must be proud."

Max glanced at his father sitting on a bench, surrounded by a group of men.

Olga said, "Max was always a clever one. No surprise that you're a man of commerce now."

"Olga, How are you? How do you fill your days?" asked Max.

"My sister and I are making cigars. We do piecework at home. Can I bring you one next week?"

"No, thank you. I've never acquired a taste for them," said Max. "You all enjoy your day." He moved on to the next family and worked his way around the courtyard, talking with each group. His sisters Marie and Helene brought out plates of food and set them on a table next to the building. The trays included ham and roast beef, sausages, pigs' knuckles, herring, cheeses, pickles, radishes, sauerkraut and bread. After arranging the spread on the table, they moved to Max. His youngest sister, Elli, who was twelve, hugged him.

"Tell me about the steamboat?" said Elli in a slow but excited tone.

"It was grand, with fine furnishings, like a rich man's mansion," said Max. "It had two big paddle wheels that pushed the boat through the water, all the way to Pittsburgh and back. It went so fast, the fish in the river couldn't keep up with it."

Elli listened intently.

Max eyed his father sitting stooped at a table, surrounded by his friends. He looked older than his fifty-three years, with thinning grey hair, a bushy mustache and a beard. The wrinkled skin on his face hung loose, and he held a long pipe off to the side of his mouth. Karl Mueller had emigrated to America from Germany twenty-two years earlier to escape political persecution. He had read of the political freedoms and economic opportunities in America in a book by a German traveler named Gottfried Duden and persuaded several friends to join him in his migration to America. Duden's book had indicated that Cincinnati had a significant German population and boasted beautiful hills and comforts, similar to the Rhineland. They made the four-month trip and established themselves in their new home. Instead of unlimited democracy and opportunity, Karl found anti-immigrant disdain and discrimination. He had been struggling for acceptance and prosperity ever since.

"Hi, Papa," Max said.

His father grunted without looking at him and introduced him to the men at his table. Some of the men were relative newcomers to town, or Forty-Eighter's as they were called, having left Germany amidst the political unrest in 1848.

Willy Jackson, a respected owner of multiple properties and a de facto community leader in Over-the-Rhine, approached the table. "Good day to you, men. Good afternoon, Karl." He shook hands all around. "Max, might I have a word with you in private?"

"What's the secret? We're all family. Have a seat, Willy." Max's father, Karl, slurred his words and pointed to the bench.

"No, thank you, Karl. I'd like to take up a matter with Max. No need to bore the rest of you on a Sunday." He eyed Max with seriousness and nodded toward the saloon's interior.

"Let's go into the sitting room, then." Max led Willy into a small room with a wooden table and benches. Like most saloons, the Eichen Garten had a sitting room used for private meetings. It was open to the regular neighborhood patrons for gatherings. Over the years, many business matters had been agreed to, and neighborhood legal, political, or family problems had been addressed within its walls. Willy closed the door behind them.

"Max, I want to talk about the upcoming mayoral election. This election is important for our community and our ability to hold on to our German heritage. The nativists believe we're a threat to America and will do anything to win this election. The Know-Nothing party is organizing to promote Pap Taylor. To gain support, they are leading their campaign message with anti-slavery rhetoric, but many Know-

Nothings are anti-German, anti-Irish, anti-Catholic and anti-alcohol. They play down these aspects of the party to gain the support of our neighbors. What do you hear downtown?"

Max said, "Talk I hear is that they're positioning Pap Taylor as the man to clean up the corruption in government and move us away from acceptance of slavery in the city. It's a risky campaign strategy. Plenty of businessmen are hesitant to draw too firm a line in the sand against slavery. Many businessmen's customers are in the South, where slavery is crucial to their livelihood. If Cincinnati openly supports the restriction of the Southerners' rights in this area, they may look elsewhere to buy their goods—Louisville or Saint Louis."

"Do you think the democrat, James Faran, has a chance to win against Taylor?" said Willy.

"I don't know," said Max. "Some city leaders are becoming more openly pro-Know-Nothing. The superintendent of Public Buildings advertised this week for laborers to build the new courthouse, indicating that American Protestants would be given employment preference. The Know-Nothing-leaning press aligns Faran with Popism and a supposed plot to take over the American west—in order to recoup the influence the Catholics have lost in Europe. It's sensationalist propaganda meant to influence the uninformed, but it can be reassuring to those receptive to the message."

"They're using the anti-Catholic message to divide us," said Willy. "They are adamant that if you don't look, talk and pray like a native, you're not an American. This country was built on the premise that we are all created equal, and it's our right to live our lives within the law."

"I know. I feel it every day," said Max. "I try to fit in. I cut my hair and dress like them. I hold my tongue. I want to make a good living and prosper, but to get it, I need to be more like them, or they won't accept me. I struggle. I have to change myself every time I walk across that bridge over the canal.

Here, I'm German-American. Down there, I'm an American."

"It sounds like you're learning how to win at their game," said Willy.

"I'm trying, but I wasn't born into their ways. I have to work twice as hard and swallow my pride at times. We have to elect politicians that keep the doors of opportunity open to people of all backgrounds. Voting against the Know-Nothings in this election is crucial."

"I figured you knew the score, but I wanted to make sure," said Willy. "I hear that a group of them are planning to stir up trouble in the German wards next week. They know we are likely to be a block of Democrat votes that can make Faran the winner. We've formed a group we're calling the Say-Nothings or 'Sag Nichts'. Our objective is to protect Catholics and foreigners at the polls. Can we count on your support?"

"Of course. I'm working on Monday, but send for me if you need me," said Max.

Willy said, "We have plenty of men ready for trouble here uptown. Our militias are on alert. I just need you to send word to me if you hear anything downtown that we need to know."

"I'll do that," said Max.

"Keep the faith," said Willy.

Willy stopped to say goodbye to Max's mother, Katharina, behind the bar on his way out. Max returned to the courtyard. The crowd had thinned, but his father still sat singing songs with a few patrons at his table.

Katharina came up beside Max. She looked exhausted. Her dress was damp with sweat and beer, and hair strands stuck to her forehead and cheeks. "What did Willy want with you?" she asked Max.

"We were discussing the election. He's worried about the Know-Nothings making trouble. They have it in for us and may try to stop some from voting in the German wards."

"I've heard. Who are these Know-Nothings?"

Max explained, "They started as a small group in secret. They would feign ignorance about the existence of their party, saying they 'know nothing,' but as their movement grew, they organized as a new national party—an alternative to the Whigs. Their members swear an oath to promote the interests of native-born Americans against Catholics and immigrants. The Know-Nothings would just as soon we all went back to Germany. The English-born who arrived in America only a few years earlier have no more claim to being American than we do, yet they act so entitled. I know; I see it downtown every day."

"Can you convince your father to vote for the Democratic candidate? I've read about the Know-Nothing candidate, Pap Taylor, in the newspapers. He is a vile, bigoted man. Some of his editorials are uncivil against the Church and immigrants. Your father believes the Know-Nothings are on his side because his friends tell him they're anti-slavery. It's a ruse. They're are afraid of losing their grip on life in this country. I've tried to make your father understand, but he doesn't respect my opinions.

"He listens to those men he sits with every day. Some are liberal Forty-Eighters who despise Catholics as much as the natives. They're so scared by the church's strong influence in Europe that they don't want to see the Church gain any power here in their new country. Your father looks past that, but he doesn't see that if the Know-Nothings get their way and stronger temperance laws come into play, this saloon and our livelihood are at stake. Less drinking means less money to feed his family. He's no mind for business."

"You're upset with him today?" said Max.

"It's not intentional, but the beer clouds his judgment and makes him lazy. I am tired of it. He enjoys the days as they come, doesn't worry about a thing, and leaves it to the rest of us. Maybe you could talk to him?"

"I don't think he will listen to me, either."

"Try. You're a man. You may get through to him."

CHAPTER 4

The next morning, Caleb opened another wooden barrel in the parlor, and he and Caroline unpacked the items. Caleb arranged the books on the bookshelf while Caroline carefully removed the cut-glass goblets and china plates from the straw and set them on the floor. They chatted as they worked.

Their mother came into the room. "You're making good progress. How many crates remain?"

"Just two more," said Caleb."

"Mother, three goblets broke in the barrel," said Caroline.

"I'm surprised it wasn't more. What about the plates?"

"One broke."

"Where is Annie?" said Sarah.

"She's still in bed," said Caroline. "She tossed and turned all night. I had trouble sleeping next to her."

"Did you tell her you'd begun the chores?" asked Sarah.

"Neither of us wanted to poke the sleeping bear," said Caleb.

Sarah scowled. She went upstairs, knocked on the bedroom door, and opened it slowly. Annie lay asleep, hugging the bedclothes in a rumpled bunch. Several crates were on the floor, and clothes were strewn about the room. Sarah pulled back the covers from Annie's face, exposing her to the late morning sunlight. Annie didn't move. Sarah sat next to her, reached over to the bundle, and began to shake Annie's arm. "Annie," she started quietly. "Annie, it's time to get out of bed."

Annie twitched violently and grunted.

"Come on now, Annie."

Annie let out a short defiant moan and twitched again.

"Annie."

Another twitch and moan.

"Annie, get up," Sarah said more firmly, anger in her tone.

Annie pulled the covers over her head.

"Your brothers and sister are well into the tasks of their day. I've taken Anthony and John to their new school. Caroline and Caleb are unpacking. You need to get up and do your part. You can't sleep the day away."

"What's the point? There's nothing in this city for me. Am I to be a prisoner in this house with nothing to look forward to but unpacking, mending, cooking and making things nice for my brothers and step-father?"

"Don't be so dreary. There is plenty for you, here. It will be what you make of it. You've always been curious and eager for adventure. This city is full of new opportunities."

"Hmph," she said, still under the covers.

Sarah pulled them back again.

Annie opened her eyes, slowly adjusting to the light. She sat up in bed. "There's plenty for a man to do in this city, but what can I do? My literary acquaintances, my salons, the city I knew are all back in New York. I'm stuck here."

"We'll get around to meeting new friends. Stephen has arranged for us to meet some of the proper families. You have the chance to start fresh. You need to think about your future. Make yourself a more eligible young lady."

"What does that mean?" said Annie.

Sarah picked up a paper from the nightstand. It was a cartoon drawing of a man with a large body and a tiny head pushing down a woman with law books and a ballot. The woman stood amongst a group of Black men and women, wearing a dress with large eyelashes and a fan covering her face. Sarah picked up the drawing and held it in front of Annie. "You can start by refraining from this sort of expression." She shook the paper. "This will get you nowhere. It will only make your life harder. Accept your place. It's not so bad. We are blessed to have Stephen and this beautiful home and its comforts."

"I can't accept this. This is not right. Not for me," said Annie.

"What am I to do with you?"

"Why did you bring me here?" Annie screamed and began crying and pulled the covers back over her face.

"Enough of this," said Sarah. "Stop sulking. Stephen and I have decided you will go to work as a teacher. He has arranged for you to meet with the Board of Examiners in the Cincinnati common schools."

Annie pulled the covers from her face, looking at her mother. "What? Did you decide what I will do, now? What if that's not what I want?"

"If you won't act enough like a lady to attract a suitable husband, then you need to position yourself for another life. I think you'll like teaching. You've always wanted to contribute beyond keeping a house."

"But not teaching children. Really, of all things to pursue."

"You have limited choices. Teaching is a respectable profession for a woman, and it won't preclude you from entertaining a suitor."

"There are other things I can do," said Annie.

"Those may come later. Right now, you need to get out of bed and face the day. Calm yourself and get over your melancholy. I want you to take a walk today, get some air. Caleb will escort you." Sarah stood up and yanked the covers back from Annie.

Annie put her pillow over her head and screamed into it.

Her mother ignored her. "Now get up, get dressed and come downstairs." She slammed the door as she left the room.

Annie reached down for the covers and pulled them back up over her head.

CHAPTER 5

Annie, her sister Caroline, and her mother, Sarah, sat in the parlor of Alice Key Pendleton, wife of George Pendleton, a prominent Cincinnati attorney and Ohio State Senator, drinking tea. There were half a dozen other women in attendance.

After Annie, Caroline and Sarah introduced themselves to the group, the hostess, Mrs. Pendleton, suggested the other ladies introduce themselves and offer their thoughts on clubs or activities they recommended to the new Cincinnatians.

Mrs. Clark, whose husband was a doctor at the Medical College, said, "I would be happy to introduce you at the Daughters of Temperance meeting. We meet every Thursday afternoon in Union Hall. It is a way for us to promote the value we as women bring to the cause of civility. In certain parts of the city, such as Over-the-Rhine, where the Germans live, and Rat Town, where the Italians live, the immigrants flaunt our temperance laws by opening their saloons on Sundays and encouraging immoral behaviors. Debauchery spills onto the streets. It's no wonder there is so much crime in those neighborhoods."

"What kinds of things do you do at your meetings?" asked Caroline.

"We take a stand against the injustices we see. Last week, we drafted a letter to the newspaper supporting the mayor in enforcing Sabbath laws. We encouraged him to restrain the breaking of liquor laws and contributing to moral depravement. Nearly all the coffee houses and pleasure gardens across the canal are open and busy on Sundays. Parents even bring their children into these places. Our society promotes moral living and the protection of women from men's abuses of alcohol."

"We would appreciate the introduction, thank you," said Sarah.

"What other ways do the women of Cincinnati promote the causes of women?" asked Annie.

"What do you mean, dear?" said Mrs. Clark.

"Are there other opportunities to promote women? For instance, in New York City, I attended lectures that aimed to raise the awareness of the injustices against our sex."

"What injustices needed to be addressed in New York?" asked Mrs. Clark.

"The same ones that exist here in Cincinnati," said Annie.

"To what do you refer?"

"Property laws, subservience in marriage, the right to use our brains to pursue education or employment."

"Annie," said her mother sternly.

Annie continued, "The right to vote on things that impact us."

Several of the women laughed. One said, "My dear, we don't know enough about politics to vote."

Annie came back, "I have met many men who vote without being adequately informed about the implications of their ballots. Fools are not prevented from voting, yet women are."

"My, aren't you progressive?" said Mrs. Clark.

Annie's mother interjected, "Annie was exposed to diverse opinions in New York."

"Where were such things discussed?" asked Mrs. Clark.

"I used to attend lectures and discussions at Mrs. Margaret Lynch's salon. She hosted some of the most fascinating and progressive people in New York. I heard Edgar Allen Poe read his poem, *The Raven*. I also heard Margaret Fuller speak on the great questions for women."

"What great questions?"

"First among them is what were we born to do? Are women satisfied with our position in life? Does 'all men created equal under God' literally mean men alone?" Annie said.

"My, those are great questions, but hardly worth wasting time on them given the blessings we have and the more pressing issues," said Mrs. Clark.

"We were given a brain and free will. Why not use them to question?" said Annie.

"Annie, I think these ladies have heard enough of your thinking, for today," said her mother, who was now red in the face. "I'm sorry, ladies if our New York liberal attitudes have offended any of you."

Caroline subtly shook her head at Annie to indicate she should stop. Annie closed her mouth and looked at the floor in frustration.

"What church are you attending?" asked one of the ladies.

"We've joined Mr. Neltner in worshipping at the Wesleyan Chapel," said Sarah.

Mrs. Evans said, "How wonderful. That's my church. It is a vibrant and well-placed congregation. We have many charitable programs. One cause that you may find of interest, Annie, is the Ladies' Home Missionary Society of the Methodist Episcopal Church. We find too many girls in the city that haven't received the proper moral instruction and thus find themselves destitute, intemperate, imprisoned or worse. If we don't address the problem before they have children, the problems multiply. To combat this, we have created several Sabbath schools to expose the misguided girls to Christian ways. Our charity's approach is unique in that we, the members of the society, go into the tenements, hospitals and the county jail to meet with the girls. We find that a woman's sympathy and counsel to another woman is especially effective in their receiving the message and changing their ways."

Annie said, "I question that many of the girls you are trying to help will be aided solely by a woman's sermon or religious instruction. Girls' moral ignorance is hardly the primary cause of women's poverty, but I applaud the woman-to-woman personal approach and your endeavors to assist them. I would like to learn more."

"Would you like to attend one of our upcoming meetings? I can present your name to the society for consideration?"

"Yes, thank you," said Annie. "That is kind of you."

Mrs. Renfro changed the subject, turning to the hostess. "Mrs. Pendleton, what is your husband's position on the upcoming mayoral election?"

"George supports states' rights and a man's right to vote his private conscience. He has stated that the Know-Nothings' nativist perspective is not right and thus can't support Pap Taylor, so he's supporting James Faran."

"Is your husband an abolitionist?" asked Annie.

"Annie," her mother attempted to silence her.

"It's all right, Mrs. Neltner. As a state senator in Columbus, George's politics are in the public's interest. Like many, George finds the idea of slavery abhorrent, but he respects the rights of the states to decide the matter for themselves."

"Isn't that kind of thinking what allows the division across our country to continue?" said Annie. "The Kansas-Nebraska Act was in that vein and a step backward for our country by allowing settlers of a territory to decide whether slavery would be allowed within a new state's borders. Morality doesn't allow for compromise on the matter." Annie raised her voice.

"Enough, Annie," said her mother.

The ladies quieted and looked around the room awkwardly, unsure how to proceed.

"Mrs. Pendleton, please forgive Annie. I fear she has offended you and your gracious hospitality. We will take leave of you ladies and let you finish your afternoon in peace. Please excuse us."

"Of course. It was a pleasure to meet you and your daughters," said Alice.

Annie, Caroline and Sarah descended the steps of the Pendleton house and climbed into the carriage. Once the driver departed, Sarah scolded Annie, "I was appalled by your behavior today, Annie. You cannot speak your mind so openly, especially in the company of new acquaintances and women of such a place in society. You offended Mrs. Pendleton, embarrassed us and put your stepfather's good name in poor light. You will write a letter of apology to Mrs. Pendleton."

Annie said, "I don't understand how someone can say that they support a person's right to private conscience and know that slavery is a moral tragedy, yet can condone a state's right to continue to allow it."

"Annie, politics are complicated. It's not always so straightforward."

"Are you saying politics are too complicated for my delicate brain to understand? I may not be schooled in the intricacies of politics; however, the matter of slavery is simple, Mother. It is not right. These ladies worry themselves about men having a few drinks and teach Sunday school for the poor to raise women out of poverty, yet are indifferent to the continuation of laws that allow people to enslave their fellow men. Why, because I am a woman, can I not speak my mind on matters of such importance?"

"It's not a woman's place. And if you must speak, you must use appropriate language to remain ladylike. Subtlety and understatement are skills that you must learn and employ."

"Father always spoke his mind and never hid behind half-truths or withheld what he believed in matters of importance."

"That's different. He was a man. Those qualities made him a principled man. In a woman, it is just brash."

"It's not fair. It doesn't make sense. Why should half of the population suppress themselves from speaking their mind?" said Annie.

"The world isn't fair," said Sarah. "If you don't accept that and move on from your stubborn positions, you'll never find a man willing to be your husband."

"Why would I want a husband? Someone who doesn't need to restrain himself in thought or actions, telling me what to do, and limiting my ambition to making his life successful and his home comfortable. Look at you. You've accepted your subservient place in marriage and blindly passed the ruse along to your daughters."

"I've had a good life. I'm not so ungrateful for the Lord's gifts that I would ask for more. I beg you to let these notions go. They will only make you unhappy. We can't change the world."

"Mother, the world needs to change. Who will change it for us? For you, Caroline, me, our daughters and granddaughters? Are we to wait for men to make the world fairer and more equitable toward women? Why would they do that? We will be waiting a long time. I cannot passively let things stay the way they are."

Caroline spoke, "Annie, please leave me out of your campaign to change the world. I want to find a good man with a respected profession with whom I can build a life. I will be content with a happy marriage, a beautiful home, and God's role for women—to care for children in a way that men cannot. Why do you insist on making ugly scenes out of nice conversations?"

"Bahhh! Bahhh!" Annie made a loud bleating noise. "You're like a sheep, just blindly moving with the herd."

"You're awful. No man would want you," said Caroline.

"Enough, girls!" said their mother. "Not another word from either of you the rest of the ride home."

CHAPTER 6

Max stood in the mansion's long hallway, admiring the eight massive murals painted on the walls. Each was approximately six by nine feet and depicted various tranquil nature settings in soft colors. He found them soothing and beautiful. Max was aware that Mr. Longworth, now in his sixties, was one of the city's wealthiest men and lived in one of the finest houses in town, called Belmont. But he wasn't fully aware that Mr. Nicholas Longworth's art collection was finer than any in the city, including the museums with small but growing collections.

Max thought back to the day he met the man. He was ten years old. Before dawn, he would get up and walk the mile to the newspaper office to wait with the other boys for the morning papers. Each of the dozen boys would be given a bundle of newspapers and expected to go to their assigned locations around town to sell them. Once sold, they returned to the office with the money and kept any tips they received. Because Max was polite and trustworthy, he was given one of the best locations in town, the east end of the central market.

Max would observe the men on their way to work each morning. He admired their clothes and how they walked with purpose, acting as if they owned the streets. He longed to be like them and dreamed of being a business owner. He built a rapport with some of the regular customers, asking them what they did for a living or which barber they went to—anything to become familiar with their ways, earn a tip or learn about the world downtown. After months of selling Mr. Longworth his morning paper, they became acquainted. Mr. Longworth was impressed by the small boy's work ethic, conversation and friendly attitude that came with a smile.

Nicholas Longworth was a lawyer by education but had made his money through real estate in the developing city and the growing of Catawba grapes to produce wines. He was the richest man in town and had given significant sums of money to support various causes—from bread doles for German widows to scientific associations. He was a fan of the arts and helped young, promising artists by underwriting their studies, funding their trips abroad or buying their works.

Longworth became young Max's mentor, and at age 11, he arranged to have Max enrolled in Saint Xavier College just a few blocks from the mansion. He paid for Max's board and tuition for the program which combined a classical with a mercantile education.

Jesuit priests and brothers ran the school, following the European models—six years that combined primary school with a college education. The classical curriculum included Latin, Greek, Poetry, Rhetoric, Chemistry, Botany, Mathematics, Physics, Psychology, Moral Philosophy, and German. Max also studied Accounting and Bookkeeping from the newly established mercantile curriculum. After six years, he earned a Bachelor of Arts degree.

The days were grueling. The boys awoke at 5:30 AM for prayers, then breakfast, classes all day, a short recreation period, dinner, study time, then evening prayers at 8:30 before lights out. They had Thursdays off and often spent it at Archbishop Purcell's mansion in the rural suburb of Walnut Hills, just north of the city. Max loved the fresh air, trees and playing rounders, a game like baseball. The boys were permitted one visit home per month. Max would spend it with his family, then visit Mr. Longworth before returning to the boarding house.

Max took his schoolwork seriously and performed well. His natural inclinations were further encouraged by the

Jesuits, whose teaching philosophy focused on developing well-rounded young men. Upon graduation, he had adopted beliefs, mannerisms, and aspirations more like the emerging American middle class than his immigrant family.

Max fondly remembered the walks in Longworth's garden and vineyards. He would pepper the man with questions about commerce and his investments, and Longworth provided words of encouragement and advice.

The door across from Max opened, and a bearded man with greying hair emerged with Mr. Longworth. "Max, let me introduce you to Hiram Powers. Hiram is a world-renowned sculptor. He created several presidential busts now on display in Washington and many beautiful pieces owned by collectors across Europe. He has come to visit from Florence, Italy. Hiram, this is Max Mueller. Max is a graduate of Saint Xavier College, and now, he builds railroads."

Max and Hiram shook hands. Max said, "Pleased to meet you, sir. I manage the books at Niles & Company. We make steam engines, locomotives and ironworks. Mr. Longworth has been a supporter of mine since I was young."

Hiram smiled at him, then Longworth. "You're in good company. Old Nick supported me in the days when I was unknown and penniless. He's an angel here on earth. We are lucky to know him."

"Indeed," said Max.

"Safe travels," said Longworth to Powers.

Powers bowed, walked down the long hall, and exited through the front door.

Longworth moved back into his office. "Come in. Update me on your business ventures. How are the Niles brothers treating you?"

"They treat me well," said Max. "The steam engine and sugar mill manufacturing business remain steady. The locomotive business is strong, but the competition is stiff. I have won the Niles' confidence, and each month they trust me to do more. They have asked me to supervise the ironworks. Without focus, Miles Greenwood's Eagle Iron

Works and other larger shops will drive us out of that business. I don't want to see the people who have given their lives in the trade lose their livelihoods, so I'm motivated to find a way to make it thrive."

"Good man. Take care of the men who work for you, and they will take care of the business. Have they given you a raise in salary as you do more?"

"Not yet."

"You need to convince them of your increased worth. Don't let them take advantage of you. A man of your education, drive and character could do many other things and be paid commensurately.

"You're drawing a good salary, but to have financial independence, you must own something. Look for your opportunity within the Niles businesses or somewhere else. Become an owner of property, an enterprise—an investment that will work for you. Always keep your eyes open for an opportunity."

Max thought out loud. "There may be opportunities at Niles. The locomotive business is tied to the western railroad expansion, so there is an upper limit to that business once the buildout occurs between here and Saint Louis. And the sugar mill machinery; I'm less comfortable working with the southerners in that end of the business. I have trouble looking them in the eyes, knowing slaves power their sugar plantations."

"I understand. It's hard to stomach. With your conscience, you need to steer toward businesses you can work in without compromising your values. It will eat you inside out. You will know when the opportunity is right for you. How is your family?"

"They're getting along, thank you. The saloon does well. More Germans are moving into the neighborhood every day. It's good for business, but I worry about some of the newcomers. They don't speak the language; many don't have skills. They can barely afford to live. They watch out for each other, but will they reach a breaking point? I see my brothers and sisters. They work hard, but what is their future?"

Longworth listened.

Max continued, "It's as if there are two Americas. One for the educated and well-to-do and one for the rest—the immigrants, Negroes, women. I'm blessed and thankful for the education you provided me."

"I'm glad I could do it. Make sure you put it to use and do some good on this earth. The Jesuits taught you that, didn't they?"

"Yes, sir. They drilled it into us—'Men for others'."

"Don't forget it."

"I won't, sir." Max could read Longworth. Their time was up. He stood and shook hands with him. "My best to Mrs. Longworth."

Longworth nodded.

CHAPTER 7

Max admired the newly constructed brick house as he approached it. He stood in the cobblestone street and unrolled the drawing showing the wrought iron fence, gate and front stair railing that Niles & Company was to build and install. The specifications looked correct and complete. He walked up the stairs and heard energetic piano music coming through the door. He knocked. The music continued, so he knocked more loudly, to no avail. The music tempo increased and then ceased with a final pounded chord. Max seized the opportunity and rapped during the break in the music. He heard footsteps.

The door opened, and there she stood. "What is your business?" said Annie.

"Miss Annie. It's you," said Max.

"Why, you, from the steamship." She smiled.

"Yes, good morning. It's nice to see you again," he said, removing his hat. "Max Mueller."

"What a surprise. This is a small city. I never dreamed I'd meet you again."

"Nor I," he smiled. "But I'm glad."

"Why are you here?" She pulled curls of hair back from her face.

"I'm here on business. Is Mr. Neltner at home?"

"No, he's gone to his office for the day," she said. "He's my stepfather."

"I have the final drawings for the gate and fence in front of his house. I have one question, and then I need final approval before we begin building it." He held up the rolled drawing.

"May I see it?" Annie asked.

"I need Mr. Neltner's input and approval, ma'am."

"Don't worry; I wouldn't dream of speaking for him. Let me see your drawings, for goodness' sake. I'm interested."

He handed her the drawing.

She unrolled it and looked at it. "It's very plain. It seems a shame. He could have made his house stand out with it."

"It's what he asked for," said Max.

"I'm not surprised." She looked at the price quote. "Well, you earn a pretty penny for forging some metal into insipid shapes. I would never have guessed you were so prosperous."

"The terms are between Mr. Neltner and Niles & Company. I don't think you should concern yourself with the money."

"Why is that? Because I am a woman?"

"No, it's just his private business. I shouldn't have divulged it."

"Well, you have, and I find it hard to believe you're charging him that much," she said.

"That is a fair price. No more or less than we charge other customers. It covers the cost of the iron and other materials, the labor to make it and install it and an appropriate allocation of administrative costs, plus a reasonable profit."

"Administrative costs?" she asked.

"That's to pay me and the foreman and such," he said. "So, don't get any ideas that I'm a rich man. I work for Niles to earn a wage."

"I presumed nothing of the sort. I'll see that Mr. Neltner gets the drawings."

"Can you relay one question for him?"

"I can," she said.

"Which side does he want the gate latch on? We build most with the latch on the right side since most people are right-handed, but I want to confirm before we construct it.

Sometimes there are obstacles or other reasons people want it on the left."

"You have to pay attention to many details. I wouldn't have thought to ask that question," she said, stepping past him and down the stairs to where the gate would be. She walked to the street and looked at the house, then pretended to push open the gate and climbed up the stairs. She stopped when she was one step above him, eyes level with his. "I don't see any obstacles with the right side, do you?"

"No, I don't," said Max.

"But I'm left-handed. The world wasn't made for people like me," she said. "When I was a child, they tried to make me right-handed. I've had to fight the world every day."

"I'm left-handed, too. I find it more productive to find ways around the world's obstacles rather than fight them." He touched her left hand with his.

"I'm sorry. I don't know why I reveal my thoughts so easily to you," she said, pulling her hand away.

"I like talking with you. I'd like to call on you again and talk further," he said.

"Call on me?"

"Yes, isn't that what your family would expect? I haven't done this before."

"My mother would love it, but I have no intention of sitting in our parlor and having my family listen to our conversation. Let's go somewhere."

"Wouldn't your mother frown on that?"

She laughed heartily. "My mother frowns on most of what I do, and I don't care. She will be happy that I am in the company of a gentleman. Besides, Mr. Neltner knows you and your reputation. I assume he will vouch for you?"

"He has no reason not to."

"Good, then. Where shall we go?" she asked.

"How much of the city have you seen?"

"Very little. My brother and I have walked the immediate neighborhood. I've called on a few families and browsed the Fourth and Fifth Streets shops, but that's about all."

"I shall give you a proper tour of Cincinnati then. I'll hire a carriage. Sunday at 1:00?"

"I would be delighted to have you introduce me properly to the city you spoke of so highly," she said.

"1:00 Sunday it is, then. Will you please give the drawing to Mr. Neltner and ask him about the gate latch?"

"What if we just decided for him—switch it and put the latch on the left side for left-handers. One little piece of the world made for those who don't belong in the rest of the world?"

"You are mischievous. I'm sorry, Annie, but I cannot do that. Mr. Neltner is paying us to build his gate, and my reputation relies on his satisfaction. I think we can find other ways to make the world more hospitable to those who aren't uniform."

"Of course. You are a man of honor," she said.

"As soon as Mr. Neltner sends confirmation of the drawings to our office, we can begin building," said Max. "It should take us five or six days to complete and paint it. If he is agreeable, we can begin installing after that."

"I will relay the message."

"Thank you, Annie."

"I look forward to Sunday." She reached out her left hand to him.

He smiled as he realized her intentional break with typical protocol and took her hand.

She watched him descend the stairs and walk down the street.

CHAPTER 8

Annie sat in a corseted dress, playing the piano with Caroline. Her siblings sat around the room. The sisters finished a classical duet, and her family applauded. Annie increased the volume and tempo with a quick playing of "Camptown Races." Her brothers joined in singing, and she pounded the keys at its conclusion. They laughed and applauded.

"Annie, enough of the bawdy songs. Play another nice one," said her mother.

"Annie is in a good mood today," said Anthony.

"That's because Annie has a boyfriend," teased John, the youngest. "Are you going to marry him?"

"Mr. Mueller is not my boyfriend. He is a man and a friend, but that isn't the same as a boyfriend."

"Anthony said you were with him on the lower deck of the steamship on the trip from New York," John said.

"What? Is this true, Annie?" said her mother.

Annie glared at Anthony. "I met him on the steamship, yes."

"What were you doing with him on the lower deck?" asked her mother. "I wasn't aware of this."

"I was investigating the steamboat mechanics and the paddle wheels, and he happened upon me. We struck up a conversation, that's all."

"I hope you maintained proper behavior," said her mother. "How did you connect with him more recently, then?"

"It was pure coincidence. I never expected to see him again. I told you, he knocked on the door this week with the drawings for Mr. Neltner. He invited me on a tour of the city."

"It's so romantic," said Caroline. "Fate brought him to your doorstep."

Annie suppressed a smile. "You make too much of this, all of you. It is an afternoon carriage ride."

"Stephen, in light of their meeting on the steamship, do you think we should let her go?" asked her mother.

"I am a grown woman. Isn't this what you have been pushing me to do?" said Annie.

"Yes, but you can't be seen with the wrong kind of people," said her mother. "Stephen, do you think it's all right?"

Stephen said, "Jon Niles employs Mr. Mueller at a respected establishment in the city. I have heard nothing ill of him, but you need to be careful, Annie. He is a German; his politics and behaviors may be more liberal than ours."

"We shouldn't let her go, then?" said her mother.

"I'm only riding in a carriage with him—in broad daylight," said Annie.

"Yes, but I've heard things about the Germans in this town. The drinking, the debauchery," said her mother.

"Mother, I am quite capable of retaining my morals amongst people who believe differently than we do. I was amongst people of many different backgrounds and faiths in New York."

"Yes, I recall. That's hardly a comforting, supporting argument for your case."

Annie scoffed.

There was a knock at the door. "I'm going," said Annie, grabbing her bonnet and moving quickly toward the front hall.

"Oh, no. You will bring this young man in so we can meet him," said her mother.

"I want to see him," said John.

"Me, too," said Caroline.

"All right," said Annie. "Stay. I will bring him in for the interrogation."

After a few minutes, Annie returned with Max, dressed in a fine jacket, waistcoat, and tie, hat in his hands. They stood in the doorway to the parlor.

"Good afternoon. I'm Max Mueller." All eyes were on Max. "Good to see you again, Mr. Neltner," he said, shaking hands with Stephen.

Annie introduced her family.

Her mother said, "It's very nice of you to show Annie the city. She hasn't met many young people her age yet. We understand you're with Niles & Company. Where is your family from?"

"My parents came to Cincinnati from Germany before I was born."

"What is your father's occupation?" said Mother.

"He runs a business across the canal."

"What business is that?" she pressed.

"He owns the Eichen Garten on Vine Street. It's a family gathering place in their neighborhood."

"I see. Is that where you live?"

"No, I board with a family downtown on Fourth Street— the Carsons," said Max. A silence filled the room as no one was sure what to say next.

"You brought Annie flowers; how thoughtful," said Caroline. "Would you like me to put them in a vase for you, Annie? You don't want to take them out in the sun all day. Their beauty will fade quickly." She took them from Annie.

"Yes, thank you," said Annie, pulling several stems of flowers from a vase on a marble top table and handing them to Max. "For you."

"What? Why?" said Max.

"Well, a small token of my appreciation in return for your flowers and your invitation today."

"Thank you, I've never received flowers," said Max.

"Max, that's a handsome jacket you're wearing," Caroline noted. "Did you buy it in New York?"

"No, I employ the best tailor in town."

"Evidently, you are a man who takes pride in your appearance. I'll bet your customers appreciate that," said Caroline.

Annie glared at Caroline. "We shall be on our way, then."

"It was a pleasure meeting you all," said Max.

They made their way to the front door and down the steps. Max helped Annie up onto the carriage and then climbed on. He shook the reins, and they started down the street.

"I'm sorry for the inspection you had to endure," said Annie. "My mother is very concerned with appearances and wanted to understand who I would be seen with across the city today."

"I understand her concern. I hope she found me acceptable," said Max.

"I am not concerned with her opinion."

"Mr. Neltner's new house is beautiful and very spacious. The woodwork on the stairs and around the doorways is fine craftsmanship. Does the house have all the modern conveniences?"

"Yes, hot and cold water, a modern coal furnace, gas lights. He bought the latest icebox. It's all very nice. You're interested in home furnishings?" she said.

"Yes, beyond the mechanics involved, I like nice things. I didn't have many growing up. Someday I will own a house like his."

"I believe you will," she said. "Where are you taking me, today?"

"I have a general plan in mind, but we can let the day lead us where it may. We'll start downtown, then Over-the-Rhine, and end with a picnic on Mount Adams. Is that acceptable to you?"

"It sounds wonderful." Annie felt lighter than she had since leaving New York.

"How have you found the city? Encountered any savage Indians, yet?" Max asked.

"As you predicted, I have not. I have found Cincinnati to be surprisingly civil. It lacks some of New York's cultural institutions, such as museums and theaters, but it appears to have a sufficient selection of shops and markets. I have found the smoky air on some days to be unpleasant."

"Yes, it gets worse in the heat and humidity of the summer. Those are the days I appreciate the hilltops and the suburbs. You'll see. What have you been doing to occupy yourself?"

"My mother and sister and I have set about to furnish the house. We've been to many of the shops along Fifth Street. We found some beautiful fabric and wallpaper for the parlor. I am tired, however, of the endless search for the perfect lamp. I finally told my mother just to pick one that lights the room. The conversations with the furniture maker about the curio cabinet were more interesting to me. I took him a sketch based on the one we had in New York. It was my father's. We had to leave it behind."

"You design furniture?" he said.

"Not really. Although it interests me, I haven't been trained in design or mechanical drawing. I just drew what I wanted. I'm sure the dimensions are off. Do you do the drawings for your ironworks?"

"Like you, I can rough sketch. I know enough to do an initial design, but then I turn it over to our draftsman. What else have you been doing since your move here?"

"I've walked about the city, some. I like to go to the public landing and watch the people when the steamships come in. The crowds remind me of New York."

"You walk down there alone?" he said.

"Sometimes, but usually with my brother Anthony. He's fourteen and as interested as I am in the city. He wants to be a lawyer."

"I recommend you don't go down there alone. Some rough men might get the wrong idea about a solitary lady."

"I haven't had a problem with them, yet. I've had more stares from the women eyeing me, looking down their noses. Honestly, I'm not sure what they have to be so high and mighty about living in this pig town. Like some of the ladies we had tea with at Mrs. Pendleton's house."

"Mrs. George Pendleton, wife of the state senator?" he said.

"Yes, she was gracious, but it was a group of women who are like-minded with my mother when it comes to a woman's place in the world."

"What do you mean?" said Max.

"My mother does whatever society expects of her and she wants my sister and I to do the same. She is unwilling to question, let alone challenge, the way things are. The ladies at Mrs. Pendleton's house seemed comfortable enough with their positions as respected wives that they couldn't even imagine that a woman might want to do something different."

"What would be something different for you?" asked Max.

"What if I went to school and studied mechanics? If I learned to design beautiful furniture and then hired men and women to build it in my factory. What if I built furniture that was smaller and more comfortable for women or had drawers and shelves suited to storing women's clothes and accessories?"

"Is that what you'd like to do?" he said.

"I don't know," she started raising her voice. "How would I know? No one permits me to explore the idea. I like dreaming up better ways to do things. I like drawing. I think I would be good at it, but I can't get the formal training to do it, and even if I did, no one would let me open my own business, hire people, or hire women. Who would loan me the money? Maybe I want to be a doctor or a lawyer. I dream of these and other things, but because I'm a woman, they're just dreams."

"I've never met any lady doctors or lawyers. Where do you get these ideas from?" Max asked.

"I've always been interested in doing things for myself, figuring things out, trying new things. The idea of cooking, cleaning, sewing and staying at home every day is enough to suffocate me."

"I hear your passion, but why do you think you can do some of those things? That's not the way the world is," he said.

"I don't accept the way the world is. It can be different. I have to try to change things. Men aren't going to change it for women."

"It sounds daunting. I'm glad I wasn't born a girl."

"Praise God, you weren't. But I'm not the only woman on this earth to feel these things. Others like me are trying to change things. I spent the summer after my father died with his cousin, Elizabeth Cady Stanton, in Seneca Falls in New York. Cousin Lizzie and her friends organized the first National Women's Rights Convention. They presented a Declaration of Sentiments that spoke to this country's injustices against women and women's rights, including the right to vote."

"What?" he scoffed. "Women will vote when pigs fly."

"I know, it's hard for you to imagine, but the fact that they said it. It was discussed and voted on by men and women in the room. It gives me hope that someday, maybe… The ability to vote is key. If women had the right to vote, we'd have a voice in the things that impact us. Today, we're at the mercy of men. Hoping and praying that men might want to give up some of their advantages to make women's lot a little better."

"That's a little cynical toward men, isn't it?" said Max. "We're not that bad."

"Individually, some of you aren't. My father was compassionate and open-minded, but our government, schools, businesses, and even our homes have all been built around a man-centered world. It's not your fault. You've become used to the way things are, and there's no incentive for you to change."

"So, what did the ladies at tea think of your women's rights?" he said.

"They thought I was bold—and unwomanly. Mrs. Macke turned so red I thought she was going to explode. They thought I was complaining and ungrateful for what I have and wasting my time when there are more pressing problems. Mother was pretty upset with me. She said I damaged Mr. Neltner's reputation."

"Sounds like you made quite an impression on the ladies of Cincinnati," said Max.

"I don't think I'll be invited to Mrs. Pendleton's any time soon."

As they talked and moved along, Annie focused more on Max and his voice than the scenery he pointed out. Max drove by the Niles & Company workshop and their new foundry building. He turned onto Sycamore Street, pointed and said, "That's Saint Xavier College and Saint Xavier Church. I lived in the boarding house there when I was in school."

"It's a Catholic school?" she said.

"It's run by Jesuit priests. Good men, wise men. They were strict but kind. I graduated with a Bachelor of Arts degree."

"Did you like it there?"

"I loved it. I was challenged but supported. I enjoyed my commerce and accounting classes more than my Latin or Greek. I have some close friends from my years there."

"We have something in common. then," she said.

"What's that?"

"I didn't enjoy Latin. either." They both laughed. "Was it hard for you to live apart from your family at such a young age?"

"No," he said.

"Didn't you miss them?"

"No."

"Wasn't it strange living in a dormitory?"

"My house was very different from the ones you're used to, like the one Mr. Neltner built. It was an adventure for me to live in the dormitory and meet boys from many different backgrounds. I loved being among them. I wanted to be like them."

He pointed out the sights as they rode along. As they moved down Broadway along the eastern edge of the commercial district, he pointed to a block of crowded wood buildings. "That's Bucktown, a nasty place that you should avoid. The lowest of whites, Negroes, and mulattos live and stir up trouble there. Rag-pickers, prostitutes, thieves, and lazy men. It's a dirty, crowded place that borders on lawless."

"We had similar places in New York. Five Points was home to some of the most unfortunate and the immoral. New York has a constant stream of immigrants who arrive with no skills, no English, and they live in squalid conditions with little opportunity. It sounds as if Cincinnati has similar challenges, but on a smaller scale."

He drove along and pointed toward the slaughterhouse district. "Cincinnati has become the largest pork processing center in the west. Last year, one-half million pigs were slaughtered here."

"That's a lot of bacon." She laughed.

He chuckled. "There are other industries that use the rest of the pigs. Other companies produce lard and make candles and soap from pork by-products."

"Soap is made from pigs? It doesn't sound very clean," she said.

"It's one of the ingredients," he said. "A whole economy revolves around the pigs of Cincinnati. Some call Cincinnati Porkopolis because of the large number of pig-related businesses. This part of town comes alive starting in mid-November when it's cool enough for the processing season. Ohio, Indiana, and Kentucky farmers all bring their hogs to the slaughterhouses. You'll smell it in these parts when it starts. It's not pleasant. My brother is a seasonal worker in one of the slaughterhouses. He earns a good wage during the short season. It's long days and hard work in the factories."

Max worked his way through the city, showing Annie the theaters, public buildings and other sights. He stopped when they came to the canal. "The Miami and Erie Canal was completed about ten years ago, connecting Cincinnati with the city of Toledo, Lake Erie and the other Great Lakes. The canals plus the Ohio River provided the transportation that made Cincinnati such an important city as the western territories opened up. The river was a natural way to get people and goods across the country. As Cincinnati grew, more and more businesses were located here because of the easy access to supplies and the economical way to distribute to markets in the west and the south. The canals provide access to northern Ohio and on to New York."

Annie looked at wooden bridge spanning the forty feet across the muddy brown canal. She put her handkerchief to her nose, using its perfume scent to mask the smell of sewage from the water.

"You ready to go Over-the-Rhine?" he asked.

"Yes, the ladies at tea warned me."

"What did they warn you of?"

"The sins of Over-the-Rhine and Rat-town. They said the temperance laws are ignored on Sundays."

"Did they say anything else about it?"

"No," she said.

"I'm not surprised. To a native, it's a foreign land that intimidates. Don't worry. I'm with you."

"I'm not worried. I'm interested to learn about your childhood neighborhood."

He hesitated. "You won't see so much of me over there. I lived at Saint Xavier from the time I was eleven. I love my family, but I'm an American, now."

"All right, Max. On with the tour."

Max guided the carriage along the canal and crossed the bridge at Elm Street. They passed a cemetery that extended over a city block. Large shade trees covered the grounds, and several hundred headstones peppered the lawn. "The Episcopals and the Presbyterians own the cemetery. There's talk that the city is planning to buy it and turn it into a park."

"What about the interred buried there?" she said.

"They'll move the remains to other cemeteries. There's an expansive new cemetery four miles north of the city called Spring Grove. It has a beautiful arboretum. We don't have time today, but it's a beautiful ride for some Sunday."

"That seems like a lot of trouble for a park. Why not just leave them be?"

"A park will be a welcome respite for the city. Our population continues to grow rapidly. There is very little grass or trees. The city is landlocked in the basin by the surrounding hills and the river. I think it's a forward-looking idea that families will appreciate."

They rode north of the cemetery into a mixed business and residential neighborhood. The buildings were built adjacent to the sidewalks with no yards, some with a small stoop at the front door. They were two and three-story wooden or brick structures that abutted each other. Some had narrow walkways between them leading to back courtyards and stairs to upper apartment porches. They rode past bakeries, coffee houses and saloons, stables, a coal yard, a cigar box factory, and an ice house. Many new buildings were under construction. People walked the sidewalks, and children played in the streets.

As they crossed a major street, Max said, "This is Liberty Street. It used to be the city's northern boundary, and it was named because of the liberties taken outside of the city laws. Several years ago, the city annexed these streets, so it's all part of Cincinnati, now."

They approached a cleared lot with piles of dirt. "This is the site of one of our projects. The city is building a new market here on the Findlay property. It will be a large market serving all of Over-the-Rhine. We're casting the iron support structures for the market house. It will be the grandest of any in town—more ornate than the central or lower markets—and built to last."

When the street came to a dead-end in front of a steep hillside, Max turned right and drove past a large brick building. "This is the Hamilton Brewery. Johann Sohn and George Klotter started brewing about ten years ago, and they've now grown their business into this. Lager beer has a much smoother taste but requires cooler temperatures. They dug out the hillside to create a big underground storage cellar to keep the lager beer barrels cool. George and Johann have an investment in my family's saloon, and in return, we sell their beer and no one else's. They've been loyal partners to us."

"What do I smell?" she said.

Max laughed. "It's the brewery. When the wheat and hops ferment in the water, it gives off that smell. Do you like beer?"

"I've never drunk alcohol. It's against the laws of my church and a vice that contributes to social ills, including the mistreatment of women."

"Sorry for you. I have enjoyed beer since I was a young boy. But I know of what you speak. Some men drink to excess and cause trouble, and some men are haunted by the drink to the point of their ruin. But the saloon is my family's means. I won't turn my back on it. I am moderate with my drink. I pass no judgment on you for your beliefs, but in return, ask that you not ask me to infringe upon the rights of men to take a drink to make their days a little brighter, so long as they aren't hurting anyone with it."

"You have a word or two to say about the subject, I see. I have little experience with spirits or anyone who does."

"Maybe you need first-hand knowledge so you can judge for yourself," said Max.

They proceeded south on Vine, the main street in Over-the-Rhine. Many buildings had residences on the second and third stories above the street-level shops. People crowded the sidewalks, and many businesses were open, even though it was Sunday. They passed a large brick school building and another large building with a red, gold and black flag depicting an oak wreath and snake. "That's Turner Hall. The Turner Society is an organization dedicated to promoting German culture. It's a gathering place for the German community. They have a chorus, a gymnasium and library.

"That's quite a combination of things going on there," she said.

"There are other German societies here in Over-the-Rhine. The men formed them, beginning with the first wave of immigrants that arrived, fleeing the German unrest in the 1830s. We call that wave of immigrants the Thirty'ers. That's when my parents arrived in this country. The societies provide immigrants with support and a sense of community among people like themselves that speak their language. In addition to choruses and gymnastics, some of the societies host lectures and sponsor militias."

"Militias?" she said.

"It's as much about marching in formations and demonstrating discipline and heritage, but the men are trained and ready to defend their community and country if called upon."

"Are you a member of any of the German societies?"

"I'm not active in any of them. My father and my brothers are. I grew up with many of the men and still see them at the Eichen Garten."

"What's the Eichen Garten?" she said.

"That's the name of my family's saloon. It means Oak Garden in German. There's a big oak tree in the backyard. It's just ahead on the right there." Max pointed to a neat, brick three-story building with a wooden door. Three windows spanned across the second and third floors, each capped by an arched stone lintel. A wooden sign with an oak leaf and 'Eichen Garten' hung out over the sidewalk.

Max stopped the carriage. "That's it. The saloon is on the ground floor, and we lived on the second and third floors. They still live there."

"Can we go in?" asked Annie.

"Let's not today. If you'd like to, we can come back some other day."

"I'd like to see it, yes."

Max shook the reins to move the horse along the cobblestone street. "You disapprove of drinking. Are you sure you'd be comfortable going?"

"I'm curious. I think it would be fun. I'd like to see where you grew up and meet your family."

"Are you sure you want to endure an inspection that will make your mother's look like a passing glance?"

"I've had many eye me critically. I have a thick skin," she said.

"All right, then. We'll come back. Maybe you'll taste the beer?"

"Perhaps. You may get me to try many new things."

CHAPTER 9

Max drove the buggy back across the canal into downtown. On Pike Street, Max pointed out some of the most luxurious homes in the city. They pulled up in front of a white mansion with tall pillars across the porch. A tended garden surrounded the house, enclosed by a black wrought iron fence. The rhododendrons were budding but not yet in bloom.

"It's beautiful. Who lives there?" asked Annie.

"Old Nick."

"Old Saint Nick?"

"No. Mr. Nicholas Longworth. The richest man in Cincinnati. He owns this house and those vineyards up to the top of that hill over there. Old Nick was my benefactor. He paid my expenses and tuition at Saint Xavier. He met with me through the years of my youth and guided me to graduation. I still meet with him. He's like a father to me."

"That was incredibly kind of him."

"Yes, it was. I'm just one of his causes. He also donated the land for the observatory up there," he said, pointing at the top of the hill.

Max led the horses up a series of roads past rows of terraced grapevines to the top of Mount Adams. He pulled the horse off the road into a small field next to the vineyard. He helped Annie down from the carriage, and they stood looking down at the city. They could see the entire basin—a grid of streets with buildings punctuated by dozens of church steeples. Most businesses were closed for the Sabbath, so the smoke was light and the view clear. To the north and west, the surrounding hilltops were dotted with homes and a few roads. Steamboats, barges, and small boats crowded the river to the south. A ferry boat made its way across to Covington. On the Kentucky side of the river, there were fewer buildings and lush, green hillsides as far as they could see.

"It's so much prettier from up here," said Annie.

Max nodded his head and took in the view.

"There's the public landing. The men look so small, like ants." Annie laughed.

Max said, "Yes. I like the quiet, up here. The city seems still until you look more closely. Then you see the movement. You can almost see it growing. See those new buildings under construction," he pointed. "A couple of years ago, none of those houses or roads were there," he pointed north of the city. They stood for another minute in silence. He reached behind the carriage seat and pulled out a basket and a blanket. "This way," he said. They walked into the vineyard, and Max spread the blanket on the ground in a secluded spot with a city view. He removed a cloth bundle from the basket, unwrapped two meat and cheese sandwiches, and laid out a bowl of pickles and some dried apples. He grabbed two tin cups and started down the hill between two rows of vines. "I'm going to the well for some water. I'll be right back."

Annie sat in silence. She realized she was calmer now than she had been for weeks. She was comforted by Max's gentle yet confident demeanor. She felt at ease with and accepted by him, making her feel more open to the things around her. Beyond that sense of comfort, she was excited by his closeness. They had bumped against each other repeatedly in the carriage ride. With each touch, she felt a charge of excitement that she liked very much, even though it made her feel less in control of herself. She had never let herself become close enough to a man to feel this way before.

As Max walked the familiar route to the well, he considered Annie. He had thought she was pretty, but now he felt even more so. Her smile, her laugh, her bosom moving up and down in her corseted dress. His mind raced over possibilities of life and love, thinking about her. He'd also felt the charges when they touched in the carriage and found himself in an extended state of excitement that became uncomfortable. He looked around the vineyard, took a deep breath, then went on to the pump. He took a drink, filled the cups, and started back toward her.

She was one of the most intriguing women he had ever met. Her unique opinions and bold demeanor kept him wondering what she would say next. He usually liked things planned and orderly, but he enjoyed her spontaneous conversation and unfamiliar background and attitudes. He hadn't courted a woman beyond a few arranged dances at college. He hadn't had the time, the inclination, or the means to do so. He went to a boys' school, taught by celibate priests, so he had no education in how to proceed. At school, they had discussed the proper behavior of gentlemen. His mother had provided him with an example of a strong female figure. His love and caring for her and his sisters taught him enough to interact comfortably with females, but he had no instruction for courting.

"Did you have to go far?" she asked.

"No, just at the end of this row. I used to run around up here as a youngster. Old Nick would have picnics, sometimes." He handed her a cup and sat on the blanket next to her.

"What do you think of Cincinnati, now?" he said.

"It's a more welcoming place now that I have a friend," said Annie.

"Is that what we are now? Friends?" he asked.

"For now. It's our first day out together. What else would we be?" she asked.

"I'm happy to have you as my friend, for now."

They watched each other. Max reached over and took her hand, placing his on top and below hers. After a few moments, he said, "Let's eat. The sun is starting to set." They ate. "What will you do with yourself once you're settled?"

"I'm interviewing for a position as a teacher in the Cincinnati common schools. It will keep me busy until I find something else that better suits me. Mr. Neltner knows members of the school board and arranged the interview."

"Have you taught school before?"

"No, not formally, but I had advanced classes in New York. My father enrolled me in a school that taught subjects beyond what women's schools normally teach."

"You don't sound excited about teaching."

"It's not my choice. My mother has insisted I do this. She feels it will squelch my urge to have a profession if I work for a year or two. She's also given up on my being restrained enough to break into Cincinnati society without embarrassing her or ruining my sister's chances of finding a suitor. I recognize I will lose my social standing by teaching in the schools." She sighed. "My sister Caroline has completed her education and is ready to court young men. She's a sweet girl, very traditional. She will be quite content to submit to the role of wife and homemaker."

"You make that sound like a bad thing," he said.

"I love her dearly. We're just very different. I won't settle for that. My mother doesn't understand me and never has. I think she's given up on me and wants me to be a teacher so I'll stay out of trouble. She's probably right. I'll dive into the work, and the mental stimulation will entertain me for a while. I'm like that. I tire quickly of things. Once I learn something and master it, I'm ready to move on to something else. Piano, Dancing, chess, drama, archery."

"Archery? You?"

"Yes, my father took me to a club in Brooklyn. There were a few women, but I was the only girl. After that, I wanted to shoot pistols, but that's where he drew the line."

"Shoot guns?"

"Yes. Target practice only. I didn't want to hunt animals. That's too masculine even for me. I don't understand why anyone would want to kill another living thing for sport."

"How were you at archery?" he said.

"I became quite good. More bulls-eyes than most of the men."

"It sounds like you and your father had a special relationship?" he said.

"Yes, I miss him. How about you and your father?"

Max hesitated. "We get along. There are seven of us. I think it overwhelmed him."

"I'm sorry. I didn't mean to…," Annie said.

"I don't mind your questions."

"Who are you going to vote for in the mayoral election this week?" she asked.

"James Faran. He's a respectable and thoughtful man."

"You've met him?"

"No, but I heard him speak during his campaign."

"I figured you would support him. I read that Pap Taylor is a nativist and anti-Catholic, so two strikes against him for you," she said.

"He wouldn't be good for my family and friends in Over-the-Rhine. I pray his tactics don't cheat Faran in the election," said Max.

"What do you mean?"

"There are rumors his party may try to strong-arm or prevent some from voting."

"Have you had issues like that before in Cincinnati elections?" she said.

"Nothing major. There have been rumors of minor improprieties in voting."

"In New York, we have Tammany Hall bosses who are corrupt and influence the elections, but they've done a lot to help the immigrants and the disenfranchised, so in some ways, they've been a good force. Good for the people, bad for democracy."

"No, nothing like that here, but I hate to see America's elections corrupted. We must guard against both nefarious politicians and the wealthy buying their influence. Both are threats to our political system."

"All I can do is watch it from a distance," said Annie.

"I've never met a woman who was so informed and motivated to cast her vote," he said.

"The results of elections impact women as much as they do men. I am subject to the outcomes of elections, so I should have a say in them. Someday—women will vote."

"You have strong convictions about women's suffrage," said Max.

"Look at that sunset. It is one of the prettiest I've ever seen. The oranges, reds and yellow," she murmured. "It's beautiful. Thank you for bringing me up here and for today."

"Thank you for accompanying me," he said, taking her hand. He leaned in and kissed her gently.

"I've never been kissed by a friend before," she joked. "I'm not sure what to think about it." Annie had never been kissed by any man. She had heard her girlfriends describe their kisses and read, but she never had the opportunity or a longing. She flushed at the charge of excitement again and how happy it made her feel.

"Did I offend you?" said Max.

"No, I liked it," she said.

"One more then?"

They kissed again and sat holding hands for a few minutes.

"We should go. The sun is almost set," said Max.

They folded the blanket together and returned the items to the basket. He stowed them in the carriage and helped her climb up. They started down the road toward the city.

"Can I see you again?" asked Max.

"Yes, I'd like that very much. Can we go to your family's saloon next Sunday?"

"Are you sure?"

"Yes. I would be delighted to join you and taste beer for the first time."

He took her hand as they approached her house. "Thank you, Annie. I enjoyed your company."

"And I yours."

He helped her down from the carriage and opened the gate. "Nice gate—fine work," he said.

"Good night, Max."

"Good night." Annie wished she didn't have to wait another week to be next to him. She wanted to kiss him again.

CHAPTER 10

Max sat at his table in the small office on Niles & Company factory's second floor, preparing the month-end accounting reports for April. Coleman Sellers, the shop foreman, came into his office.

Max put down his pencil. "Coleman. How is progress on the steam engines progressing? Any more delays anticipated?"

"No, I think we'll finish the two in the shop on time. No changes to the schedule."

"Good. Jon Niles will sleep better when he hears that. You're doing good work. We can produce four engines with the same number of men that we used to build three with before you became foreman."

Coleman lowered his voice. "Some days, I think Jon is looking for a reason to get out of this business. I've heard him grumbling with his brother James. I don't want all my improvement efforts to be for naught."

Coleman took off his jacket. "Did you hear about the ruckus at the central market?"

"No, what's happening?" asked Max.

"There's a crowd. Some men are making speeches. Word is the steamer, Daniel Boone, brought in three hundred tough men from Kentucky to make sure the votes go the way of the Know-Nothings in today's election."

"Is that true, or just a rumor?" said Max.

"I don't know, but there are a few hundred men, some drunk, some armed, at the market. One of the speakers said there were irregularities in the eleventh ward. Young German boys were allowed to vote to push the election in Faran's favor. They're debating what to do about it. A lot of shouting. One of the city officials tried to calm them, saying the votes will be checked and they need not take things into their own hands, but the crowd booed him and pulled him off his platform. Another man said he heard the Germans firing cannons on Jackson Hill to celebrate a Faran victory. The voting's not even done."

"Those cannon shots are part of the German celebration of Jefferson's birthday. I know the men who were planning that. These men are inventing stories," said Max.

"I picked up one of these. The market grounds were littered with them," Coleman said, handing him a red paper flyer. 'Pap Taylor For Americans' was printed at the top, with some text in the middle, and 'Whip the Dutch' at the bottom.

"How many men did you say are in the crowd?" asked Max.

"I don't know. Two, three, four hundred. It was hard to tell who was there to shop and who was there for the speeches."

Max said, "The Know-Nothings have positioned Pap Taylor as a pure American and non-natives as a pox. Did you see the cartoon in the paper this morning? Pap Taylor is himself the son of Irish parents. What a hypocrite. It's all a ruse to try and play into people's fears—unfounded."

"It's politics, Max," said Coleman.

"It's politics until they start disrupting every man's right to vote, then it borders on tyranny. I'm worried about these Kentucky toughs brought in from the outside and what they might be meaning to do. I'm going over to the market."

"Be careful. They won't take kindly to your kind in the crowd."

"I look and dress enough like everyone else to avoid trouble," said Max.

Max told Jon Niles about the trouble brewing and asked to be excused, promising to make up the missed work. He took one of the Niles' horses and rode the half-mile to the market at Fifth Street. As he neared, he saw men walking toward the open-air market with the red flyers in hand.

He moved closer to hear what a man standing on a crate was saying but couldn't get close enough to understand. There was a large crowd of men. Several held up a banner that said 'Pap Taylor for Americans.' He heard shouting and chanting, "Hurrah for Pap Taylor." Max asked a man walking away from the crowd. "Sir, what is the crowd about?"

The man said, "The Germans are trying to steal the election for mayor. They stuffed the ballot box in the eleventh ward and possibly the ninth and twelfth. The Dutch are heavily armed and may try to stop others from voting. There's a call to take the votes from those wards by force if necessary."

A mass of men in their black hats filled the plaza. Some had guns or knives. The group started swarming toward him like a disturbed hill of ants. There didn't seem to be a leader-just chaos. He moved back out of their way and listened to voices as they passed. He heard "To the eleventh ward," "Burn the fake ballots," "Ninth Ward," "Dirty Germans," and "Kill 'em and their women, too."

Max raced ahead of the mob moving north on Main Street toward the canal. Once clear of the mass of people, he urged his horse into a gallop. He reached the polling place at the engine house in the ninth ward within ten minutes. He dismounted and went inside. He knew one of the men working the polls and explained what he had heard at the market and that a mob had formed and was headed north. "You need to protect the ballots," he said. "Some of the men are armed. Send someone for our militia. I'm going to the eleventh ward to warn them."

He ran outside, mounted the horse and made his way toward the polling place at the Mohawk engine house. As he approached the fire station, he saw a mob of men on foot and horseback moving toward him. Several men and boys hung from a buggy in the middle of the crowd. One of the boys fell off and screamed as the wheel ran over his leg. The toughs ignored him and kept moving toward the polling place.

Max rode along the side of the road, staying out of the way. He rode past several German women, with their backs against a building, watching the melee on their street. He heard a gunshot and several screams but couldn't see the source.

As he approached the building, an angry crowd parted to make room for a man running out of the fire station carrying the ballot box over his head. The crowd surged toward the man but retreated as another waved his gun. One of the rioters shouted, "Burn the corrupt votes."

As several Germans rushed the man with the ballot box, he attempted to throw it to one of his cohorts, but it crashed on the street, splintering into several pieces. Paper ballots scattered across the road, and the crowd erupted in a frenzy as men from both camps went for the ballots. Some grabbed them, some ripped them, and others threw them into the air. It was a mass of men and sailing papers.

More Germans came out of the polling place and went at the rioters, fists flying. The commotion of the mob increased as more men joined in the fighting.

Max sat atop his horse and watched the spectacle in horror. He wasn't a fighting man and knew better than to move into the throng.

A man ran from the center of the crowd and screamed, clutching his stomach; his clothes reddened with blood. Max recognized him as George Roder, the foreman at the Links Brewery. Max dismounted and pushed his way through the crowd to assist George. As a man fled holding a bloody knife, Germans descended on him and began beating him.

Max reached George, took him in his lap on the ground, and applied pressure to his bleeding midsection. A small circle of men formed around them. George lost consciousness. "Is there a doctor?" Max shouted. "This man needs a doctor!"

"Hold on, George." Max continued to push on his abdomen and hugged him. "Help, someone!" Others repeated the call for a doctor. George breathed several heavy breaths and then stopped breathing. Max shook George and called his name. He felt his neck for a pulse. "Dear Jesus," Max prayed.

The crowd around him grew. Someone shouted, "He's dead," Screams. The concerned and the curious pushed in to get a glimpse. Max leaned further over George, attempting to shield him from the gawkers.

The fighting subsided, and the Germans and the Know-Nothings stood in pockets in a standoff. Some Know-Nothing men pulled a cannon they had stolen from the Jefferson Birthday celebration up the street. The crowd parted and cheered as they placed it in front of the building. Several men posed beside the cannon with guns held across their chests. One climbed atop it and held his rifle above his head; another waved a stars and stripes flag. Two men stood behind it and waved a banner for the Know-Nothing candidate.

A brick flew from the crowd and hit one of the men, causing another round of fighting. It went on for twenty minutes, resulting in more stabbings and shooting. The nearby residents watched from their second-story windows, stunned by the violence in their peaceful neighborhood.

The armed mob outnumbered the Germans, so they eventually backed off. The Know-Nothing crowd began to move, dragging the cannon with them. "To the Ninth Ward." The horde cleared out, leaving the street quiet, except for the echoes of a woman crying and a few distant voices. Paper ballots, pieces of the ballot box, red flyers, broken glass from store windows and other debris littered the street.

Max sat holding George in his lap and prayed while a few hovered around him. George's wife pushed through the circle and kneeled, wailing, "Georgie, no, not my Georgie!" Max gave him to her as she fell on top of him, crying into his still chest. Max stepped away as several women comforted

George's wife. He stood for a moment in silence, watching the grieving huddle.

Helpless to do anything more, Max went to find his borrowed horse, but it was gone. He began walking south toward his family's house. The mob had broken shop windows and looted stores. Two men stopped Max in his bloody coat, asking if he needed help. He shook his head and continued walking.

Max found the saloon door locked, so he walked around to the courtyard. He stood at the entrance, still in shock. His father sat at a table talking with his cronies.

"Maxwell, my God, are you all right," he spoke in German. "Katharina, come quickly."

Katharina came outside, "Max, my child. What happened?" She ran to him and felt his bloody shirt.

"I'm all right. I'm not hurt. It's not me. It was awful. Chaos everywhere," Max said.

Katharina held him. "Tell me what happened. We heard the shouting and gunfire. Why were you there?"

His twelve-year-old sister Elli came over to him. She spoke with slow, slurred speech. "Hi, Max. Why are you sad? Do you want a hug?" Elli asked him.

"A friend of mine got hurt. I tried to help him," he said. "I'm sad for my friend." He hugged her.

"Elli, will you please go get a beer for Max?" said his mother.

Elli went inside.

Max took a deep breath. He walked over to the men and his father. "Papa."

"Tell us," Papa said.

Max and Katharina sat at the table with the men listening to him relay the afternoon's events.

"I pray for George's soul," said Katharina. "His poor family, now without him. The girls and I will send some food over tomorrow."

Papa said, "Are you sure it was the Know-Nothings?"

"Yes, Papa. They proudly displayed banners of the Know-Nothing party's candidate. They are staunch nativists."

Papa shook his head.

Max said, "I can't believe that these men would resort to violence and lies to elect their candidate. I thought democracy allowed for differences of opinion and civil governing according to the majority."

Papa said, "My son. You have been sheltered by the illusion of egalitarian democracy in America. The greed and power-seeking of the ruling class and their political parties corrupt the republic. You have only lived in peaceful times surrounded by the coddling Jesuits. Men are capable of violence, evils and cruelty much more intense than this."

"But why do they hate us so much?" said Max.

Katharina spoke, "Fear. Fear of those different from them. Fear of losing their control. Man is capable of so much evil toward his fellow man. We left the Fatherland to escape this, but it is everywhere, just in different flavors."

"I need to go. Mother, please be careful. I don't know where the mobs went and if they'll be back. I'm going to try to find Willy to see if there's anything I can do."

Katharina walked him outside. "Do you want to stay here tonight? It may be dangerous for you to go downtown."

"I'll be safe. I dress like a native. I have to work tomorrow."

"Max, you've always been sensitive to the injustices around you, and I know today was difficult for you. Your father is the same, and we left Germany because he couldn't face it any longer. You're stronger than him. Don't forget that."

#

Max found Willy at the Freeman Hall meeting with a group of men from the German community.

"Max, what happened to you? Are you injured?" said Willy.

"No, I was at the eleventh ward when the mob attacked. I went to the brewer George Roder's aide after he was stabbed, but to no avail."

"A terrible thing. Witnesses reported that Dr. Brown stabbed him. After the mob beat Brown up, they took him to the Bremen Street station house, where he was arrested. Unfortunately, the authorities have already released him. He has friends in high places."

"Were any others killed? I haven't heard," said Max.

"No, but dozens were injured. It could have been a lot worse. It may get worse."

"What do you mean?" asked Max.

"The mobs are still running around town in pockets. They're south of the canal now. We're not sure who is directing them. We don't know if it's locals or the roughs they imported from Kentucky," said Willy.

"I was at the central market when the mob started forming today. There was no one in charge, only plenty of angry people. Stories of ballot box irregularities seemed to light the fire. Is it true? Were boys voting?" said Max.

"No! That's hogwash."

"I saw the mayor try to calm the crowd. Several other officials at the market tried to appeal to common sense. The crowd has a soul of its own."

Max and Willy turned their attention to a German community leader, Dr. Fries, who spoke to the assembled group, "Keep the peace for God's sake, but if your rights are violated, shed the last drop of blood in your veins rather than submit. We will have our militias at the ready until things calm down."

Max said to Willy, "I agree we have to be ready to fight, but we have to combat the misinformation that's out there. These men used reports of untrue events to whip up the mob."

Willy said, "People hear what they want to believe, but there isn't time to address that. For now, we need you to keep us informed if you hear anything else. Because of your quick action today, the Ninth ward removed the ballot boxes before the mob got to them. The mob also went for the Fourteenth Ward ballots, but the Irish held them off with shotguns and stones. The Irish were the ones who took our cannon back from the Know-Nothings as well."

#

The following day, Max was in his office before dawn, catching up on his work. Jon Niles agreed to let Max pay off the cost of his lost horse over time but was not sympathetic to Max's cause or any involvement in the politics of the day.

Max walked through the central market on his way to check on a project job site. He bought two different newspapers from the boys in the market, tipping them well. The reporting was incomplete and inaccurate or biased based on the paper's political position. A crowd had again assembled. He talked to men standing around to get an update on the day's events. "What are you hearing?" he asked a well-dressed man in the crowd.

"Oh, it's bad," said the man. "In the twelfth ward, they counted more votes yesterday than male residents living there. This morning, our American patriots seized the fraudulent ballots from the firehouse and destroyed them. Damn Germans; they cheat any way they can to win an election. They can't be trusted."

Max started to sweat, thinking of a repeat of yesterday's violence, this one in his family's ward. He pushed his way closer to hear the speaker perched on the crate.

"We demand the Germans return the cannon. They cannot be trusted with heavy artillery. They have threatened to turn it on the women and children of our city."

"What lies," Max said under his breath as he pushed his way back through the crowd. Someone shoved a red handbill in his chest. He grabbed it. "March Over-the-Rhine, take the Freeman Hall and the Turner Hall. Disarm the German militias."

Max headed north toward the canal. He walked briskly but didn't run so as not to draw attention to himself. He saw several men harassing a young German boy. One was holding him while the other was slapping him on the chest and face.

Max pulled the man off the boy. "Leave the boy alone," he yelled.

"He's a dirty Dutch. They're all cheats and criminals," said the man.

"He's just a boy. Fight your battles with men," said Max. The boy ran off.

"What's your problem? Are you for the dirty immigrants?"

"I'm for human decency," said Max, and he ran on his way without giving them a chance to respond. When he crossed the bridge over the canal, two German men eyed him suspiciously. Max greeted them in German, gave his name, and explained that he had information about the mob at the Fifth Street market. They sent him to Freeman Hall.

A line of men with guns stood guard in front. He went inside and showed them the handbill. They had already been warned and were organizing a defense. Men stood on alert throughout the Over-the-Rhine neighborhood, ready to warn the central command if trouble started.

Most of the shops in Over-the-Rhine were closed again today. After checking in on his parents, he had to get back to work, so he ran the two blocks south until he got to the canal, then resumed walking for the last mile. He saw groups of men hanging around, some armed. They eyed him but left him alone. By the time he sat down on his office stool, his clothes were drenched with sweat. He felt unsettled. The serenity of his life was shattered.

Max left work at about 7:00 PM. It was still daylight. He overheard a group on their way to a gathering of the Know-Nothings at a meeting hall. He went inside and stood in the back of the large crowd. There were several speakers. They were angry that the immigrants had tried to steal the election and defile their American electoral process. They formulated a plan to storm the Freeman Hall and the Turner Hall in

Over-the-Rhine. They had tried earlier in the day to march up Vine Street, led by a fifer and drummer. When they'd approached the canal, the German sentries shot at them. Several of their men were killed, forcing them to retreat. They now had more men and more guns and planned to storm Over-the-Rhine after dark. The group debated how to proceed. A professor stood and warned them that if they insisted on attacking, they must be ready to fight with arms, as the Germans would use their weapons to defend themselves. Max took deep breaths. He knew the German militia was prepared, but he didn't want to see more bloodshed.

He slipped away from the assembly and went back to Freeman Hall to report what he had heard. Then he went and sat in the courtyard with his family. His sister brought him some food and a beer. Around 10:00, he decided to go home. As he approached the canal, he heard gunshots. He stepped behind a tree and watched.

The Germans had blockaded the canal bridges with carts and wagons. On the far side of the canal, he could see a mob of black hats, many with torches in hands. They were shouting, "Kill the Dutch." And "Hurrah for Pap Taylor." The German militia fired shots over the crowd's heads. The group scattered for cover. Max watched the torches move south in retreat. He stood in the dark of the night and scanned Canal Street; only a few black hats remained. He breathed a sigh of relief but felt he couldn't safely go into town tonight.

He went back to the saloon and gave his family an update. His mother and sisters prepared food and growlers of beer for the militiamen, and Max and his brother took them to the sentry guards. Max stayed with the men on patrol.

As things quieted down, Max stepped into a yard behind one of the brick buildings. He leaned against a tree, closed his eyes and started his nightly silent prayer in his mind. "Dear God, please be with me and guide me. The past two days were the most frightening of my life. The passions and evils of men swarmed into actions that tested the citizens of this city and me. I am grateful for the opportunities you have given me—my position at Niles and the freedom to go to the aid of others. I am grateful for the German men who were there to defend the polls and fight the Know-Nothings, these militiamen who stand guard over our families and property, my mother who consoled me, made me feel safe for some moments and gave these men food. I am thankful that more people didn't die or suffer harm. I pray for the soul of George and ask you to watch over his wife and family. I am grateful I was here, and I did what I could.

"I am afraid for this country; the peace and freedoms we have are in jeopardy. You gave me the courage to act. I feel helpless to fight the forces that are so much larger than any one man—the organized politics that lose sight of what's good and just and right—they forget the humanity of the people they govern.

"I know my mission is not to take up the sword but rather to use the intellect you have given me. Tomorrow, help me stay vigilant to keep my brethren safe and deny the aggressors a victory. Talk sense into men who will listen. Watch over my family. Stop the violence. In your name, I pray, Amen."

He opened his eyes and scanned the streets. All was quiet. He slid down the tree trunk and dozed. Around 2:00 AM, he awoke to the voices of the sentries and a small group of Know-Nothings approaching the bridge with torches and guns. Max joined the sentries who stood with guns pointed at the advancing men. He shouted across the canal, "There's nothing to be gained by your attempt to cross the canal tonight. We're all Americans, but you insist on firing on us. We will defend our homes and our families. Proceed at your own peril. A larger group of men tried this earlier tonight, and several lost their lives. Go home and hug your wives. They will be happy to see you."

Max heard voices amongst the mob, then saw the torches move away from the canal. The rest of the night was peaceful.

CHAPTER 11

On Sunday, Max opened the door of the Eichen Garten for Annie to enter the bar. She noted the unfamiliar smell of beer and stopped as the men quieted and eyed her suspiciously. Faces relaxed when Max followed and closed the door behind him. "Good day, everyone," he said in German as he entered with a smile. Max gave Annie a reassuring nod and took her elbow, leading her through the room to the back door. As they passed, the men greeted him and resumed their conversations.

They emerged into the sunlight and fresh air of the rear courtyard. All the tables were full, and again, the men, now joined by women and children, eyed the fancily dressed stranger at Max's side.

Elli ran to them and hugged Max. "Max!"

"Hi, Elli," he said with a smile. "This is my friend, Annie."

"Hi, Annie. Your dress is pretty."

"Thank you," said Annie. "I brought this for you." She handed Elli a doll with a porcelain face.

Elli lit up and took the doll. "Her dress is pretty, too. Thank you." She hugged Annie and then ran to the table to show her father. Annie and Max followed.

Papa stood as they approached.

"Papa, this is Annie Bennett," said Max.

"Welcome," Papa said in thickly accented English. "You are the girl who finally gets Max to look away from his books and his work. Many German girls here today are envious of you," he said.

"It's a pleasure to meet you, Mr. Mueller."

"Beware the jealous women," said Papa.

"It's not so," Max whispered to Annie.

Papa introduced them to his friends at the table—several men from the neighborhood and then, "This is Karl Heinzen, from Louisville."

They sat at the table with the men. Max's middle sister, Helene, dressed in a simple dress and an apron with a rag hanging from its pocket, approached and introduced herself. Annie started to get up.

"Don't trouble yourself. I'm here to serve. May I bring you a beer?" said Helene.

Annie looked at Max with a smile and then nodded. "Thank you, yes."

"Annie's a Methodist," said Max. "She's agreed to have a beer with us today to find out what she's been missing."

Helene said, "Are you now? I didn't think my brother had it in him to corrupt anyone. But he's a man, like the rest of them, so I shouldn't be surprised. I trust you'll find beer to be a lot of fuss about nothing."

"Where's Mother?" asked Max.

"Upstairs in the kitchen. Marie's up there helping."

"My brothers?"

"They're about. Peter is serving at the bar, and Albert's over there with some friends," Helene said, pointing to a table of young men and women laughing and talking. "Mother sent Oskar to the baker to get the bread," and she was off to get the beers.

Max provided the family rundown, "Peter is 18, works here in the saloon and is a carpenter when he can get the work. He's the one who works at the slaughterhouse during hog season. Albert is 17; he works at the cooper shop, where they make barrels for the breweries. Marie is 15; she keeps house for a family down on Seventh Street. Helene is 14; she is a seamstress who does piecework, sewing here at home, and works in the saloon. Elli is 12, and Oskar is 10. He helps out around the saloon, delivers growlers, runs errands, and sweeps up. He's in school at Saint Mary's."

"Sounds like a family affair, then; everyone does their part," said Annie.

"I also put in my time during the summers when I wasn't at Saint Xavier. Beer runs in our blood and is an important part of German culture. We feel the Sabbath is a time to enjoy life and each other. Having a beer and singing and dancing to music are traditions that our parents brought with them from Germany."

Helene set two large steins of beer on the table in front of them. Annie looked at the beers and then at Max.

He picked his up and toasted to her, "Zum Wohl. You raise your mug and toast before you drink. Zum Wohl means to your health, or you can just say, Prost."

She picked up her stein, smiling and looked around.

Eyes were on her. The men at the table raised their beers, "Zum Wohl!"

"Zum Wohl!" she exclaimed heartily and took a sip. She puckered her cheeks.

The group cheered and laughed.

"It's good, yes?" said Max.

"Yes. A bitter taste, but good, yes," said Annie, smiling.

"You will get used to it. I don't remember what it was like to taste it for the first time. I drank it from the time I was a young boy. Drink it slowly."

"Max tells me you are new to Cincinnati? Tell me your story," said Papa.

Annie said, "My father, Charles Bennett, was raised in Saratoga, New York and moved to New York City after he graduated from Rutgers College and became a banker. My mother was raised in Boston. I grew up in New York City and attended a finishing school there. After my father passed, mother remarried Mr. Stephen Neltner, an attorney here in Cincinnati, in February, and we arrived here several weeks ago."

"I passed through New York when I came to America. An amazing city. I read that it has changed and grown dramatically," said Papa.

"Brother," said Marie, holding a large plate of food. Max introduced her to Annie. "Mother said to come up to the kitchen. She is busy preparing the Sunday food and wants to meet your friend."

Max led Annie up a narrow staircase and into a kitchen that filled the back half of the house. Two windows overlooked the courtyard. A large stove and a dry sink ran along one wall, and a large table with benches filled the middle of the room. Max's mother stood over the table, slicing bread on a cutting board. She looked up when they entered the room. Max walked over and kissed her cheek.

"Mother. This is Annie Bennett."

Her mother nodded and smiled briefly.

"I'm pleased to meet the mother of such a fine gentleman as your son," Annie said.

She grunted and nodded and went back to slicing.

Helene came up the stairs and said something in German to her mother. Annie heard her name.

Katharina scowled at Max and reprimanded him in German, shaking her head.

Annie looked at Max.

"She says she will have my hide if I corrupt you with beer and all that comes with it. She's not joking. She doesn't think your mother will look favorably on me if she learns of it."

"Mrs. Mueller, I assure you my mother knows that I am not influenced by any man against my will. I am responsible for my conduct." Max translated for his mother.

Annie continued, "I believe a woman should have equal rights as men under the law as under God and have equal opportunity to pursue her inclinations."

Katharina studied Annie for a moment. "I wish her luck," his mother grunted in German. She turned to Max and continued rattling in German. They conversed seriously for a few minutes. Marie and Helene came in and carried several more plates of food down the stairs.

"Shall we go back outside," Max said.

"It was so nice meeting you, Mrs. Mueller. Thank you for your hospitality," Annie said.

As they moved to the top of the stairs, Annie glanced into the room in the front of the house. Three windows faced the street. One wall had a large fireplace. The room was sparsely furnished; no rugs, several benches and chairs, a cabinet and bookshelves. A single vase of flowers hung from a cord in front of one of the windows. Newspapers and books were piled around the room.

When they returned to the courtyard, an accordion player moved around the grounds, blaring music while the patrons sang and clapped to a German folk song. When the musician finished the song, the crowd cheered and applauded. He started another one. Max's brothers Peter and Albert came up behind Max, pulled him from the bench onto the ground, and dragged him to the courtyard's center. They began dancing in a circle, stomping their feet and clapping in a traditional German dance. The patrons clapped to the rhythm of the music. Other men joined in the dance. When the song was finished, the brothers hugged, and the crowd applauded. The brothers accompanied Max back to the table and introduced themselves.

"That was joyous," Annie said to Max. "You dance well."

"Ha, he hardly remembers how to do it," said Peter. "Do you want to try the next one?" he asked Annie.

"Only if Max will teach me."

"Come on," said Max. He took her hand, and they stepped toward the group of men and women dancing in pairs and moving in a circle. Annie watched the other dancers for a minute, then turned toward Max. He took her hand and guided her. They awkwardly danced a beat or two behind the others, laughing and smiling. When the music stopped, he leaned in and touched his forehead to hers, both smiling. He held her hand as they walked back to their table.

Max drained his beer. Annie took several sips. "Are you hungry?" Max asked Annie.

She nodded her head. He walked her over to the table and explained the German food. Helene set down a plate of warm wiener schnitzel and potato pancakes.

"That's what you must try. My mother's wiener schnitzel is delicious."

Annie put a piece of the breaded veal and a pancake on her plate.

They sat at a table with Max's father and his friends. His father's acquaintance, Mr. Heinzen, had an audience with some neighborhood men. He was one of many German travelers who stopped at the Eichen Garten to be among their countrymen and talk politics.

"He spoke in English for Annie's benefit. "I was born in Grevenbroich, where I attended school, then studied medicine at the University of Bonn. After completing my military service, I worked at various jobs, wrote books, and moved about, living in Prussia and Switzerland. When the 1848 revolution happened in France, I returned to Germany to support the working man's uprising. When the insurrection was crushed, I had to flee, and that's how I ended up coming to America.

"I wrote for a paper in New York before moving to Louisville, Kentucky, two years ago. I publish a German newspaper from Kentucky called *The Pioneer* that advances our German causes. Max, I understand you were part of the defense against the Know-Nothings during the elections here last week?"

"I was in the middle of it," said Max. "I wasn't part of the armed defense but found an opportunity to provide information to the Turners and militias due to my position downtown. I saw the violence of the mobs and our defense first hand."

Annie looked at Max surprisedly, unaware of his role in the election riots.

Heinzen said, "I read accounts of it and have spoken with the men at the Turner Hall. I am concerned that our elections in Louisville in August may encounter similar aggressions. The American republic is being corrupted by the Federal government's passive reactions to slavery and advancing the elite class that suppresses the working class, immigrants, women and Negroes. How involved were the Know-Nothings in coordinating last week's activities?"

Max said, "The local party members had support from the national organization. Prior to the election, the Know-Nothings adjusted their message in response to local perspectives and played into their prejudices. They emphasized the anti-slavery message and de-emphasized the anti-nativist and anti-Catholic sentiments in the German wards. They brought ruffians in by boat to stir up the crowd and spread falsities on election day. The violence then became an unorganized mob that fed upon the initial sparks. Thankfully, Faran won the election, and at least in Cincinnati, the Know-Nothings haven't won out."

Heinzen said, "It appears the Know-Nothings are becoming another force against the preservation of our German heritage. I can't support them or the Democrats."

Annie said, "Mr. Heinzen, I've heard your newspaper is a strong voice for personal liberty and supports women's rights?"

"We do. We profess that women are among those individuals who are created equal and try to be a platform for diverse voices including women's rights advocates. We have published several lectures by German-American Mathilde Franziska Anneke. Do you know of her?"

"I have read some of her lectures," said Annie. She is a friend of my father's cousin Elizabeth Cady Stanton."

"I am familiar with Mrs. Cady Stanton's work. In March of last year, a group of German men met in Louisville, and we created a similar but broader platform than her Declaration of Sentiments. I was sharing it with these gentlemen before you arrived. Would you like a copy?"

"Yes, I would very much like to read it," said Annie.

He handed Annie a printed page. She scanned it, "Oh, it's in German."

Max said, "I can translate for you later. I think we've had enough of this talk of politics. It was a pleasure meeting you, sir."

Heinzen said, "I hope to exchange ideas with you in the future, Max. We must stand united in our fight. You are welcome to visit me in Louisville any time."

"Thank you," said Max. "Good luck to you in your elections. I hope yours is a more peaceful election day than ours."

"Sometimes, it is worth fighting for what we believe," said Heinzen.

"Annie, I think it's time we departed." They said their goodbyes to the men at the table. They left the patrons talking and singing in the courtyard, with Max's father asleep, his head on his forearms on the table.

Annie and Max walked along the streets toward her house.

"How were you involved in the violence during the elections this week? It sounded dangerous. The paper said that the Germans stirred up the trouble," said Annie.

"That was one paper's account of the events. I assure you that's not the case. I've read several different accounts. None of the papers reported accurately the events I saw," said Max.

"I had no idea you were part of it."

He relayed the events of the days and his role to her.

"That sounds horrible. Did you take up arms?" she said.

"No, violence is not in my nature. I'll leave that to other men. It was awful. Citizens were killing and maiming fellow citizens. I did what I could and will continue to do so in my own way. I understand it is necessary to defend ourselves when aggressors threaten our lives, but I advocate political resolutions to matters where possible. Men such as Heinzen insist on German ways and even German superiority of values beyond what most Americans will tolerate. It can be dangerous."

"You don't like Heinzen, do you?" asked Annie.

"It isn't a matter of liking or disliking the man, but I disagree with some of his positions. The Germans of America are not of one mind about how to best fit into their new country. He is at one extreme—a mini-German society within America. I believe that becoming more assimilated into American society and culture is the only way we will be accepted. Immigrants should become part of American culture while keeping some of our traditions, rather than maintaining our cultural identity as a separate subgroup within America. It will lead to better outcomes for German immigrants."

Annie said, "I was happy to hear his sympathies for the plight of women. We need more men to speak up for women. I'd like to learn more about his politics. What does this say?" She handed him the printed flyer.

They stopped while Max skimmed the flyer. "The platform contains twelve declarations that free Germans believe should become part of an integrated America."

"What are they?" she said.

Max's lips moved silently as he read in German. "Let me summarize for you. 1- Slavery is a moral cancer and should not be extended to any additional territories, the Fugitive Slave Act should be repealed, and slavery should be gradually eliminated in America.

"2- Freedom of religious expression. It says Sabbath laws, prayers in Congress and Legislatures, the oath upon the Bible, the introduction of the Bible into the free schools, the exclusion of the word "atheists" from legal acts, etc., are all open violations of human rights. He's apparently not a Christian and certainly not a Catholic."

Annie said, "Do you know that? He may be a Christian, yet believes that imparting even his own beliefs through the government violates human rights. Just like he can advocate for women's rights without being a woman."

"Hmm." He looked at her. "Well, it goes on to say that we, therefore, consider the recognition of the Roman hierarchy in this country as anti-Republican, its position as anti-democratic and its continuance as highly dangerous." He skimmed down the page further, "They fear the history of the clergy and its past influence in Europe; it will bring ruin to America. They advocate that Catholic bishops and Jesuits not be allowed in America. Well, so much for religious freedom. He seems to want it both ways. He is an extreme radical."

Annie said, "I have read that the Pope's influence is counter to democracy, and those within the church plot to infiltrate and run America."

"What papers are you reading? Editors write what they believe people want to hear if it aligns with their position. I spent six years living among the Jesuits. The Jesuits believe that reform in the Catholic Church begins with the reform of the individual. They teach a doctrine of 'Men for others,' sharing our gifts, pursuing justice, and having concern for all men, regardless of their stature in society. I agree the hierarchy of the Church in its history has its dark spots, but what you read is preposterous."

Annie said, "You were raised by men at Saint Xavier who taught you 'Men for others.' I'm not enamored with the slogan."

"It's a philosophy; the word translated doesn't mean only the male sex. Its meaning is people, not just men."

"I look forward to you educating me first hand as to why the Catholics are not evil and trying to usurp America. Regardless, I agree with his point that we must respect religious freedom and separate it from our government. I believe we can respect each other's beliefs and practices as long as we do not harm each other. What else does it say?"

Max continued reading and paraphrasing for her. "3-Welfare of the people. Hmm. The government needs to stop granting land to wealthy speculators and instead give land to people who need it. It proposes a national office of colonization and emigration to provide for immigrants, who are exposed to so many sufferings, wrongs and abuses, and so on. Rights of workers. Free schools, including the teaching of German—we already have that here in Cincinnati.

"4- Direct elections by the voters, rather than the electoral college, 5- Free trade. 6- Internal improvements, 7- Foreign policy, 8- Women's rights." Max read directly from the document, "The Declaration of Independence says that all men are born equal and endowed with inalienable rights including life, liberty, and the pursuit of happiness. We adopt this principle and believe that women, too, are among 'all men'. That's all it says about women's rights."

"It's a start, and I'm glad they have it as part of the platform," said Annie. "Anything else?"

Max continued reading and highlighting, "Rights of the Negroes, Penal laws, Military laws, limits of legislation. Individual freedoms; it mentions temperance laws as a specific example of challenge to personal freedoms."

Annie said, "His positions are far-reaching."

"As I said, he doesn't speak for all Germans. I applaud his defense against the forces detrimental to Germans and other immigrants, Negroes and women. Still, his radical positions and insistence that there be an identifiable German community within America is a futile objective."

"But taking a stand and advocating for what he believes is admirable."

"As is his right in this country," he said.

"Will you write out a translation of the entire text for me? I want to understand where the interests of women and the interests of this Louisville platform intersect. There may be opportunities to collaborate in the future."

"That sounds like a great assignment for one of my brothers," said Max. "I'll get it for you. So, what did you think of your afternoon in the Rhineland?"

"It was like nothing I've ever experienced. The families all seem to know each other as if they're relatives. It was very relaxed and devoid of formality. I liked it. I didn't know you could dance. I liked watching you."

Max blushed. "I'm glad you enjoyed it. What did you think of my family?"

"Your mother works very hard, as do your sisters and brothers. Your family doesn't have means, but they provide a place that brings comfort to many people. I don't think your mother liked me."

"She has never been one to express affection liberally. She bears the burden of the family, and it has hardened her. She manages the saloon business, keeps the house, and raises the children. My father is not strong-willed, drinks too much and lacks motivation. She accepts it."

"Her English is limited," said Annie.

"She understands more than she speaks, but yes. Because of her limited English, she rarely ventures south of the canal. She's a hard-working, bright woman. Papa owns the saloon and is the head of the household in name only. She is often frustrated with him, and his conservative nature has limited their prosperity."

"Is she proud of you and what you've accomplished?"

"She wants her children to rise above our family's position. She is happy for my rising stature but wary of my American values at times. I feel guilty moving away from the German way of life and for what I have while she and my father struggle. My brothers and sisters will also struggle to earn a decent wage and take advantage of America's opportunities. I wrestle with whether I should pull them out of the neighborhood or let them be."

"I understand your concerns for them. The immigrant's concerns in this city are your family's concerns—it is very personal to you. Next week, I am interviewing for a teacher's position in the Tenth District School. If I teach there, I will see the children of this neighborhood first hand."

"That is wonderful. You will be a good teacher and a progressive influence on the girls."

"And on the boys," she said.

"Of course."

Annie said, "The boys become the men. The men hold the power. Women's lot in life cannot change without altering the perspective of men. Pointing out what's unfair or what needs to change from the outside isn't enough. Men make the rules."

Max stopped them at the corner of Annie's street and took her hands. "Thank you for coming with me today. I enjoyed your company."

"Me, too. You are the sole warmth I feel in this city. You brighten my day when I am with you."

Max looked around to ensure no one was watching, then kissed her. Annie eagerly returned the kiss.

"You still missing New York?" he asked.

"Yes. New York, people with open minds, new ideas. I appreciated the conversation with Mr. Heinzen today—hearing an educated man with a propensity to act against injustice. It's encouraging. In New York, I attended lectures and discussions and had vehicles for expressing my ideas. I'm still searching for those, here."

"I need to go. I have accounts to review before tomorrow morning," he said. "Thank you for the flower. Max touched the daisy in his breast pocket and gave her a lingering kiss. Good luck with your interview this week."

"Thank you. Can we see each other again next Sunday?" said Annie.

"I will look forward to it."

He escorted her to the gate of her house, opened the gate and watched her ascend the stairs.

"Good night," she said before going inside.

CHAPTER 12

Annie sat in the large room across a table from three men dressed in coats and ties. They introduced themselves and explained they were from the board of examiners, charged with assessing and hiring the best possible teachers for Cincinnati's common schools.

Mr. Brooks began. "I see Mr. Neltner, a lawyer of sound reputation and standing, has referred you to the School Board and vouched for your character and qualifications. We respect Mr. Neltner's recommendation, but given he is a relative by marriage to you and our duty to entrust the education of Cincinnati's children to qualified teachers, we will proceed with our interview. Do you have any letters of recommendation?"

Annie handed him a letter. "I have this from the Thacker Collegiate School in New York, where I finished my education."

"Any others?"

"No." She shook her head.

"Did you bring the requested writing sample?"

Annie provided a letter she had written, demonstrating her grammar and penmanship.

"How old are you, Miss Bennett?" asked Mr. Brooks.

"I am 18 years old."

"What is your marital status?"

"I am unmarried."

"Good. Do you have a betrothed?"

"No."

"Are you courting a gentleman?"

"Does that matter?"

"It does. We need to understand your availability to commit to a position. If you marry, we expect you to resign from your position."

"Why?" said Annie.

"Married women have responsibilities to their husbands and households that prevent them from teaching in the schools."

"Are married women prevented from teaching by law?"

"Not by law, but by common practice in the Cincinnati schools."

"Are married men prevented from teaching?"

Mr. Brooks looked up from his paper over his reading glasses. "No, of course not. Men earn the wages to provide for their families. It is not a conflict for them." He glanced at the other two examiners, then continued. "What is your previous teaching experience?"

"Would you allow a woman such as myself to continue in her position after marriage if she could demonstrate that her arrangement in marriage allowed for her to continue to fulfill her responsibilities to her students and the school board?"

"That is an improbable situation that doesn't warrant an answer."

"What aspect is improbable?" Annie asked.

"I beg your pardon?"

"Which part is improbable? That you would allow a married woman to continue teaching or that a married woman could capably fulfill her duties to the school?"

"Both. It isn't done."

"It may not have been done in the Cincinnati Schools, but I assure you that it is not impossible. You disqualify half the population and lose experienced teachers with this policy," stated Annie.

"Thank you for your perspective. Your previous teaching experience?" he asked again.

"I have tutored my sisters but have not taught in a formal classroom."

"What is your religious practice?"

"I was raised a Methodist."

"Are you a member of a church?"

"I attend services with my family at the Wesley Chapel."

"The Bible is one of the nine sections of the Cincinnati School curriculum. Are you schooled in the King James Bible and equipped to teach its lessons in your classroom?"

"Yes."

"You may be asked by parents of some students, especially Catholics, to allow their children to read other versions of the Bible. At this time, the school board has agreed to this accommodation."

Mr. Knowlton took over the questioning. "Where did you receive your education?"

"I was schooled in my home in New York City by tutors until the age of 16. At that point, I attended the Thacker Collegiate School for Women."

"I see you completed courses in astronomy, geometry, algebra, and even Latin. That's unusual for a woman. Did you grasp these concepts?"

"Of course. I received high marks. It's there in the letter."

He asked her a few basic questions to test Annie's knowledge, which she readily answered. "You have more education than most of the female teachers in our primary schools. You won't need those subjects in your position, but you're well qualified. I have no further questions."

Mr. Brooks spoke again. "Thank you, Mr. Knowlton. Miss Bennett, we have an open position teaching the lower grades at the Tenth district school on Vine Street in the German neighborhood. Most of the students are German in that school. The salary is $28 per month, given your experience. After one year, your pay will be $30 per month. You are expected to be in your classroom 15 minutes prior to the day, which begins at 9:00. You will take direction from the school principal, Mr. Nye. Can you begin next week?"

"I have a few questions," Annie said.

Mr. Brooks looked over his glasses at Annie. "Yes?"

"Am I required to teach in German? I don't speak the language."

"No, those students enrolled in the German curriculum will spend half of each day reciting their lessons with a German teacher. This is how it is done across all of the Cincinnati schools."

"If a position becomes available in the upper grades, will I be considered for it? I prefer the mental challenge of the more advanced subjects," said Annie.

"We find that the male teachers are better suited to handle the discipline of upper-grade students."

"May I be considered?"

"That is something you will need to take up with Mr. Nye once you have established yourself. Anything else?"

"What is the pay for a male teacher with commensurate experience to mine?"

"That is not your concern."

"I am not asking what any individual is compensated. I ask what the public school pay rates are?" said Annie.

"Still not a concern of yours. Do you accept the position?"

"I will not accept the position without understanding if I am to be fairly compensated for my experience and the work I will perform."

"Your salary offer is consistent with other female teachers and a fair wage for the work." They sat silently.

"Consistent with other females," Annie said, her voice quivering. "Are men with similar qualifications paid more?"

"Men have families to support. They bring more education and rationality to the position."

"They do the same work and bring the same qualifications. How is it equitable that you pay them more? It appears that the Cincinnati school board subsidizes the families of the men they employ with citizen's tax dollars."

"Miss Bennett, please be rational. We are the Board of Examiners. We do not set the pay scale for the teachers. Your tirade today only makes us question whether you have the demeanor to sit in front of young minds. I implore you to silence yourself. Do you accept the position?"

Annie took several deep, slow breaths and calmed herself. "Yes."

"Very well, then. Please step out to the secretary's desk, and Mr. Light will assist you with preparations to begin. Good day, Miss Bennett."

CHAPTER 13

Several weeks later, Max and his friend from his school days, Patrick Sweeney, sat in a saloon downtown eating dinner.

"Molly is with child again," said Patrick.

"Shannon is only a year old. You've wasted no time," said Max.

"I hope it's a boy this time. I need a son to carry on the Sweeney name."

"Congratulations, my friend."

"How about you? Isn't it about time you take a wife?" said Patrick. "You won't meet any of my family's friends I offered to introduce to you. You're not interested in German girls, either. You're very discriminating. Are you above most of the girls, now?"

"No," said Max.

"There's no one worthy of your interest?"

"Well, yes, there is one."

"Do tell."

"Her name is Annie Bennett."

"She doesn't sound German," said Patrick.

"No. American. She moved to Cincinnati from New York City in the spring. She comes from a well-to-do family."

"How well-to-do?"

"Not Longworth rich, but educated and cultured. She's rich enough to live in a fine house on Clark Street."

"What's a respectable girl like that see in a Dutchman like you?" laughed Patrick.

"She doesn't see my heritage or care about my family's position."

"Well, it can't be your face nor your incessant need for order. What's she like?"

"She's atypical," said Max.

"What do you mean?"

"She's pretty. Red hair."

"Sure she's not Irish?" joked Patrick.

"I'm sure. She's strong-willed, an independent thinker. She wants to do more than most women. She's educated in mathematics, Latin, things that most women have no use for."

"What does she want to do with an education like that?"

"She wants a profession just like a man."

"Why? Didn't you say she comes from a well-to-do family?"

"She has a mind and creative spirit that doesn't accept being told that she can't do things. She refuses to be limited by the expectations for polite women and wants to seize the opportunities around her. It's funny. She's strong, independent and ambitious, yet is beautiful and easily converses. It's like she's a perfect combination of a man and a woman."

Patrick said. "That is an odd way to describe a woman. She doesn't sound like someone who would make a good wife. She sounds too interested in herself to take care of a husband."

"She's not traditional, but I can't help myself. When I'm near her, my heart quickens, and my body wants for hers. I want to be with her all the time."

"You are in love. Are you going to propose marriage, then?"

"I don't know," said Max. "I don't know if she wants that. There's so much I don't know about her yet. I'm not sure I ever will. She's unpredictable."

"You do not like unpredictability. You hated it if I interrupted your studies to have a little fun. I don't understand your attraction, but I would like to meet the woman to see for myself. Bring her over for dinner," said Patrick.

"That would be nice. I'd like that."

"What does her family think of you courting their daughter?"

"I don't think they're excited about my family background or religion, but she doesn't care what her family thinks. Her father died, and her mother married Stephen Neltner, the attorney. They disapprove of her independent nature. They may see me as an extension of that."

Patrick said, "She may not care, but they care. Families of that stature always care. The families they marry into are of utmost importance as it affects their place in the community."

"I know," said Max.

"Have another drink?" Patrick ordered another whiskey for them.

A handsome, tall, well-dressed gentleman approached their table. "Well, well, look at you two. Still thick as thieves, I see. How are you?" The man reached out and shook hands with Patrick. He turned to Max, his blue eyes looking intensely into Max's of the same color. Max hesitated before shaking the man's hand and then looked down at the table.

"What keeps you busy?" the man asked Patrick. "I haven't seen you since graduation. Has it already been four years?"

"I have ownership in the O'Neil furniture company. I am married with a daughter and another baby on the way," said Patrick.

"Congratulations on both accounts. That's respectable. How about you, Mueller?"

"I manage the accounts for Niles & Company," said Max.

"Family?" said the man.

"No."

"Living Over-the-Rhine?"

"No, I'm downtown," said Max.

"I was just admitted to the bar. Two children myself, a boy and a girl. We just bought a new home."

"That's grand," said Patrick.

"Please excuse me," said the man. "My friends are departing. Nice to see you, boys."

"Good to see you, Aaron," said Patrick.

Max nodded his head.

"What's wrong?" Patrick asked Max after Aaron departed.

"I never liked him." Max downed the remainder of the whiskey in his glass.

"He was arrogant, and he liked to pick on us, but it was just schoolboy banter," said Patrick.

"It was more than that for me," said Max. "He was cruel. He went out of his way to ensure I didn't forget where I came from. Almost everyone else at school accepted each other for who we were. Not him. He felt entitled to look down on the rest of us because of his family's money. The brothers and priests looked the other way because of his family's influence."

"I guess I had thicker skin than you. I'm getting you another," said Patrick. He took Max's glass to the bar.

Max thought back to his third year at Saint Xavier.

#

Max was thirteen, studying alone at night in an empty classroom. Aaron came in.

"I thought I smelled something in here. Must have been your farts from all that sauerkraut you eat. God, you stink," sneered Aaron.

"What do you want, Aaron?" asked Max.

"Why are you in here all alone? No one can stand the smell of you. I can't stand the smell of you. Why don't you go back to where you came from?"

"I was born here, just like you were," said Max.

"Your mamma may have borne you in this country, but you're not a true American—born of poor immigrants that don't speak the language, hide across the canal and form secret clubs. I hear they sacrifice pigs on the altars of your churches up there."

"I am an American, the same as you."

"Oh, you're not the same as me," said Aaron. "You're not fooling anyone. You'll never be the same as me, no matter how much you want to be. You may think that if you come to this school with people like me and get better marks than me, you might be on the same level, but it will not be so. The priests know it, and you know it. You can't study your way into a respectable family. Admit it. You're Dutch scum, not American."

"I am," said Max.

"You wish," Aaron sneered.

"I am," Max insisted.

"Never." Aaron kicked Max's bench away from the desk and pushed Max to the floor. He picked up Max's papers from the desk, tossed them onto Max's chest and ground his shoe into them. "You can pretend, but you'll always be a dirty German inside." He leaned down, spat in Max's face and left the room.

Max curled up and cried silently.

#

"Max, you all right?" said Patrick, pushing the glass of whiskey across the table to him.

"Fine. I'm fine." Max took a sip of the whiskey. "Thanks," he tipped his glass toward Patrick.

"I've got some good news," Max said.

"What's that?"

"I sold some railroad stock this week and made a handsome profit."

"You're investing in railroads? That's a risky proposition. So many railroads have gone bankrupt. How did you choose the right one?" said Patrick.

"I've dealt with several railroad companies through my work. We started making steam engines for locomotives about five years ago. In the last couple of years, we started building entire locomotives. I've been studying the railroads. In looking at Cincinnati, I noticed that the business leaders and government have been hesitant to fully embrace the railroads because many are protective of their investments in the canals and the steamships. They're afraid to invest in railroads, thinking that railroads will take away traffic and revenue from the waterway transportation. But the railroads are coming, whether they like it or not and whether they invest in them or not. Someone is going to make money off of them. I decided I wanted in. Unfortunately, other cities have pushed for railroad investments more than Cincinnati, so I predict that some cities in the west will overtake Cincinnati's leadership position in commerce."

"Maybe so, but it will take years," said Patrick.

"Not as many as you think, unfortunately. Once the railway lines are laid, Cincinnati's reign will be overtaken by Chicago, Saint Louis, and even southern cities such as Louisville. Cincinnati will remain a leader in some areas, but even in pork production, Chicago is posting larger numbers of late."

"No," said Patrick.

"Yes, Cincinnati has peaked in the annual number of heads of pork slaughtered."

"But the Deer Creek valley streets are flooded with the beasts in the fall," said Patrick.

"Production numbers are reported each year, and the declining trend is clear. Never mind the pigs—the railroads. Three major East-West Railroad companies are investing in tracks to the western lands: The Baltimore & Ohio, The Ohio & Mississippi, and The Cincinnati & Belpre. Many smaller railroad companies invest in lines from these major arteries to other cities north and south. As you've said, plenty have gone bankrupt already. The Little Miami is the only one that has completed lines out of Cincinnati so far.

"At Niles, we've done business with several railroads. I got to know the men at the Marietta and Cincinnati Railroad. The Marietta and Cincinnati was formed about seven years ago to build a rail link between Cincinnati and the western end of the B&O. Two years ago, many railroads went broke, so railroad stock prices were substantially deflated. I took all my savings and bought stocks in the Marietta and Cincinnati."

"That was reckless. Weren't you afraid of losing all your investment?"

"I was petrified," said Max. "But I knew these men, and they were buying equipment from us. I prayed on it, and then I did it. Last month, Marietta and Cincinnati placed an order for ten locomotives from Niles. Ten! I knew that if they had secured the credit to buy ten new locomotives, the market was confident in them. Their stock price had soared. I don't believe that they will maintain their independence in the end, and I don't see their rail lines as being important enough to sustain their profits, so I sold the stocks this week for multiples of what I paid for them."

"You're a financial genius. You fox!" said Patrick.

"I'm no genius. It was luck and the grace of God that He decided to bless me with this fortune."

"What are you going to do with the money?"

"Invest it."

"In what?"

"I'm going to buy out Niles & Company. I think I can convince them to sell part of the business to me. It's a business that I know. I have ideas on how to make it grow. This is what I have worked for, all these years—I will be an owner, not an employee."

"Congratulations, I'm happy for you," said Patrick.

"Thank you. Please keep this all confidential. I haven't approached the Niles brothers, yet, and I haven't shared this with anyone other than you. I am meeting with Longworth next week to seek his advice. The negotiations, owning a business, who to trust, bankers and lawyers. There's so much to learn and do."

"Of course. My friend, Max Mueller, proprietor of one of the largest ironworks and machine fabricators in town."

CHAPTER 14

As Max walked out of the meeting with Conrad Windisch and Christian Moerlein, he was excited. He was confident he had convinced the two men that Niles & Company could manufacture all the iron fixtures and components for the new, larger brewery building they were planning in Over-the-Rhine. Max had known the Moerlein family since his youth, and the Niles reputation made them receptive to his proposal. He gained agreement in principle. His next step would be to meet with the architect and create a proposal. His mind raced as he walked and thought about all the components he would need to include in the bid. He envisioned creating a master schedule of items by category for the new building that he could re-use on future proposals. That would make the process much more efficient and accurate, he thought.

He detoured to Saint Xavier Church on his walk back to the office. He needed some spiritual encouragement to handle his next discussion. Max opened one of the large wooden doors in the center of the church and stepped inside. It took a moment for his eyes to adjust to the dim light. He removed his hat, dipped his hand in the bowl of holy water on the table in the vestibule, crossed himself, and walked down the center aisle toward the altar. His footsteps echoed in the nearly empty church. He passed a woman kneeling in a pew, shawl-covered head down, praying the rosary. He genuflected, crossed himself again and knelt near the front. He folded his hands, closed his eyes and rested his head on them. He breathed slowly and deeply as he prayed. After a few minutes, he stood and retraced his steps back outside.

He walked into the Niles building through the foundry and blacksmith shop on the first floor to the back stairs. He scanned the activity in the machine shop on the second floor, then approached the foreman.

"Max. How did it go with Moerlein?" said Coleman.

"I think we'll get the work," said Max.

"That's good news. You're a great salesman."

"Can we talk in the office?" said Max.

They sat across from each other at a table.

"Coleman, I am seeking your advice in confidence. You are the most critical man at Niles & Company. Without you, we wouldn't have the reputation or profitability we have. The three hundred men who work here look to you for direction."

"Thank you, Max. I appreciate your compliment."

"I know you have worked many hours over the last two years since you became foreman, and you've made many efficiency improvements. You and I have discussed our frustration with Jonathan's and James' managing of the business—their hesitancy to expand and our belief that they ultimately would like to sell the business and move back east. I would like to buy the business from the Niles brothers, and I want to gauge your interest in joining me."

Coleman looked confused. "Are you serious?"

"Yes," said Max.

"But how can you afford it? We did close to one-half a million dollars in business last year."

"I recently made a significant sum from investments. I have the capital to secure a business loan that will allow me to buy a large portion of the business. If you are interested in being a partner with me, I would be honored. If not, I'd like to retain you to help me run the business. I need your expertise. I know the financial and sales aspects, but I do not know about design and production."

"This is good news. I think your progressive nature will be good for business," said Coleman.

"Are you interested in buying in as a partner?" said Max.

"I appreciate your offer and trust in me, but I must decline. My cousin, William Sellers of Philadelphia, has asked me to join his business as chief engineer of his company. It is a good opportunity for me. I promised him I would join him within a year. I'm sorry. Had I known of this opportunity, I might have chosen otherwise."

"Is there anything I might do to persuade you?"

"Nothing Max. He is counting on me," said Coleman.

"You have a brilliant mechanical mind and are a committed man. It will be difficult to replace you. Do the Niles know of your intention?" said Max.

"No, I have not divulged my intent."

"If you will allow me, I may be able to use this in negotiating a more advantageous price. Your value is great to either them or me."

"I appreciate your confidence. I will allow it."

"Thank you. How long can you delay your move to Philadelphia? I may be able to offer you a financial incentive to stay longer."

"I will need to write to my cousin, but possibly mid-next year."

"I am putting together a proposal for the brothers. I have no interest in the sugar mill business—the southern sugar plantations have the blood of the enslaved on their hands. I will not own a business that is so directly tied to them. I see the greatest growth opportunities in the machine tool business—lathes, planers, borers, milling machines, and other heavy machinery. Beyond the casting of the equipment we do today, this business will grow as new and advanced steam engines are developed to power a multitude of new machines."

"I agree with you," said Coleman. "It is a relatively small portion of the business today, but the greatest opportunity."

"What are your thoughts on the rest of the business?" Max asked.

"The locomotive business is limited for us. Our market is the western railroads, and the overall financial health of many railroad companies is questionable. Some railroads are buying from eastern builders due to lower prices, even though the *Railroad Advocate* magazine reported that our locomotives are the best construction. So, I think this business will not grow for Niles. The other business to consider is the repairs and maintenance. We did $130,000 in repairs last year, so there is a significant ongoing opportunity there."

Max said, "If I buy the locomotive business, it's a short-term play. I could streamline the business further and then sell the business to another manufacturer at a profit. What do you think?"

Coleman said, "It's a gamble. The railroad business is going to continue to move west. Without the growth to support scale in a manufacturing shop, the operations will become less profitable."

"Ah, I see your point. I hate to think of the men who work there if those jobs go away. What about the decorative ironworks?"

Coleman said, "It was Niles's original business, and as you know, we have a great reputation in Cincinnati that gives us some advantage. The work is more custom and still relies on artisans. Although Eagle Iron Works is a tough competitor, with some of the efficiencies that I have been trying to implement, I think this can continue to be a valuable line of business but will shrink as a percentage of the profits over time."

Max summarized, "So I should offer to buy the machine tool and ironworks business, and this building from the Niles brothers and leave them with the locomotive, sugar mill and related businesses on Congress Street. I want to do more analysis on the maintenance business."

"That sounds like the best opportunities. Do you think they'll agree to split up their business and sell the pieces to you?" asked Coleman.

"Jonathan has confided in me that his wife is in poor health and would like to return east to Hartford. It's only a matter of time. If I bring them a solid offer, I can entice them. Furthermore, if they learn of the risk that you and I may exit the business, their prospects for future years will not look as good. Blymer & Morton have expressed interest in buying the sugar mill business. I'll propose the brothers sell it to them. I think I can put together an attractive offer."

"You sure you want to do this, Max?"

"I'm excited about the growth opportunities, and yes, my dream is to own a business, make it better for the people who work for me and build it into something bigger. Are you comfortable with my putting you in the mix of the negotiations?"

"I'm happy for you. It's been difficult working for the brothers. I gave them my sweat and tears for too many years before they made me foreman. You've been a great partner since you've been here. I will be fine. If this deal blows up and they discharge me, my cousin would be happy to have me sooner."

"Thank you, Coleman. Will you please keep this between you and me, for now?" They shook hands.

"I will."

"Coleman, one more thing," said Max.

"Yes?"

"Have you heard anything about the project to build the new suspension bridge across the Ohio River? I hear things are picking up again. Do you think we should try to bid on the iron work?"

Coleman said, "We looked at it about five years ago when the Ohio Legislature approved its construction. There continue to be delays in getting started. Ferry boat operators are fighting against it. Some influential businessmen in Ohio are opposing the bridge because of fears of lost business to Kentucky merchants. Others oppose it because they're afraid slaves will flood into Ohio for freedom. It will be a beautiful structure and an engineering marvel, but it will be a drawn-out project that will take years. Miles Greenwood, the owner of Eagle Iron Works, is on the Bridge Committee, so he has the advantage in winning the work. I'd pass on that one."

"I tend to agree with you, but the bridge architect, John Roebling, will be in Cincinnati next week. I am meeting him to discuss the project," said Max. "I am reluctant to pass up any opportunity to grow our business."

CHAPTER 15

Max sat in the parlor with Annie's family in response to her mother's insistence that he formally call. The girls, dressed in their receiving dresses, sat in the chairs. The boys sat on the floor. Max presented Mrs. Neltner with a box of chocolates from a confectioner downtown and Annie with flowers. Annie pulled a flower from the vase on a side table and tucked it in Max's lapel.

Annie re-introduced her brothers Anthony and John and her sister Caroline. "Caleb is away at West Point."

"You must be very proud of Caleb," he said to Mrs. Neltner.

"Yes, he has been a good role model for his younger brothers. A good student and citizen," said Mrs. Neltner.

"Where did you study, Max?" asked Anthony.

"I attended Saint Xavier College here in Cincinnati. I studied both classics and commerce."

"I want to study law, like Mr. Neltner," said Anthony.

"Good for you. A good lawyer is an invaluable man," said Max. "I am looking to retain a lawyer for a business proposition."

Mr. Neltner said, "Max, I am happy to discuss your proposition. If my firm is not practiced in your area of need, I can refer you to a reputable firm. We can step into my study before you leave to discuss business."

"Yes, you men need to shut yourself in the study to discuss such complicated matters privately," Annie said sarcastically.

"Annie, it's not appropriate to discuss private business during a social visit. Besides, we have nothing to contribute to topics of law," said her mother.

"I have read Blackstone's *Commentaries on the Laws of England*," said Annie. "I would have plenty to contribute to a conversation."

"You have?" said Mr. Neltner surprised.

"Not all four volumes, but I've made it through the rights of persons and the rights of things."

"What's that?" asked Caroline.

"Blackstone's is one of the foundational texts that law students study. Much of American law was derived from it," said Mr. Neltner. "Where did you acquire the books?"

"From your study. I hope you don't mind," said Annie.

"I don't mind. I'm just surprised. Why would you read them?" said Mr. Neltner.

"I wanted to understand the rights of men and women. I must say, as a woman, it is very disheartening to read, but I felt it important to understand our current standing if I mean to help change it."

"My word," said her mother.

"No wonder you can't remember your stitches. You fill your head with all that legal information you'll never use," said Caroline.

"I don't remember my stitches because I find embroidery work mindless," said Annie.

"All right, girls, I don't think our guest is enjoying your banter. Caroline has had several young men calling on her. Perhaps you know them, Max?" said Mrs. Neltner.

"Who are you seeing?" asked Max.

Caroline walked to the credenza and picked up a stack of calling cards. She read one, "Mr. Oliver Wright, he is an attorney at law. He boards at the Washington House but is establishing his practice and soon will have his own home."

"No, I haven't met Mr. Wright," said Max.

"Mr. Levi Wickersham. He is a dentist who is in practice with his father," said Caroline.

"No, I'm afraid I haven't met him either."

"That's enough," said Annie.

"Well, these gentlemen are most handsome and from fine families. I feel fortunate to have fallen in with such an attractive circle of acquaintances soon after moving here. Annie, we should arrange an afternoon of games with Max and one of my callers. It would be fun," said Caroline.

"Let's wait until you know more about them than their occupation before we arrange a family social gathering, can we? It doesn't sound like a way I want to spend my day off," said Annie.

"Max, how did you enjoy *Uncle Tom's Cabin* at the theater last week?" asked Mrs. Neltner.

"It was an intriguing performance. I found that the stage version of the story softened many of the more direct illustrations of the injustices in the author's text. I believe the play intended to introduce the book's questions without offending. It didn't have the same impact on me as the book did. Have you seen the play or read the book?"

"No, I have not had the opportunity. I have been so busy setting up the house. I understand the author, Harriett Beecher Stowe, resided in Cincinnati?" said Mrs. Neltner.

"Yes, her father was the president at the Lane Theological Seminary, which hosted a series of debates on slavery in the 1830s. I understand she found much of her inspiration for her writing while living here," said Max.

"Mother, I have a copy of the book if you want to enlighten yourself?" said Annie.

"Thank you, Annie. You and I are in firm agreement in our anti-slavery point of view. I don't need to be convinced."

"Are we? Limiting the further spread in new territories and total abolition of slavery are not the same," said Annie.

"Enough, Annie. Let's keep our conversation polite. We've talked about this. Why don't you tell us about your first week of teaching?"

"I am enjoying it so far. I have a class of twenty-five girls. Some of them are so timid I can hardly get them to speak up in class. It will take some time for me to help them build up their confidence."

"You are doing admirable work, Annie," said Max.

"I had an argument with the principal," said Annie.

"Over what? You didn't mention this," said Mrs. Neltner.

"He's pig-headed, and I told him so."

"Annie, why would you say such a thing to a man and the head of the school?"

"I told him that all of the classes needed to be mixed classes of boys and girls immediately. The school board authorized a trial of this model for this year to test whether it will help girls' learning without impacting the boys. It's ridiculous to wait another year to mix all the classes. The girls are hampered by separate classrooms that do not have as rigorous a curriculum as the boys. I have to teach a class of all girls, and he refuses to consider taking the issue to the schoolboard but is content to wait another year for more progress. Ridiculous."

"That didn't take long," said John.

"What?" said Annie.

"You defying authority and getting yourself in trouble," said John.

"John, enough from you," said Mrs. Neltner. "But Annie, he's right. You need to be on your best behavior and show more respect for the principal."

"He was condescending and treated me like an idiot. I have more education than he does," Annie said, raising her voice.

"Annie, you have to control yourself at school. If you are terminated from this position, your reputation in Cincinnati will be ruined. You insist on working, and you'll have limited options if you burn this bridge," said Mrs. Neltner.

"Why don't we discuss this later," said Mr. Neltner. "Let's give Annie and Max a few minutes to themselves. Max, would you like to discuss attorney services before you leave today?"

"Yes, thank you, sir."

"Knock on my study door on your way out, then."

"Thank you."

The rest of the family excused themselves, and Mrs. Neltner closed the door to the parlor on her way out.

"They all gang up on me," said Annie. "They never attempt to look at things from my perspective. I can only do so much for these girls if the school continues to separate them and treat them as frail half-wits—these poor girls. I can't do it. How am I supposed to do it?" Annie began to cry. She turned away from Max.

He touched her shuddering shoulder. "Annie, it will be all right."

She turned and let him put his arms around her. "Shh."

"I feel like everything I try to do is an uphill battle. The world is against me; my family is against me," said Annie.

"I am at your side." He hugged her. "I see your struggles."

She looked up at him. They kissed.

"I don't know if I can do it," said Annie.

"Do what?"

"Continue at school. Continue fighting against the world. All of it."

"Annie, I don't know what it's like to have my opinions, actions and very being questioned just because of my sex, but I've had to face bigotry and beliefs that presume a place in the world for me. Can I share with you some of the ways I try to deal with it?"

She nodded her head.

"I know you're not one for rules, but I have a code of Max's rules to live by. I won't bore you with all of them, but one that has helped me avoid frustration is to leave things that I can't change and instead focus on the things within my sphere of influence.

"The world has placed men above women for centuries. It is ingrained in our culture, government, and institutions, such as education. You won't be able to change it by yourself, but you can start with Mr. Nye—he's in your realm of influence. But to change him, you need to work with him, not fight him. And you need to be calm and rational, or he'll disregard you as a fanatic. Build his trust in you and find ways to help him, and once you've established a rapport, you can start to influence him. Try it this way. He may prove that he cannot accept you; some men can't. If so, he's a lost cause, and you move on to a different battle. It will take time. In the meantime, do what you can within your circumstances."

"You make it sound easy, but it's not," said Annie.

"I know it's not, and patience comes more naturally to me than you. But you have so much passion for changing things for the better. It saddens me to see you so unhappy. Can I share something else with you?"

"What's that?"

"When I was at Saint Xavier, they taught us a simple way of praying called the 'examen of consciousness' to help reflect on your day, see the good in your life and focus on tomorrow. I have done it every night for the past ten years. It helps me be more appreciative and intent in my life. I think it could help you."

"I don't think I can pray like that, like a Catholic," she said.

"Don't think of it as a prayer, then." He took her hands in his. "Close your eyes. There are five steps. I'll write them down for you, but let me guide you through them. Are you willing to try it with me?"

"I don't know what you mean, but yes," she said.

"Trust me. Breathe slowly. Step 1 is gratitude. Give thanks for the things in your life. What are the blessings you have? The people who matter to you. The home and the food you enjoy. The beauty you see around you."

He spoke slowly and softly and paused at each step. "Step 2 is asking for God's help. Open yourself up to his love and support. Step 3 is to review your day. What did you do today? What stands out? Who are the people you were with? What emotions did you feel? Step 4, reflect on your shortcomings. Where did you fall short of your expectations or God's expectations? What could have gone better?

"The last step is renewal. Look ahead and think about what you will do tomorrow or maybe what you will do differently. Is there a specific thing you will do?" Max remained silent for a minute. He saw a tear roll down Annie's cheek. He wiped it with his finger.

She opened her eyes.

"That's all it is, but if you take a few minutes every day, it might help you feel better."

"Do you consistently do it every day?" she asked.

"I've missed a few, but yes. We did it as a group when I was young. I continued on my own after that. Do you feel any better? Calmer?"

"I always feel better when I'm with you," she said.

"Me, too." They kissed.

"I have exciting news." He told her of his railroad stock purchase and windfall.

"Max, that's wonderful. I'm happy you are realizing your dreams of owning a business. How can you remain so calm with so much to think about and do?"

"The examen helps. This is why I wanted to talk to Mr. Neltner about a lawyer. I need to consult someone on some legal aspects as I put together the proposal for the Niles brothers. The proposal has to be complete and compelling so that they will accept it. I must think through all alternatives, pick the right combination and contemplate their objections in advance. I have so much running through my head and only have the mornings and evenings to work on it."

"Max, I can help you," Annie said.

"You've read Blackstone's law books, but I think I should retain a practicing attorney. Thank you, but I'll talk to Mr. Neltner."

"No, not with your legal questions. I was very good at writing persuasive arguments when I was in school. Would you like me to help you write your proposal?"

"Would you?" said Max.

"I'd love to. You dictate all the elements that need to be considered, and I can draft them into a letter. Or you draft it, and I will review and critique it."

"It is urgent that I approach the brothers before conditions change or I lose my courage. Can you start tonight?"

"Yes," she said. "I couldn't imagine you losing your courage. My impressive business merchant."

"We need a place to work together. I can't have you to the Carson's house. That would be improper. So would working at the Niles office. It can't be any place too public, either. Let's plan on the sitting room at the Eichen Garten. It's not too far from here. If others are meeting in it, we can go upstairs in my family's house."

"Are you sure it will be all right?"

"It's the best plan I have for now. Let me talk to Mr. Neltner. I'll come back here at 7:00 this evening to walk you to the Eichen Garten.

CHAPTER 16

Max met with Stephen Neltner's law partner to discuss company structure and other legal parameters to consider in a contract to buy a portion of Niles' businesses. He also met with his mentor, Nicholas Longworth, who gave him advice on negotiation. He consulted with his friend Patrick Sweeney regarding personnel matters and Coleman Sellers on alternative organizational structures and accounting figures. Finally, he met several times with his banker about the terms of the loan.

Over the next three weeks, he and Annie spent many evenings with papers spread across the Eichen Garten sitting-room table. She quickly picked up the business concepts and was good at generating ideas for Max to consider. He would take these and methodically analyze them, discarding all but the best options. Annie kept a log of the aspects of the purchase that would go into the offer and then drafted a beautifully written proposal that was clear, concise and compelling. They became comfortable challenging and teasing each other. When Max would become disillusioned or less confident about the venture, Annie would paint a picture of his success or cheer him up. When Annie became frustrated at school or with something else, Max would tease her or help her put things into perspective.

They sat at the table next to each other with the proposal in front of them. Annie read out loud, making final edits. Max had his sleeves rolled up, and his hair was disheveled from repeatedly running his fingers through it.

Elli brought in two steins of beer and a plate of bread and mustard. "Mama asked me to bring you this."

"Hi, Elli." Annie hugged Elli.

She stroked Annie's dress.

"How high can you count tonight, Elli?"

"One two three four five six seven eight nine ten," said Elli.

"Eleven," said Annie.

"Eleven," Elli repeated.

"Twelve."

"Twelve."

Annie continued to fifteen, with Elli repeating.

"Good. Now, how many fingers?" Annie held up four fingers.

"One, Two, Three, Four."

"Well done. Good job Elli."

Max smiled at Elli. "Thank you for bringing us the beers, Elli."

"And the bread and mustard," said Elli.

"And the bread and mustard," said Max. "Annie and I need to finish our work, so please leave us alone, now."

She hugged Annie, hugged Max, then skipped out into the saloon.

"I think you've set the price too high," said Annie. "Based on the projections you calculated for the machine tools, your profits are meager."

"I want to be fair. They've been good to me."

"You're too kind. Take the emotion out of it."

Max noticed a man eyeing Annie and him from the bar. He got up and closed the door. "Annie, you of all people. Asking me to ignore the impact on people."

"This is business. They are wealthy men. It's not like you're squeezing pennies from a wage earner," she said.

He thought about it silently, chewing his nails.

"Stop that," she said.

"What?"

"Biting your nails."

"I didn't realize it."

"Max, your projections don't account for a reduction in business that might occur should there be a war."

"I know it could happen, but I don't know how to account for it," he said. "The machine tool business might increase if we need to build artillery or supply an army. Maybe even the ironworks, too. On the other hand, if we go to war with the South, we would lose some customers. If there's a war, there will be a reduction in overall commerce. Will military business offset that?

"How are we to know? We have to pray the war would be short-lived. Besides, the Niles brothers will not take less than their business is worth based on my wild prediction of a war." He bit his nails and thought. "I'm leaving it as is."

Annie pressed him. "If they don't like the price, you can negotiate. You're not competing with anyone but yourself. Start with a lower offer."

"All right. You've convinced me. You are a brilliant woman." He scratched through the numbers in several places.

"What a high compliment for a woman."

"I didn't mean," he said apologetically.

"I'm teasing you."

He looked up from the paper and shook his head, laughing. "Thank you. He kissed her."

"For what?" she said.

"For all the help you gave me over the last three weeks. For all your ideas, your honest criticism, which you gently presented. Your beautiful penmanship. Your support."

"It's been one of the most satisfying things I've ever done," Annie said. "I've cherished the mental stimulation, the trust you placed in me and the time we spent together. I am going to miss our evenings together."

They kissed again, holding the kiss longer. Max brushed his face against hers. "Oh, Annie. I—we need to stop. We still need to finish." They broke apart. "Will you rewrite these two pages we changed while I read through it one more time?”

#

The next evening, Max asked his parents to talk with him in the sitting room at the Eichen Garten.

“What is so important we have to sit down in this room behind a closed door?” Max’s mother sighed, speaking in German. “I have customers to take care of.”

“Peter will serve the customers. Take a break, Mother, please,” said Max.

“Does this concern Annie? You two have been spending too much time together alone. People are talking. I don’t like her,” slurred his father.

“Papa, you hardly know her.”

“She’s opinionated and outspoken,” his father declared.

Max took a deep breath and started to address his father’s remark, but his mother interrupted him, “I don’t think that’s what he wants to discuss, Karl. Let the boy talk.”

“Annie has been helping me put together an offer to buy a business. I made an offer today to buy out part of Niles & Company from the Niles brothers.”

His father said, “By yourself? Do you have other investors? That is a substantial business. How can you afford to buy it?”

“I have been saving my money since I started working there. I invested my money in railroad stock, and now I have enough to secure a mortgage to buy it. If they accept my offer, I will be the sole owner of a company with 150 employees. The business has good growth opportunities. I will pay off the loan in five years.”

His mother put her hands in front of her mouth. “I can’t believe it. My son will own such a large successful enterprise.” She closed her eyes. “When we came to this country, we dreamed of what America might hold for us. We found political freedom but not success beyond supporting our family day-to-day. When you were born, and every day since,

I prayed that my children would find happiness and enough success to be truly free. One of ours has done it, Karl." His mother wiped tears from her face.

His father remained silent.

Max went on, "Something else I want to discuss. I have enough money now that I want to pay for Oskar's tuition at Saint Xavier. He's young enough that he can enter there and get a degree. They have closed the dormitory, so he'll live at home, but he'll get the same education as I did."

His mother continued to cry. "Thank you, Max."

His father stood up. "No. I won't let the Jesuits corrupt my son. Look at you. You're ashamed of your German family, our language, our culture. You're too good for us. Saint Mary's will give Oskar an adequate education."

His mother shook her head back and forth. "No, we should let him. It is an opportunity for him. Look what it has done for Max."

"Yes, look at what it has done for Max. He's an American aristocrat now," said his father.

"Papa, I am only trying to fit in enough to be a success."

"Your definition of success—Focus on money; become one of the elite who will have others toil for you. Speculate in stocks, taking profits while other men lose their shirts."

"Papa, that's not who I am," said Max. "I will be a fair employer and create new opportunities for men. I acknowledge the realities of the country I live in but work to change things. What would you have me do? Sit in the saloon and drink all day and hope that the world changes to help me?"

Papa slapped him across the face, then stood and left the room.

Max fought back the tears, his face red, and stared at the table.

His mother said, "Max. I am proud of you. We all do what we have to do. We each have to live our own life. You are a good person. Papa is a good person, too. He hoped America would be better for him, but it has defeated him. He thinks you have rejected your German heritage and become part of the American establishment that rejected him. He resents you because he sees you chasing American materialism, but inside, I think he sees you are succeeding where he failed, and he is too proud to be happy for you. I am happy for you and wish you good fortune." She stood and squeezed his shoulder.

"My boy," she kissed his cheek, then left him alone in the room.

A few minutes later, Max's brother Peter came in. "So, you're a rich businessman, now. Is our life not good enough for you? What's this? Papa says you want to take Oskar and feed him the same manure they fed you at that school. Teach him how to look down his nose at us and throw us some table scraps, too?"

"No, Peter. Why do you say that?"

"What's wrong with you? Why have you sold out to the high and mighty? You have to have fancy clothes and live downtown, ride in carriages with your fancy girlfriend, while we work our asses off just trying to survive."

"Peter, you don't understand."

"Oh, stop. You think you're the smartest German to walk the streets of Cincinnati. What don't I understand?" Peter was shouting now.

"Calm down. Let's go for a walk," said Max.

"No, I need to get back to work. Somebody has to do the work around here," said Peter.

"Peter, I'm sorry I was the one Mr. Longworth picked to go to Saint Xavier. It could have been you if he had gone to a different corner to buy his paper. He picked me. I don't know why—I know it was nothing I did. God put me on that corner, and I thank him every day for it. Mother and Papa left their families to come to America so that we could have a better chance at a good life. Mother has worked hard every day to give us as many opportunities as possible, but there's only so much she can do. The world is not fair, and many of our friends and family will work their entire lives here in

Over-the-Rhine and never have enough money to do anything beyond getting by. Things are no longer as they used to be. It doesn't work here the way it did in the Fatherland. There isn't enough from the saloon to support Mother and Papa, you and the others. You have to prepare to take care of yourself.

"You're not destined to do what our parents did. You can choose, and it can be something that you enjoy doing. You can have satisfying work, a sense of accomplishment for yourself."

"What are you talking about? You read too many books," said Peter.

"Don't you have dreams? Something more than working here at the Eichen Garten?"

"I don't know."

"You have dreams. When we were young, you wanted to go west to California," said Max.

"I was a kid. I can't leave Mother to fend for herself."

"You can, Peter. You're a man, now. You're allowed to be what you want to be. It's uncomfortable, I know, but it's also exciting. America has so much more to offer you. Don't be like him and let it defeat you."

"Don't talk about Papa that way," said Peter.

"I'm sorry. He's our father, I know, but he's given up. You're too young for that. Look around you at other men for other possibilities. I'll help you. Education is one way. I can help you go to college if that's what you want. If not that, then find a trade, go west, do something. Don't stay here."

"What about the girls? I can't leave them," said Peter.

"We'll help them find their way. It's harder for girls. Their options are much more limited, and their fate rests in many ways in the hands of others. It's not fair, but hopefully, it will get better for them. We'll help them figure it out. You can't let that stop you."

"And Elli?" said Peter.

"Oh Jesus, talk about unfair," said Max. "Society discards people who are slow like her. She's family, and we'll make sure she always has someone. I'll make sure. It's not all on you."

"You're asking me to be like you and abandon the family."

"No, not abandon them. You have to take care of yourself so that you can help them." Max went on, "Please don't hate me. Yes, I've made compromises and had to make choices that pulled me away from my heritage and family. I struggle with that. I still love my family and always will. The world is moving forward like a herd of buffalo. We need to adapt or be stampeded by it. I'm doing the best I know how in this rapidly changing world so that I am in a position to help you all and as many other people as I can."

Peter looked at the ground. "I always looked up to you. We were together every day. You were smart and fun to be around. When you left for school, I cried at night for weeks. I felt like you wanted to get away from me and us. I resented you for it."

"I didn't know. I was eleven years old. I'm sorry. Can you understand why I did it?" Max asked him.

"Yes."

"Can you forgive me for hurting you that way?"

Peter stayed silent.

"Will you think about what I said? What your dreams are, and why you have to do something about them?"

"Maybe," said Peter.

"Think about it. We'll talk next week."

"But Mother and Papa."

"They'll be sad, but they'll understand."

CHAPTER 17

Annie's carriage pulled up in front of the Burnet House Hotel, billed as the grandest hotel in all of America. The massive, five-story structure spanned an entire block and was capped by a gold dome with an American flag flying atop it. Basement windows spanned the lower level along Third Street, with a large stone staircase in the center leading up to the Corinthian column-flanked entrance. Annie saw Max leaning against the stair wall, reading a newspaper. "Max, here," she called out the window to him.

Max folded his paper, placed it under his arm, and walked to the carriage. He took her hand and helped her down. She wore her school attire—a gray dress with a corded petticoat and boots.

"Using every moment of the day, I see," Annie said.

"It was nice to breathe the fresh air while reading the news for a change. How were your students today?"

"Very good. I'm seeing some of the shy girls start to open up."

"And Mr. Nye?" asked Max.

"He and I are still getting used to each other."

"But you're smiling today, so it's a good day. Shall we go in?"

"Look at this building? It's grander than the Astor House in New York," said Anne.

"Old Nick is one of the major investors in it. He says it's the finest hotel in the west. A showpiece that will attract more commerce to Cincinnati," said Max.

They walked up the stairs, and a doorman held the door. They entered the large, elaborate lobby rotunda, furnished with imported furniture, Turkish carpets, and crystal chandeliers. They moved out onto the veranda that looked down onto Third Street, the riverfront and across to Kentucky. They retreated inside to explore further. Max studied the modern lattice-work iron bridge across the courtyard and the iron steps leading downstairs to a bar, cigar shop, barbershop, and other small stores. They made their way back upstairs to the entrance to the dining room.

The host greeted them. "We can seat you right this way in the family dining room." He led them to a side dining room where several families were already dining.

"Excuse me, sir," said Annie, "but we would like to eat in the main dining room. It is more elegant."

"I'm sorry, ma'am, but that is the gentleman's dining room. If the two of you are dining together, the family dining room is your only option unless you want to dine in your hotel room."

"We're not registered guests of the hotel. We're here to celebrate Mr. Mueller's new business deal over dinner. I promised him a lovely meal." She moved toward the main dining room.

"Ma'am, I'm sorry, but women are not permitted. I assure you the food will be as delicious," the host said.

"I am surrounded by children all day long. I don't care to pay for a fine meal and try to enjoy it in the company of children."

"Sir, if you could help here." He looked at Max.

Max said to Annie, "Annie, it will be fine."

"No, it won't. This is ridiculous," she said.

"We have our reputation to maintain, and it would be improper to admit you. It would offend the gentlemen in the dining room. You must understand, sir," said the host.

"Why are you addressing him?" she said. "Are these gentlemen so faint of heart that they would be offended by the presence of a woman while they dine? Do they make their wives and daughters eat in the pantry with their servants at home? What do they think I will do to offend them—open my corset and flash my bosom at them?"

"Ma'am, now you are being coarse. Sir, I am sorry, but I must ask you and the lady to..."

Annie cut him off, "Stop addressing him as if I were a child and he were my father. He is not in charge of me."

A small crowd of men had formed in the restaurant and lobby and watched the escalating scene. The hotel manager came over. "Mr. Matthews, can I be of assistance to our guests?"

The host said, "Sir, this lady has requested to dine with her companion in the gentlemen's dining room. I have offered them a table in the family dining room, but she has rejected it."

The manager turned to Max, "Sir, you must understand that in a fine establishment such as ours, we must maintain the integrity of the gentlemen's dining room. It would not be proper to admit a lady. Please let us serve you a meal in the family dining room tonight, and perhaps you would like to return another evening with your associates to dine in the gentlemen's dining room. We also have a lovely ladies' ordinary."

Annie screamed, "Why are you ignoring me? I'm standing right here in front of you."

Max took her elbow and whispered, "Annie, calm down. You're not going to get anywhere, like this."

Annie glared at the manager and then at the host. She yanked her arm from Max's hand and walked across the vast lobby toward the exit. Max fell in a few feet behind her. The crowd of men parted as Annie walked toward them. They were laughing. One of the men said to Max, "You need to take that bitch home and pound some sense into her."

Max stopped, turned, and swung at the man's face with all his might. The man ducked, stood, and punched Max, knocking him to the floor.

Annie heard the scuffle and men's shouts, turned, and saw Max on the floor, blood coming from his cut lip. "You beasts!" She ran back to help Max. He shook his head. She helped him up and toward the door.

One of the men muttered, "Well, we see who wears the trousers in that family."

They stepped out into the evening light and slowly walked down the stairs. When they reached the sidewalk, Annie asked, "Are you all right?"

"I'm fine."

She tried to dab the blood on his lip with her handkerchief, but he pushed her away.

"God, you're just like the rest of them," Annie said.

"What?" said Max.

"You men are all the same. You wouldn't let me speak for myself." In a low manly mocking voice, she continued, "Annie, calm down. This isn't getting you anywhere. Mr. Man. I'm in charge. Tell the woman what to do, just like a child."

Max shouted, "What did you think was going to happen? Did you think that all of a sudden, the manager would reconsider and say, 'oh, I'm sorry, ma'am? You're right, our long-standing policy of only admitting gentlemen to the gentlemen's dining room is outdated and unjust, so in front of all these men, I'm going to make an exception for you because you're a righteous woman from New York who has made me see the ills of society's ways. Please do come in and sit among these gentlemen and enjoy your dinner.' Is that what you thought would happen?! That wasn't going to happen, and if it did, wouldn't that have been a lovely celebration for our business venture? You're not going to make progress for women if you don't know when to push and when to show self-restraint. You're smarter than that. Use your brain." He calmed and slowed, "You can do so much. I know you can; I've seen it. But you spoiled tonight for us. The dinner doesn't matter to me, but I don't want to be with someone who spits venom and carries a dark cloud about us all the time. You'll bring me down. I can't do it."

He started down the sidewalk, her following. "There's a hack stand just down the block," he said. She caught up to him, and they walked in silence to the taxi stand.

Max gave the driver the fare. "Please drive the lady to Clark Street. It's just past the bend in the canal off of Western Row."

He helped her into the carriage, then pulled an envelope from his breast pocket. "For you. Goodnight."

He watched the cab pull away, then turned to walk home.

Annie cried quietly in the carriage. She wondered if her temper tonight had ruined her relationship with Max. She was used to it. Her moods, bluntness, emotional outbursts, resistance to accepted behaviors and conviction that the world must be fair had scared away every other man or boy in her life. Everyone except her father. She had thought Max was different. He was accepting of her, encouraged her and treated her as an equal. He was gentle, kind and patient. When they had differing opinions, they seemed to accept it without it degrading their friendship. Had it been a mirage? Had she wanted this companion so much that she missed the signs of his masculine entitlement?

She noticed the envelope in her hands. 'Annie' was printed neatly on the front. She turned it over and fingered the wax seal with his initials, 'MM'. She thought of his smile, blond hair and calming blue eyes, soft, reassuring voice, easy-going laugh, and lips when they kissed. She opened the envelope and removed a single sheet of paper.

In Max's draftsmen-like, perfect block letters, it said:

ANNIE,

PERFORM THE EXAMEN OF CONSCIOUSNESS DAILY
TO HELP YOU IN YOUR MISSION TO BRING JUSTICE
TO THE WOMEN OF THE WORLD.

    1. GIVE THANKS
    2. ASK FOR GOD'S SPIRIT
    3. REVIEW THE DAY
    4. FACE YOUR SHORTCOMINGS AND ASK
        FOR HEALING
    5. LOOK TOWARD THE DAY TO COME

I LOVE YOU,
MAX

Annie closed her eyes and sobbed quietly in the carriage.

CHAPTER 18

Max stood at the Eichen Garten bar several days later, eating and drinking a beer.

His mother stared across the bar at him.

"What?" Max asked.

She pointed to his swollen lip.

"Just a little scuffle," he said.

"It's not like you to fight. Did Annie cause this?"

He took another bite without answering her.

"She's a wild one dressed up in a pretty package," she said.

"Yes," he smiled. "She is that."

"Mrs. Beck told me that her daughter, Lina has Annie as a teacher in school. She said that Lina is getting high marks. She must be a good teacher. Why haven't you brought her around lately? Elli has been asking about her?"

"We had words."

"Men and women have words. You move forward," said his mother.

He changed the subject, "Where's Papa? Will he speak to me, yet?"

"He is already upstairs sleeping for the night. He accepted that it would be good for Oskar to go to Saint Xavier, but then Peter told him about your conversation."

"Oh." He took another bite and chewed. "Mother, you understand that Peter has to leave."

She nodded. "Yes, I know. In America, children leave their parents to pursue their fortunes and adventures. The family is secondary to personal and economic pursuits."

Max finished his beer. "Thank you for supper, Mother. I have to go back to the factory. Now that it is my business, I have more to do."

"Yes, I understand this," she said.

#

Annie sat in the parlor after dinner with her family. Mr. Neltner chuckled aloud as he looked at his newspaper.

"What makes you laugh out loud, dear?" asked Mrs. Neltner.

"This cartoon. There was a report in the paper several days ago about an incident at the Burnet House Hotel. A woman tried to eat in the gentlemen's dining room. Her escort attacked the host to try to gain admittance for them. There was a scuffle, and then they threw the two of them out on the street. This cartoon turns the woman into Oliver Twist as if she's been neglected and outcast." He handed her the newspaper and pointed to the cartoon depicting a young woman standing at the doorway to the Burnet House dining room, bowl in hand. A group of well-dressed, fat men sit in the dining room, smirking. An imposing man stands before her, looking down, scowling. The woman says, "Please, sir, may I come in." Underneath the cartoon caption reads, "Olivia Twist banished to the ladies' ordinary."

Annie's brothers moved to their mother's side to look at the cartoon. John snickered and looked at Annie, then at Caroline.

Annie sternly eyed John and shook her head.

"What's going on?" said Mrs. Neltner.

John started laughing.

"What's so funny?" said Mrs. Neltner.

"It's Annie," said John.

"What do you mean?" She looked at Annie.

"That's Annie's cartoon," said John.

"What do you mean? Annie, is this true?" said Mrs. Neltner.

"Yes."

"How did the newspaper get it?" said Mr. Neltner.

"I submitted it to them anonymously."

"It's a good drawing," complimented Anthony.

"Why?" said Mrs. Neltner.

"Because the Burnet House policy and the men in that dining room are ridiculous, and it needed to be called out," said Annie.

"Why did you insert yourself into their affairs like this?" Mr. Neltner said.

"Oh, no. Annie, please tell me it's not so," Mrs. Neltner covered her mouth with her hand in astonishment. "It was you?"

"Yes, it was, but it didn't happen as the paper reported," said Annie.

"My word." Mrs. Neltner covered her face with her hands. "What have you done? This family's reputation."

Caroline said, "You'll have me shunned along with yourself if you're not more careful, Annie. First the behavior at Mrs. Pendleton's, and now this."

"No one knows it was me," Annie said.

"Did you try to enter the gentlemen's dining room?" asked Mr. Neltner.

"Yes."

"With Max?"

"Yes."

"Did he assault the host?"

"No. A man insulted me as we were leaving, so Max tried to defend my honor."

"He instigated a, what did it say, a scuffle?" said Mr. Neltner.

"No, a man said something derogatory about me, so Max and he exchanged blows. Then it was over," said Annie.

"What did the man say? Tell us. It must have been bad to result in a fight," said Mr. Neltner.

"Something about me being a bitch. I don't know; I hardly heard it."

"Annie, such words," said Mrs. Neltner.

"They're not my words. You insisted I tell you. Max came to my defense. Can you blame him?"

"Did they throw you out of the hotel?" said Mrs. Neltner.

"No, we proudly walked out."

"Proudly? Hardly? It sounds shameful," said Mrs. Neltner.

"I thought Max Mueller had more sense than that," said Mr. Neltner. "To allow himself to be drawn into a fistfight in a public place. You may be an unknown in this town, but he is not. Did anyone identify him?"

"I don't know. I don't think so," said Annie.

Mrs. Neltner said, "Why did you put him in this position? Your unorthodox behaviors. This was your idea to challenge the decorum at the Burnet House, wasn't it? Is this unfortunate incident why Max hasn't called on you lately?"

"Yes."

"I don't blame him, but it's just as well. He's a fine young man, educated but not educated in the ways of proper society. If you kept up with him, you would lose your standing," said Mrs. Neltner.

"I regret the whole incident. I didn't mean to cause Max or anyone any harm. Mother, I don't have much standing in Cincinnati society. Caroline's reputation and standing are forming and fragile right now, I know. I apologize if my behavior put that at risk."

Mr. and Mrs. Neltner exchanged glances, surprised at Annie's apology.

Her mother said, "Annie, you can have a place in Cincinnati society, but you must be willing to work for it. You've chosen to teach in the schools for now, but we can still arrange for callers if you desire it. You've been so down the last few days. It might be just what you need."

"Not now, Mother, thank you."

"The rest of you. You are not to breathe a word of this to anyone outside this family, is that understood?"

"Yes, ma'am." the children agreed.

"Annie, this letter came for you in the post. It's from Seneca Falls," said Mrs. Neltner.

"Cousin Lizzie." Annie tore open the letter and read it. "She says there will be a Women's Rights convention here in Cincinnati in October. She isn't coming, but her friend Lucretia Mott and others are. I met Mrs. Mott the summer I spent with Lizzie. She suggests I attend." Annie perked up.

"That's nice, dear. Something to take your mind off of things. Maybe channel your energies into a more proper form of advocacy besides breaking decorum in public and slipping anonymous cartoons into editor's hands?"

#

The boy knocked at the door to Max's office.

"Excuse me, sir, I have a letter."

"Yes, come in," Max stood and moved to him. "Who is it for?"

"Dunno. I can't read. Lady told me to bring it here."

Max took the envelope from him. "It's for me, thank you."

"Yes, sir." He started to leave.

"Wait, boy." Max took a coin from his drawer and gave it to him.

"Thank you, sir."

"You're welcome." Max returned to his desk and sliced the envelope with a letter opener. He recognized Annie's neat handwriting. His heart quickened as he read the letter.

Dear Max,

My soul has ached of late for your companionship. I fear my outburst in public has pushed you away from me, and for that, I am deeply regretful.

I have reflected on your words that evening and used your examen to inspect my own sentiments and behaviors. It has been enlightening, and I long to converse with you about it.

Your outburst brought forth your true feelings, which I am grateful to now know. Your revelation of your feelings has caused me to acknowledge that my nature is to excite quickly, and this may injure the emotions of others. There is wisdom in your counsel to consider how to convey my feelings and achieve my objectives.

I am troubled by your characterization of a dark cloud. I long to rid myself of these melancholy feelings, which overwhelm me at times. I have found that your company and encouragement have helped me to lift this cloud for periods. My father had a similar influence on my demeanor. I have lost him, and now I fear losing you, too. Please don't give up on me. I can't suppress my passions, but I vow to try to temper them, considering both the impact on those around me and the likelihood of an intended outcome.

I am sorry for casting you as the same as all men. This gross characterization is unfair. You are an extraordinary man. I do believe, however, that you have instinctive behaviors like all men that, although not intentional, insult the worth of women. It is so ingrained in men—in society, everywhere—that men can't recognize it when it happens. If you could walk a day in my petticoats, you would feel the relegated place men have given women. I can't fault you for this, and you show more respect than most toward women as individuals. I appreciate your attempt to understand with as much empathy as possible without actually being a woman.

I pray that our bond can be mended and continue as I feel a part of me is missing without you.

Warmest Regards,
Annie

CHAPTER 19

Annie pushed open the school door, hoping for relief from the heat, but stepped into a blast of hot, humid air. A few children lingered on the sidewalk, and men and women passed by, wrapping up their daily errands. Max sat on the stone ledge in front of the school building. He had his hat and jacket off, collar loosened, and sleeves rolled up. When he noticed her approaching, he stopped writing in his notebook and smiled.

"Miss Bennett, the great educator of German girls."

"Max, what a surprise," she said, smiling. "Oh, I'm a mess. It is sweltering in the building." She pulled back loose strands of hair from her face.

He hopped down from the ledge. "You're beautiful." He took her chin and kissed her.

"Let's move. I can't be seen here like this," she said.

He offered her his arm, and they proceeded away from the school.

"You look like you could use a beer," he said.

"Yes, please. Eichen Garten?"

"Unless you have another favorite saloon?"

"A cool drink under the trees would be nice." They walked.

"Max, I'm sorry for that night."

"I read your letter. You don't need to say anything more. We can have differences of opinion and remain friends."

"My friend and my protector. Thank you for defending my honor."

"I attempted to. The incident diminished my manhood."

"Fighting between men is an uncivilized means to resolve differences. When has physical violence ever led to a satisfactory outcome? Men and their fights and wars. It's barbarian," said Annie.

"I agree with you, but when provoked to a certain point, one must defend himself and his honor, or in this case, the lady's. I never learned to fight properly, unlike my brother Peter, who has had plenty of street fights."

"Thank you. Did you catch what the man said as we walked out?" she said.

"What's that?"

"Something about knowing who wears the trousers in this family. I'm not sure if it was your honor or mine that he was insulting."

"Both, I think," he laughed.

As Max pulled open the door of the Eichen Garten, a tall, broad, dark-haired man stood in the doorway.

"Max," said the man.

"Officer Ficke." Max tipped his hat.

The officer eyed Annie. "Ma'am," and stepped back to let them inside.

"What's going on?" asked Annie.

"That's one of the ward watchmen," said Max. "He probably stopped in so my mother could show her appreciation."

"Does she serve him dinner?"

"No," he chuckled, "she slips him money to keep the saloon from getting in trouble for violating the temperance laws."

"Oh."

"I know it must seem nefarious to you, but it's how things work. Pay a little something to the watchmen, and they look the other way. She probably did give him a beer, but not dinner. He's a nice fellow, and it's good to have him on your side."

"I knew things like that went on in New York, but I had no idea Cincinnati had corruption," she said.

"There's plenty of unofficial politics, here."

Max made eye contact with his mother behind the counter as they walked through the bar. She nodded, and he nodded toward the courtyard. They sat across from each other at a small table in the nearly empty garden.

Peter approached them, smiling, "Big brother. Hi Annie, we haven't seen you in a while."

Max asked, "Ready to talk about dreams, yet?"

"I think I am."

"What are you thinking?" asked Max.

"I thought about what you said. I want to go away, but not to California. It's too far."

"What then?"

"I want to go to college."

"That's good. I'll help you. Let's talk later."

"Do you want beers?" asked Peter.

"Yes, please."

When Peter left, Annie asked, "What was that about?"

"I'm taking a stronger hand in steering my brothers' futures. Papa doesn't know what's possible for them. I'm enrolling Oskar at Saint Xavier this fall. I convinced Peter that he must get out of Over-the-Rhine and follow his dreams. He hasn't felt like he could leave our parents."

"What about Albert?" Annie asked him.

"He's next. There are so many young people here whose futures will be to eke out an existence if they don't see role models to show them there can be something else. Encourage them, give them a lift."

"I see it every day at school," said Annie. "What about your sisters?"

"I know. I don't know the answer there, yet. For now, keep them from getting knocked up and marrying young."

"Max!"

"Well, it's a common path. I've seen it plenty," he said.

"You're a good soul," she squeezed his arm.

"Annie!" Elli came running to their table and bounced into Annie's arms.

"My goodness, what a nice greeting," said Annie.

"Papa said you weren't coming back," Elli said to Annie.

"Well, here I am, now."

Elli, plump and sweating, sat on the bench adjacent to Annie and set her doll on the table. Annie put her arm around her.

Peter delivered the beers.

"I hear Papa wasn't too happy with me about our conversation?" said Max.

"He was full of piss when I told him about it, but he's mellowed. Yesterday, he told me he wanted to see me be my own man, just don't become an American prig like you." Peter laughed.

"I'm happy I could take the heat off you," said Max. "Where is he?"

"I think he's up the street with his friends."

"Is Oskar here?" said Max.

"Yes. He is cleaning out the spittoons."

"Send him out here, will you?"

"The beer tastes good on this warm evening," said Annie.

"You're growing to like it, eh?" said Max.

"Don't tell my mother, but yes. My cousin Lizzie sent me a letter this week. She said the Sixth annual Women's Rights Conference will be held right here in Cincinnati in October. She wants me to attend."

"Really. Are they sure Cincinnati is ready for a Women's Rights Conference?"

"I don't know. Ready or not, here we come."

"Based on the reaction to the blasphemous cartoons I've seen of late in the newspaper, I'm not so sure." Max looked at her, smirking.

"You saw it?"

"My eyes about popped out of their sockets. That was pretty good."

"Not my best," said Annie.

"You have more?"

"They've published six of mine. I send them in anonymously."

"Well, I'll be. That's a creative outlet for your frustration. I'm impressed."

"The conference will have some of the country's leading women's rights speakers in attendance. I haven't had this type of discourse since I left New York. I can't wait. I'm going to write Lizzie and offer my assistance."

"That's good. I like seeing you this excited about something."

"My one concern is getting the board of education to approve my absence from school to attend."

"Maybe your step-father can help with that if he's willing. He knows some of the board, doesn't he?"

"I can't ask him; that wouldn't be the proper channels."

"If you want to attend, think about the most likely way to achieve your objective," said Max. "If you think going through the chain of command at school, starting with Mr. Nye will fail, it may be worth imposing on your step-father for this. Sometimes your connections are the only way to get something done."

"Oskar!" said Max, hugging him.

"Miss Annie," said Oskar.

"Hi, Oskar. Working hard, as usual, I see," said Annie.

"Yes, Ma'am. Thank you for paying for me to go to Saint Xavier, Max. Papa told me. I can't wait to start."

"It's a special place, Oskar. It's a privilege to attend, and you'll need to work hard at your schoolwork, but I think you're going to love it there. I'm here for you if you have any questions."

Oskar nodded.

"Oskar, can you run an errand for me, please?"

He nodded again.

"Run to Miss Annie's house and knock on the door. Tell them who you are and that Miss Annie is with Max at the

Eichen Garten. She'll miss supper, but she is safe with Max. Can you do that?"

"Yes."

"Tell me what you're going to say?"

Oskar repeated the instructions.

"Very good. The address is 421 Clark Street. It's just across the canal from 12th Street. Do you know it?"

"Yes."

"It is a red brick house with an iron fence across the front. 421." He placed a coin in Oskar's hand. "Be off then, and report back to me when you return."

"He's adorable and a smart boy," said Annie.

"He's watched six older siblings and is wiser for it. Sometimes we forget he's only ten." Max felt the day's heat and saw the sweat running down Annie's face and neck toward her bosom. He longed to free her from her heavy dress but settled for, "Elli, why don't you go see if Peter needs help."

Elli stood and skipped into the bar, allowing a little more air to move around Annie.

"Sorry, she can be a little smothering," said Max.

"She's fine."

Max reached across the table and interlaced his fingers with hers. "I'm happy to see you. I missed you."

"Me, too," she said.

"I have something to ask. I need your help," said Max.

"What is it?"

"I'm giving a lecture at the Ohio Mechanics Institute on Friday with my friend, Patrick Sweeney. We are presenting modern ideas for improving manufacturing efficiency. We're sharing some of the innovations we've developed together to help Patrick's furniture company make chairs and other furniture more cost-effectively. We've created new ways to make furniture by considering the assembly process when designing the furniture and creating custom tools for specific pieces of furniture."

"That sounds fascinating. Can I attend?"

"I don't think so. We don't need a repeat of the Burnet House incident. There are no women members of the Institute. Maybe someday. I would, however, like you to read my lecture and help me polish it."

"I would be happy to," said Annie.

"Thank you. He pulled his written speech out of his notebook and handed it to her. Can we meet to discuss it tomorrow evening?"

"Yes. Here?"

"Why don't I call on you at home? I think we need to get your mother more comfortable with me."

"You're probably right. She was happy when I told her that I hadn't seen you since the incident. She is worried about the impact you will have on my place in society."

"Because of my heritage?"

"Because of your family's class, your place in society," said Annie.

"Are you worried about it?"

"No, of course not. Besides, it's not as if we're betrothed. My mother gets ahead of herself."

"I am certain she has your best interest in mind."

"And hers," said Annie.

#

The next evening, Max bathed at the public bathhouse, then called at the Neltner's home. He visited with the family for fifteen minutes, and then they retreated, allowing Max and Annie privacy in the parlor.

They embraced. "You smell nice, of soap," she said. "How are things going with the purchase?"

"We closed the deal and are working through the transition. It's hard to say goodbye to the men I won't be working with anymore—the ones staying with Niles. I think they are fearful of their future, but I cannot concern myself with it. We moved all the heavy equipment and inventory this week. I've named the new company Miller Industries, spelled M I L L E R. The sign will go up next week."

"Why did you change the spelling?" she asked.

"This spelling will reduce the chance of prejudice from potential customers. Besides, I am an unknown outside of Cincinnati, and my name has no bearing." Max stretched his neck by leaning his head from side to side. "I'm exhausted, but the disruption will soon subside, and we can get back to building for customers."

"And you have this lecture to prepare in the middle of it all," she said.

"The date was set long ago, so I couldn't change the timing. This will be good publicity for Patrick's furniture company and Miller Industries—assuming it is well received by the men at the Institute. To that end, let's see the marks you have put upon my paper, teacher."

Annie began sharing her feedback. "It was interesting to read about your innovations. Artisans and craftsmen don't need to know everything themselves but specialize in doing one thing very well. You made it sound modern and noble. Some will still object. I suggest you speak to the new system's benefits first to paint the picture of the advantages to broader society and working men. Describe the ability to afford goods—in this case, furniture—that previously was only available to the more well-to-do. Once they agree with you on the merits, then elaborate on how to do this. Reiterate the benefits in summary at your conclusion, so that is the last message they hear."

"Hmm. I believe your suggestion will be more persuasive and impactful. It's brilliant."

She smiled at the compliment but continued with her feedback. "In this section, you elaborate with so much detail that I fear your audience will lose interest or not understand. I tried to edit it to get the key points across without all the details. They need to understand enough to be convinced, but not enough to create a chair-making factory themselves."

"I see your point—good. My inclination is to be thorough and precise. It's the German in me."

"Which makes you an excellent businessman but will bore your audience to tears. I corrected some grammar here and here. You're almost there," Annie said.

"Thank you. I am grateful for your assistance."

"I am happy to do it. Do you want to practice your opening?" said Annie.

"What. Here? Now?"

"Yes. It is most important to start with confidence. Stand there. Use the table for a podium." She didn't give him a chance to disagree. "Begin."

Max started awkwardly, then fell into a smooth delivery. "Good morning, gentlemen. Imagine a time when every man can furnish his home with fine furniture and goods, reminiscent of the fancy furnishings of the town's well-to-do. Every man earns a wage that allows him to buy and furnish a home, and he can spend some leisure hours with his family that he previously spent at work."

"Good. But look at them and smile," said Annie.

"What?" he said.

"Smile."

"Why?"

"How you say it is as important as what you say. I stand and speak all day long. Granted, it's to children, but I've found that if you put them at ease and engage them so that in their mind, they feel as if you're talking to them directly, they're more likely to be receptive and comprehend."

"Are you certain? Aren't the words more important?"

"Your words are important, and the transcript of your lecture will be invaluable, but most listeners can't retain all the words you say. You have this short time to leave them with an impression and some key messages. Besides, your smile and blue eyes are captivating—use them."

"To women maybe, but men don't see such things," said Max.

"Not consciously, but they do."

"Have you learned this from your pupils as well?"

"I learned this from books on oration and mental philosophy. Practice it again. This time look at me for five seconds, then move on to the imaginary man in the back of the room, then up here. Move your eyes naturally, and smile."

"How am I supposed to read my lecture if I'm doing all this looking men in the eyes?" said Max.

"That's why you should practice. Become familiar enough with your material so you can continue to speak extemporaneously if you lose your place."

Max practiced several more times with Annie critiquing, then he said, "Ich bin fertig."

She raised her eyebrows for translation.

"I'm finished. Done. Tired."

"Very good. You will be masterful."

He walked over to her and put his arms around her. "Thank you." They kissed and embraced each other tightly. He felt the tension of the day leaving his body, replaced by the warmth of her closeness.

His physical contact, his smell, and the taste of his mouth impassioned her. She pressed her chest into his. She felt their closeness and sensation of her breasts against her corset and yearned for more.

His breathing became heavier as he kissed her neck and down to her bosom.

She kissed the top of his head and squeezed to feel the muscles of his arms through his shirt. She pulled back, creating space between them. "We need to stop. It is sweet, but my family." She eyed the door.

He nodded.

"I should go. I have final editing to do tonight." He put on his jacket and gathered his papers into his notebook. They kissed again, "Good night."

"Good night."

Annie stood on the porch, watching him move down the street until he was out of sight. She wished they could spend more time together. She thought about him often when they were apart. He was the first man for whom she had such strong feelings. When they touched, the warmth inside her was pleasing and exciting, but it was more than that. When she was with him, she felt strong, as if she could do anything. He respected her thoughts and what she could do.

They were getting over their spat at the Burnett House and settling back into the closeness she had missed when they were apart. She realized that as much as she wanted a world where she could do whatever she wanted, that was a child's fantasy, and the world didn't work that way for men or women. Max was able to support her while acknowledging the realities of life in a manner reminiscent of her father. She wished all men could be like them.

CHAPTER 20

Max walked alongside Oskar across the canal and south into downtown. Oskar took two steps for every one of Max's but had no trouble keeping up. It was a hot summer day, the sun beating down.

"Will I be in class with old men like you?"

"What? No, the older boys are in separate classes from the younger boys. You'll start with a group of boys, all about your age. As you master the lessons, you'll be promoted to the next grade. Most boys will be promoted with you, but some learn faster and some slower. You'll study Greek, Latin and German, history, poetry, and English in your first couple of years. Then as you get older, you'll start your study of mathematics, sciences, and philosophy. If you want, you can study commerce as I did."

"How many years will I study there?"

"Six."

"Why aren't there any girls at the school, like at Saint Mary's?"

"All schools used to be for boys only. Saint Mary's added girls so they could get their educations, also. Saint Xavier has decided to remain boys only."

"Will they ever allow girls?"

"I don't know. Someday, I suppose they will."

"I like girls."

"Me, too," said Max. "You'll still see your sisters and friends in the neighborhood."

"Luis said that the priests beat you and try to make you a priest."

"Most of the priests are very nice. They care about their students and want to help them. If you misbehave, you might get a whipping, but I don't think you need to worry about getting a beating. And Saint Xavier isn't a school for priests. Boys who want to become priests study at a seminary. Pay attention. Here's where you turn left—at Sixth Street. That building on the corner is the Ohio Mechanics Institute. I gave a lecture there last week."

"Lecture like a teacher?"

"Not like school. I was teaching other men how to build things better in their factories. There's the school," Max said, pointing, "on the corner at Sycamore Street. Just past it is the church, with the steeple."

They stepped into the school office. "Good afternoon, I'm Max Mueller. I'm here to register my brother for classes this fall."

"Good afternoon," the young Jesuit brother, dressed in a cassock, stood and shook hands, "I'm Brother Ryan. Are you the new student?"

"Yes, sir," said Oskar.

"Welcome. We're happy to have you join us."

"Are you familiar with the college?" Brother Ryan asked Max.

"Yes, I'm an alumnus. I graduated five years ago."

"Welcome home, then."

"I've met with several of the priests about Oskar attending. I just need to complete the paperwork and pay the first session tuition and fees."

Max completed the provided paperwork while Oskar sat quietly in the hall, studying the daguerreotypes of previous classes of men that adorned the walls. Max handed over the papers and a bank check for $45 to the brother.

"We will have an orientation for new boys on Wednesday and Thursday, August 29 and 30, starting at 7:30 AM each day. Classes start Monday, September 3," said Brother Ryan.

"I would like to speak with Father Horstmann. Is he in today?" asked Max.

"Yes, I believe he is in his office. Do you know the way?"

"Yes. Is there someone who can show Oskar around the school while I meet with Father Horstmann? Maybe one of the summer school boys?"

"Yes, I can arrange that."

"Oskar, after your tour, you walk home, all right?"

"Yes, Max."

"See you later."

"Thank you, Max." He hugged his brother at the waist and then sat back down.

Max made his way upstairs and down the familiar hallways, wooden floors creaking in the silence of the empty building. He knocked on the closed door.

"Enter," said a deep voice from within.

"Max, what a surprise. Come in, please," said Father Horstmann. The two men embraced. The priest shut the door and pointed to a chair in front of his desk. "I'm updating my German class for the coming year. We have more and more German students attending, and I need more advanced lessons for them. What brings you here today?"

"I've enrolled my youngest brother Oskar to begin classes in September."

"Is he as serious a student as you were?"

"He's as intelligent and more streetwise, for certain, as the youngest child. I don't think he's as serious. This generation takes their position and future more casually, I think."

"I don't think there will be another student at Saint Xavier as serious as young Max Mueller was. You were pretty hard on yourself. I trust the more balanced personality you allude to will serve him well."

"He's a good lad. I'm happy to entrust him to the Jesuits and provide him a path out of Over-the-Rhine."

"We will not take the trust you have given us lightly," said the priest.

"I'm grateful, Father. For what this place gave me. I wish living in the dormitory were an option for Oskar. He would benefit from the environment, I think."

"Yes, sadly, we had to close the residences last year due to declining enrollment. We only had a few students from out-of-town. I think some of the civil unrest in the city the prior few years scared some away. So, now we are exclusively a commuter college. How is your family?"

"They're getting along fine. My mother works too hard. My brother Peter helps out, and my sisters, when they can."

"I haven't been to the Eichen Garten in a while. I need to visit one Sunday. The garden there is delightful. And your baby sister. Is she still with them?"

"Elli is fine. She loves people and is oblivious to the world outside her home."

"God bless her and your mother. How's your father?"

"He's no better. He's a shell. He just drinks and is angry."

"I'm sorry, Max. He doesn't hurt your mother or sisters, does he?"

"No, thank God. Drink doesn't affect him that way. Father, I don't know if I ever thanked you for your guidance and support. You helped me make sense of my situation when I was young. If it weren't for you, I probably would have kept believing that his behavior was my fault. You pushed me, and you made me believe in myself. Now, I'm trying to step in for my brothers. My father resents me for it, but he's allowing it because, deep down, he knows they deserve more than he can give them. I pray that I can do enough for them."

"Hebrews 13: God equips those he calls," said Father Horstmann. "I'm glad you're there for them. I read in the paper about your new company. You're doing well in your business."

"I'm excited about my prospects," said Max. "I enjoy the pursuit and the work, and I think I can grow the business and create more opportunities for men while enhancing my position. Sometimes, however, I struggle with my choices and the impact they might have on others."

"What do you mean?"

"For example, I bought railroad stocks a couple of years ago when the price was low and then sold them this year when the price was high at a profit. That's how I was able to buy my business. I know that my profit was someone else's loss. Is it right in the eyes of God to profit at someone else's misfortune or expense?"

"Did you break any of the Lord's commandments in buying and selling this stock?"

"No, of course not," said Max.

"Are you pursuing your business in good faith?"

"Yes."

"Are you striving to be moral and just in your business dealings?"

"Yes."

"Breaking any laws?"

"No."

"I offer you these thoughts on your moral question. This country's political and commercial systems are ripe for unscrupulous, materialistic and self-serving behavior. You can choose to join a monastery and pray that other men will rectify these flaws. That is one course of life. You, however, have been blessed with the intelligence and talents to work with people. I think God calls you to serve him by working to improve the world around you. It is a fact of American life that financial assets assist you in that mission. Making a profit need not be a sin if you do so with an honest heart, do no harm and serve others with your wealth.

"This is one priest's opinion. We could study and debate this forever, but you must provide for your family. Continue to pray on it."

"I don't have a family yet," said Max.

"You have your brothers and sisters and your community."

"There is a woman that I met. I may love her."

"Tell me about her."

"She's a remarkable woman. One of the most intelligent and imaginative I have ever met. It's strange. She's unconventional, but I've never been so attracted to a woman."

Father Horstmann said nothing, so Max continued, "She's strong-willed and independent. She was raised in New York, where she attended an advanced school for girls. She wants to have a profession and resists the traditional place of women."

"A free spirit?"

"Yes. She advocates for the rights of women and the poor, the Negroes, anyone who is oppressed."

"A principled, free spirit." Father Horstmann nodded.

"More than principled. An advocate, a fighter. Sometimes she's downright testy in advocating her position. She's not afraid to make a scene or push back against men. Even though she isn't ladylike in the traditional sense, I can't help my feelings toward her."

More nodding from the priest.

"We spent time working on my business proposition. We spent many hours together. She thinks of things that are so helpful. Says them in a way that makes me receptive to hearing them. She fills in the places where I'm less accomplished. I feel so comfortable with her, like one of my sisters, except her voice, her touch, they make me feel more alive, happy when I'm near her."

"It sounds like you're in love."

"I want to propose marriage to her, but I'm not sure she'll marry me or any man. I sense she has similar feelings for me, and we have become dependent on each other's friendship. She would be a true companion."

"I sense hesitation?"

"It's a few things. She's not Catholic. She was raised Methodist Episcopal. She's a Christian with a good soul. She teaches in the common schools in Over-the-Rhine. She shuns her mother's upper-class pretense of charity for true humane caring."

"God has blessed mixed marriages, but you could not be married in the Church unless she converted to Catholicism. You have to decide for yourself if your beliefs are compatible and consider the souls of your children," said Father Horstmann.

"Children?" said Max, as if the topic were irrelevant to their discussion.

"Would she agree to have them baptized Catholic?"

"I don't know if she wants children."

"That is God's decision, isn't it?" said the priest. "If you marry, he may bless you with children. You can't interfere with that. That would be a mortal sin on your soul."

Max lowered his head and rubbed his forehead with his fingertips. "She's a progressive woman."

"She can be progressive on many things, but on this, there is no room for debate. You know this."

Max closed his eyes. "Let's assume we get past that," said Max.

"All right." The priest looked at Max, the slightest upturn of a smile on his lips.

"I'm worried that she's so unconventional it won't work."

"Be more explicit."

"Her ideas of what a woman should do and what a man should do are so far from what's expected that I'm not sure I can do it. I don't know how she expects me to act in a marriage. I'm afraid I'll say or do something that will disappoint her."

"Her ideas are far from what's expected by whom? By her family? By your family? By you? By God?" questioned Father Horstmann.

"I don't know. I suppose I mean society."

"Is that what's most important to you and your marriage?"

"You and your questions. I feel like I'm back in school. You never give me answers," Max said, smiling.

"I don't have the answers, Max. You need to answer the questions yourself. And you and your lady need to talk about these things before you decide to marry. What's her name?"

"Annie."

"Annie sounds like an extraordinary woman and an equal to you in many ways."

"Father, help me."

"I will pray for you. Come back any time you want to talk."

They stood and embraced.

#

Max and Patrick stood at the bar in their usual downtown saloon.

"Whiskey?" asked Patrick.

"You know I prefer beer," said Max.

"Come on, don't make an Irishman drink alone."

"Whiskey, it is."

"Two whiskeys," Patrick said to the man behind the bar, who poured for them.

"Sláinte!" said Patrick as Max toasted "Prost!" in unison.

"Did you read the reviews of our lecture in the papers?" asked Max.

"Yes, we achieved our objectives of getting our businesses in the papers, but the press was mixed. The *Gazette* bought your message and made you sound like the second coming of Christ for Americans. Most of our business customers read the *Gazette* because it's pro-business and tells them what they want to hear."

Max said, "On the other hand, the *Enquirer*, which caters to the Democratic perspective, picked up on that gentleman's questions about the direct impact on skilled artisans—both wages and value of the work they do."

Patrick said, "That gentleman was Michael Gampfer. He's a union proponent who has worked his way through several trades over the last few years. He pushed for updates to the

Cabinet Maker's Book of Prices, instilling higher standard prices and wages. It's the de-facto guide that all of the Cincinnati cabinetmakers use to set our wages and prices."

"We haven't seen that level of organization in the ironworks industry yet," said Max. "I expect it's just a matter of time, and I plan to propose some ideas on how to structure wages in a way that isn't exploitive but is also flexible enough to work with some of our new production methods. I'd rather work with unions than against them. I think I've picked the right man to lead the effort for me."

"Max, I have to say I was in awe watching you up there on the stage. The audience was locked in on you and seemed to be enjoying themselves. Not sure how you did it, but you took a technical topic and made it seem like they were sharing a drink with you." He clinked glasses with Max and downed the rest of his whiskey. "Another, please," he motioned to the barman.

"Annie helped me with the speech."

"Annie did?"

"Turns out she knows a lot about persuasive oratory. She helped me restructure the speech, edited it for grammar and gave me some teacher pointers on how to better present to an audience."

"I'm surprised. How is she?"

"She's very well. She and I are even closer."

"Yeah?" Patrick raised his eyebrows and smirked suggestively.

"No, not that. I mean, believe me, there have been evenings when I wanted to explode when I was near her, but I won't soil her reputation."

"So instead, you soil your drawers."

"Bug off. Seriously though, can I ask you something?" said Max.

"Sure."

Max lowered his voice. "I've never been with a woman. I generally know what to do. I understand my part of it, but I don't know what a woman's part is. I went to the Mercantile

Library and looked at an anatomy book. There's no chapter on it."

"You did what?" said Patrick, laughing.

"You know me. I don't like leaving things to chance."

"What do you want to know?"

"How do you know where to put it?"

"It will happen naturally. She'll help you. If you're not sure, ask her. She'd prefer that over you poking around."

"I don't know," said Max.

"Spend some time exploring her. And be honest with her. She's a virgin?"

"I believe so."

"Then admit your ignorance and tell her you both will learn together. If you're extremely concerned, you could go to one of the bordellos down near the riverfront. Those girls are experienced, and no one would be the wiser."

"I'm not doing that," said Max.

"Give me your notebook."

"Why?"

"Hand it to me." Patrick opened it to the blank page at the back. He sketched a rough drawing of a woman's anatomy and pointed with his pencil. "You put it in, in between these, right here. This above is very sensitive to touch for her. Her ass is down here—don't make that mistake." The barman walked their way. Patrick snapped the notebook shut and shoved it against Max's chest. "Don't stress about it—people have been figuring it out for centuries."

"Thanks."

"Does this mean you're going to propose?" said Patrick.

"I'm not sure yet. I think so. I don't even know if she wants to get married. She's pretty unconventional. I don't know what it would be like to be married to her."

"If any man can handle and appreciate an unconventional intelligent woman like her, it's you. And no man can know ahead of time what it will be like to be married. You need to forge ahead."

"I went and talked to Father Horstmann about it."

"How is old Horseman? I'll bet his pictures weren't as helpful as mine." Patrick laughed.

"He's fine. He was good to me growing up. He's a wise man."

"Max, asking a priest for marriage advice is like asking a railway passenger how to build a locomotive engine. They have a general awareness of the subject but no useful knowledge of any worth."

Patrick pressed his finger against Max's chest, "Well, am I wrong? Was he helpful?"

"No, not really. He asked me some very thought-provoking questions."

"I remember. He was tricky that way," said Patrick. "He always turned it around on you when he didn't know the answer. That kept the aura that he was a wise man intact."

"He had some good points. The most difficult for me is the question of children. I don't know if Annie wants to have children. Father Horstmann was emphatic that anything we might do to impact God's plan for children is a mortal sin."

"Christ. I forgot how God-fearing you are. Remember how the brothers and priests used to warn us about spilling our seed and how we would burn in hell if we did it?"

"Yes."

"Did you do it?"

Max hesitated, "Yes."

"As did I. And every boy in our class. We're not going to hell. I don't know what Popist tribunal came up with that interpretation, but it's not natural. Molly and I are having our second child. If I didn't pull my Johnson out sometimes and spill my seed, we'd have five children by now. You're too good a man to worry about being punished for something like that. You listen to Father Patrick and forget the bunk that Father Horseman says. Does that help?"

"I don't know," said Max, frustration in his voice.

#

Max walked with Nicholas Longworth through the gardens surrounding his mansion. The hedges were neatly trimmed, and beds of flowers were in full bloom.

"Is your acquisition of the Niles businesses complete?" asked Longworth.

"Yes, sir, closed last month."

"How's the transition going?"

"No major issues. I retained the foreman who knows the business."

"What's next?"

"I'm going to focus on machine tools. I want to make the machine tools to build the future."

"I saw in the paper that you spoke at the Mechanics Institute. I heard you made quite an impression on the room," said Longworth.

"I hope so."

"You did. I spoke to a man who said you lulled them into a trance, and they drank in your message. A talent like that, you could run for office."

"Sir?" said Max.

"The skill of speaking and connecting with an audience like that is not common, especially in thinking men. Consider using it. Like we previously spoke—for good. We need moral, intelligent men like you to be in politics to keep the bad apples from ruining the country." He squatted down, pulled a few weeds from the edge of a garden bed and threw them into a pile. He guided their walk toward the front yard.

"Political office never crossed my mind, but I will give it some thought. Can I ask your advice on something personal, sir?" said Max.

The old man looked at a note pinned to his sleeve. "I have another appointment in a few minutes. What is it?"

"I've met a young lady who I am considering for marriage. She is from New York City. Her mother married Stephen Neltner, the attorney, and they moved to Cincinnati this spring. She is an outspoken advocate for women's rights. Given her strong convictions, I believe she would be a nontraditional wife, in that she disregards some decorum when it offends the female sex."

"What are you asking me? If you should marry her? How would I know? I never met the woman."

"Sir, I respect your opinion on all matters. I seek your opinion about the relative importance I should place on the lady's nontraditional womanhood. Do you think I may suffer damage to my reputation and thus success in my endeavors if I were to have a wife that did not participate in Cincinnati society in the traditional ways?"

"Son, when I came to this town, I didn't have much. I was an attorney, but I made my fortune in real estate. Due to my wealth, the town accepted me into society, but I don't bother with the fuss. I like working in my gardens and vineyards. Being a part of society has its advantages. It can connect you with influential people who can help you get things done—be it grow your business, build a library or feed the poor. If being part of the Cincinnati aristocracy is something you desire, there are norms you must follow. However, being part of it is not a prerequisite to success. There are other paths."

They had reached the front porch, and Longworth stood at the bottom of the steps.

"Thank you, sir. As always, I appreciate your advice, and thank you for your time." They shook hands.

"Think about it. Run for office," Longworth said.

"Yes, sir," Max strode down the front walk to the street.

CHAPTER 21

Annie and her sister and brothers met Max and his siblings at the corner of Canal and Race Streets at 7:30 AM. Albert carried Elli on his shoulders; she loved being above the crowd. Hundreds of families from all parts of town were headed to the city's Fourth of July celebration at the Court Street Market space, across from the county courthouse. Annie and Max had prepared their respective siblings for the meeting, instructing each to be polite. The families were curious about meeting each other and intrigued by the close-up view of how the other half lived. They fell in together, walking toward the courthouse, their difference in attire a visible sign that they didn't belong together.

The Bennett children had never attended such a public event. In New York, they had left public holiday events to the masses and instead attended private parties at a friend's estate home or club. They were interested in observing the morning events and taking in the crowd of diverse Cincinnatians on the streets. They saw everyone from the elite sitting in reserved seats near the podium to the poor, both Black and white. A few beggars moved among the crowds, hats in hand. Native and non-native alike had come out to celebrate their shared national pride, at least for a day.

Max and Anthony forged a path for the group, pushing their way as close as possible to the front of the courthouse. The makeshift stage over the steps was adorned with American flags and red, white, and blue banners. A band played marches and American folk music. The parade marching all over town since 6:30 AM that morning made its way across Court Street, led by the Rover Regiment, a historic militia in full dress and arms. They marched into the square and stood behind the crowd.

A man took the podium in the center of the stage, and the crowd began cheering. Max set Oskar on his shoulders so he could see.

"Who's that?" asked Oskar.

"That's Mayor Faran," said Max.

"Do you know him?" asked Oskar.

"I've met him—he's a good man. There was a movement by the organizing committee to limit the parade entries to native Protestant organizations only, and Mayor Faran stepped in and halted the nonsense. He said all Americans are welcome to participate. I was worried we'd have another election day riot on our hands."

"I can't hear what he's saying," said Oskar. Although the mayor spoke with a hand-held megaphone, it was useless against the crowd.

"He's welcoming us," said Max.

The band on the courthouse steps began playing, and the crowd cheered and clapped to the music. At the conclusion, a preacher stepped to the podium and removed his hat. The men in the crowd removed theirs.

"He's saying a prayer," said Oskar. "Amen. He's done."

"Oskar, what's happening now?" called Helene.

"A bearded man is reading something."

"That's Mr. George Pugh. He's a lawyer that works with Mr. Salmon Chase. He's also Ohio's new senator. He helps make the laws in Congress in Washington," said Max.

"What's he reading?" asked Oskar.

"The Declaration of Independence."

"Anthony, you know it," said Annie. "Can you recite it for us since we can't hear? Anthony wants to practice law when he gets older."

Anthony began rapidly reciting, "When in the course of human events, it becomes necessary for one people to dissolve the political bands which have connected them with another, and to assume among the powers of the earth, the separate and equal station to which the laws of nature and of nature's God entitle them, a decent respect to the opinions of mankind requires that they should declare the causes which impel them to the separation.

"We hold these truths to be self-evident, that all men are created equal, that they are endowed by their Creator with certain unalienable rights, that among these are life, liberty and the pursuit of happiness. That to secure these rights, governments are instituted among men, deriving their just powers from the consent of the governed, that whenever any form of government becomes destructive of these ends, it is the right of the people to alter or to abolish it, and to institute new government, laying its foundation on such principles and organizing its powers in such form, as to them shall seem most likely to affect their safety and happiness.

"Is that enough?" whined Anthony.

"Yes, very good, thank you," said Annie.

"Why is he reading it?" asked Oskar.

Max said, "To remind us. Today, the Fourth of July is the day back in 1776 when the founding fathers declared their independence from England to form The United States of America. The brave men decided an unjust king wouldn't rule them without their voices heard and started the revolutionary war to win their freedom. Because of their action, America was founded, and our families were able to make our lives here in the greatest country on earth."

Annie said, "It is the greatest country on earth, but there are still injustices and things that are unfair. The Declaration says all men are created equal, but in America, some men, like the Negroes and the poor and all women, are not treated equally. So, we have to continue to work to make America a great nation for everyone, not just some."

The crowd applauded, cheered and waved their flags. "He's shaking the mayor's hand," said Oskar. "Someone else is speaking now."

"I don't know who he is," said Max.

"What's he reading?" asked Oskar.

"I don't know. I can't hear him," said Max.

The crowd applauded and cheered again. "Finally, he's done," said Oskar. "The mayor again. Take your hats off; now it's the preacher again."

A burst of gunfire echoed throughout the market area as the regiment fired their rifles in salute. The crowd roared.

"That is the end," said Max. "Let's walk that way, away from the crowd." He pointed west. They started moving slowly.

"What did you think of it?" asked Annie.

"I'm not sure," said her brother, John. "I'd have a more informed opinion if I could have heard it."

"Oskar's narration was terrific. It was almost as good as hearing it all," said Albert.

"Yes, thank you, Oskar and Anthony," said Annie. "Part of it is just being together with your fellow countrymen for a day, setting aside our differences and being grateful for our blessings in this country."

"That's right, Papa and Mother had to leave their country because of the oppression and lack of opportunity in the Fatherland," said Albert.

"Where's Peter, today?" asked Annie.

"He's helping Mother at the Eichen Garten. We will have a large crowd today," said Albert.

"Are you coming to the garden today, Annie?" asked Elli.

"No, not today. I'm going to spend some time with my mother, and then Max and I are taking a ferry boat to Kentucky."

"Where are you going in Kentucky?" asked Albert.

"There's a celebration put on by the Mercantile Library. We'll have a picnic and then watch some fireworks shot from the roof of the library," said Max.

They reached the canal and said their goodbyes. The Muellers headed north into Over-the-Rhine, and the Bennetts walked west to their house.

"I'll call for you at 2:00," said Max.

"I'll be waiting," replied Annie.

Once they were out of earshot from the Muellers, Caroline said, "Annie, I see why Mother is concerned with you spending time with Max. What would Father say if he were alive to see the family of the man you are letting escort you around town. He would be heartbroken."

Annie said, "Why do you make such an uncharitable comment? I think Father would respect Max for what he has accomplished and how he treats me."

"Yes, Father would have wanted you to be with a man who treats you with respect, but not a man from his class," said Caroline.

John said, "Did you see the clothes they wore? Oskar's clothes were filthy dirty, and the girl's dresses were so plain for a morning walk in public. Besides, they're Catholic."

Annie said, "Max's parents came to America with nothing. They fled their country and left their families. Max has worked very hard and now owns his own business and is a respected man in the business community. I will not judge a man based on his family's misfortune, and I suggest you two consider whether your judgment based on your brief encounter today reflects your Christian values. Anthony, what's your perspective?"

"Annie, they're nice people, but they're not the type of people we associate with. I honestly can't see being acquainted with them. You can do better than him."

"You're privileged brats, one and all," Annie said calmly.

#

"What did you think of Annie's brothers and sister?" Max asked.

"I liked them," said Oskar.

"I liked them," said Elli. "Her sister had a pretty dress like Annie's."

"Marie, Helene?" asked Max.

"Caroline puts on airs. I don't think she likes you. She's different from Annie," said Marie.

"Anthony seems very smart. I feel like they were looking down their noses at us. They didn't talk much," said Helene.

"They're not the most talkative lot, I agree. Albert, what did you think?" said Max.

"I'm sorry, but I don't understand why, of all the pretty girls that like you, Max, you choose Annie? They live in a different world."

"I agree our families don't have a lot in common. I'm sorry if it was uncomfortable for you, but I appreciate you all being polite," said Max.

Out of the mouths of babes, thought Max as they reached the Eichen Garten and filed inside.

#

Max helped Annie down from the carriage and paid the driver. Annie wore a wide-brimmed hat to protect her face from the hot July sun. They were both already drenched with sweat. Max took her arm, and they started walking down the steep public landing toward the river. Scores of people were about, and vendors pitched food and drinks to the holiday crowd. Max guided her to the ferry boat landing and paid their fare. Packed tightly with the other passengers, they watched the steam-powered flatboat make its way toward them. As it came to rest in shallow water, two men pushed a plank from the landing onto the boat deck while a crewman dropped anchor. They waited for the passengers to disembark, then boarded the ferry. Annie sat on a bench with the other women while Max stood in front of her. The boatmen wasted no time pushing off with their poles, and they moved across the river.

"This reminds me of the day we met on the steamboat," said Annie.

"Yes, that was a chance meeting that turned into something unexpected."

"It seems a lifetime ago," she said. "My life in New York is just memories, now."

"Do you still miss it?" said Max.

"At times. I miss the women who thought like me. It's hard to be a lone voice. I miss my father, too. I know we can never turn back time. Forge ahead."

"It's the only direction we can go."

The ferry arrived at Covington's landing, and the men repeated the process of unloading and loading the passengers. Annie accepted Max's arm to avoid slipping on the muddy landing. They walked up a road leading to a hilltop, stepping to the side as horses or carriages passed. Some ladies had to stop on the ascent, but Annie was healthy and had dressed in a loose corset so as not to restrict her breathing.

At the top, they came upon a grassy clearing surrounded by shade trees. Several tents had been erected, and well-dressed ladies and men sat about on blankets. Vendors sold roasted corn, dried fruits and other food, lemonade and small handheld flags. Clowns roamed through the crowds, juggling, miming and entertaining. A small brass band played music at one end of the clearing.

Max said, "The sun is starting to fade, so we'll soon be in the shade if we sit here." He took the blanket from his basket and spread it on the ground. They sat and took in the crowd, which produced a low murmur of voices in the background and occasional cheers or firecrackers.

"What did you make of our social experiment this morning?" said Annie.

"You're referring to the forced comingling of our families?" said Max.

"Yes."

"It didn't go as well as I would have hoped," Max admitted.

"Have you and I deluded ourselves? Have we been so focused on us that we ignored our own families' prejudices?"

Max said, "I was surprised by my family's rejection of your sister and brothers. I expected it from yours, but I thought my family would be more accepting. Take people for who they are, not their status in society. But they couldn't separate the individual from their class. It's understandable. It's ingrained and reinforced in daily life and, in some ways, necessary for survival, but it was a hard realization for me. I had hoped for better from them."

"I suppose it is," Annie agreed. "Much of it comes from fear and discomfort of the unfamiliar. The only way to break through that is to get to know people personally and wear down the walls of distrust that we all put up."

"Do you think it's possible to break through it with our families?" asked Max.

"Yes, but it will take time."

"Annie, there's something I want to discuss with you."

"What is it?"

"It's about us and our future."

"Oh."

"I don't presume anything about you, so I want to understand your aspirations."

"My aspirations?"

"Annie, I love you, and I would be honored to be by your side for life in matrimony, but I don't know if that's even something you want for yourself—matrimony—with me?"

She blushed and drew in a breath, "You just put it out there, don't you?"

"I'm sorry, I don't know any other way. I'm not good at this sort of thing; romanticism, the proper ways to do things. I don't even know if you want me to be romantic."

She smiled and chuckled and took his hand. She kissed it and sat back, still holding his hand. "Yes, I appreciate your romance. Your sweet gestures and chivalry make me feel special, and everyone likes to feel special and appreciated. Just because I want to be treated fairly and given the same opportunities as men doesn't mean I don't want to be loved."

"It's hard for me to know what you want sometimes," he said.

"I don't know what I want sometimes," she laughed.

"But do you want marriage?" he asked.

"Max, I love you, as I have never loved anyone before. I was undecided about marriage as a practical matter. If I marry, the law says I lose my identity. My property becomes yours and I lose what little rights I have. I am expected to devote my life to supporting my husband and even leave my teaching position. I lose my father's name. For these reasons, I never entertained marriage until I met you. But my love for you has grown with each passing day, and my desire for you may only be quenched in marriage."

"Annie, I can't know what your experience is, but I have come to appreciate your position and your dreams. I have come to feel a sense of shared understanding with you. I am now incomplete without you, and I want us to pursue each of our dreams with each other's support. I vow to you that I will strive to grow in understanding your plight and supporting you with my love as best I can. Ours will not be a marriage with the traditional roles of man and wife, but instead, we will create a union of equals that will evolve."

Annie said, "I, too, have come to feel you are now a part of me that I need to fully live. Your offer of marriage and vow for the unconventional is not one that most men could make. I know you are extraordinary in this way, among others."

"What about children—will you welcome children?" said Max.

"I fear the traditional role of a mother will curtail my endeavors, but through my own family experience and seeing my students, I recognize the importance of a mother's love and care for her children. I accept that motherhood comes with these responsibilities. So yes, someday, but there are things I want to do before I have the additional responsibility of children."

"Would you allow your children to be baptized in the Catholic Church?"

"Max, do you have a checklist tucked in your pocket that you refer to?"

"I'm sorry, I must."

"I'm teasing you. I know you. However, now you want me to become a Catholic? That is asking too much and not something I can agree to," said Annie.

"No, not you, unless your heart calls you to, but our children. As a Catholic, it is my duty to baptize them and educate them in the Church. We can expose them to both Catholicism and the Episcopal Methodist Church. I want them to know Christ's teachings."

"I understand this is of deep importance to you, so I can agree to this. You're a Catholic, and I love you. Maybe my past is full of biases against Catholics by those fearful and ignorant of their ways. I am open to you further enlightening me."

"I am heartened by our honest discussions. My heart is filling," said Max.

"I am excited, too."

"As to the marriage. Since you are not a Catholic, it will be in your church, I presume."

"As is customary," she said.

"What of our families and their reservations and objections?"

"My mother will object, but I have disappointed her many times. Mr. Neltner will defer to her. She may distance herself from me, but that has already occurred in our hearts. I can live with her disappointment. What about your family?"

"I have forged a life for myself that is my own. They have accepted that. In time, I think my mother will learn to respect you. Most of my siblings like you. I don't think our families need to come together just because we marry, do you?"

"No, I agree with you," she said.

"And what about you? Are you comfortable with losing your position in polite society by marrying me, a man without your social standing?"

"Ha, I have done enough on my own to lose my position," she said.

"Do you truly understand what this will mean for you, and are you prepared for it?"

"You mean that some families won't receive me, and some people will think less of me due to my husband's family?"

"That and the loss of the privileges of wealth and connections that your family has today?" he said. "I aspire to be among Cincinnati's upper class, but I will never be of its aristocracy."

"I've lost much of that with the loss of my father and uprooting of my life to Cincinnati," she said. "Besides, those things aren't as important to me."

"You need to be sure."

She nodded her head.

"Your children will have German heritage and be considered non-native Americans. Are you ready for the discrimination that your children will face? To ache for them because of the teasing they'll endure from the cruelty of others, and all you'll be able to do is love them and support them and try to help them stand up for themselves?"

"Max, is that how you felt growing up?"

He nodded. "It was crushing to my soul to be hated simply because of my birth—something of which I had no control whatsoever."

"I'm so sorry that has been your experience, Max. I experienced my own version of that. Since I was a little girl, I've been treated differently because I didn't want to do what the girls were expected to do. I was treated differently by the boys, by the girls and by the teachers. I never felt like I belonged. That's why I'm so passionate about women's rights and all human rights. Regardless of who you are, we all deserve to be accepted and given a chance to flourish. So, if we have children and they feel on the outside because they have a German father or because they're a girl who wants to be a doctor, I will fight for them and work to make the world a more equitable place for them. I may have been born of privilege, and I am thankful for what it has afforded me, but I think I am aware of the relativity of everyone's privilege— there's always someone who has more than you do. Fighting for what's right is worth the fight, but I'm learning that losing sight of the joy of living, surrounded by people to love, is a trap that I need to avoid."

"I love you," said Max, as he leaned in and kissed her.

"I love you."

"I'm sorry," said Max.

"For what?"

"That I doubted your ability to know yourself and choose for yourself."

"I didn't take your comments as such."

"I just want to make sure you're not disappointed. You're a wise woman." He leaned over and kissed her. "So, will you marry me, Annie Bennett?"

"Yes, I will, Max Mueller." They kissed.

#

As dusk approached, Max and Annie stood with the crowd along the hilltop's ridge, looking across the river at Cincinnati. Most of the buildings were dark, gas lights lit some of the streets, and distant lights of hilltop communities created a sparkling pattern against the darkness.

"It's beautiful at night," said Annie. "It feels like home, now."

He took her hand. "Our home. Where we'll build our life together and grow with the city."

She squeezed his hand.

The first fireworks exploded over downtown, filling the sky with red and white cascading sparks. The crowd exclaimed and clapped as the fireworks boomed and lit up the city.

CHAPTER 22

Annie arrived at the Smith & Nixon Piano Hall early, hoping to meet Lucretia Mott before the convention began. She paid twenty-five cents to the young man collecting admission fees. When she entered the lobby, several women greeted her and gave her a flyer for the two-day Sixth National Women's Rights Convention. She inquired as to Lucretia's whereabouts.

"Lucretia is in the hall with her sister Martha, preparing for the session. You may go in."

Annie opened the heavy wooden door and entered the large performance hall. Three pianos were pushed against the walls, and more than one hundred chairs filled the room. Three women and a man were on the stage, where a row of chairs and a podium faced the room. She recognized Lucretia, now in her early sixties, wearing a modest dress and bonnet on her head. Annie climbed the stairs onto the stage. "Excuse me, Mrs. Mott. I'm Annie Bennett, Elizabeth Cady Stanton's second cousin. It's been five years, but I met you at Elizabeth's house in the summer of 1850. I was just a girl of thirteen at the time."

"Good morning, dear. Elizabeth told me to look for you. Yes, I remember; the girl with the red curls. It's so nice to have young women such as yourself join us. You live here in Cincinnati, now, I understand?"

"Yes, my family moved here this past spring from New York. I'm a schoolteacher in the common schools."

"Wonderful. Were you here yesterday? I don't recall seeing you," said Lucretia.

"Unfortunately, I could only attend today due to my responsibilities in the classroom. I read some of the reviews in the paper this morning. It sounds like I missed some passionate speeches and discussion," said Annie.

"It was lively. We'll provide transcripts to the newspapers. If you can't find a full transcript, write us, and we can send you one in the post. Let me introduce you to my sister, Martha Wright, president of the convention. Martha, Martha, come. Martha, I want to introduce you to Elizabeth's cousin, a young advocate here in Cincinnati."

"I'm Annie Bennett."

"Martha Coffin Wright." Martha had worked with Lucretia Mott and Elizabeth Cady Stanton to organize the first women's convention. She was also an abolitionist who assisted escaped slaves in her Auburn, New York home, a stop on the underground railroad.

"It's an honor to meet you. I've read about the other conventions since the first meeting in Seneca Falls. I'm grateful for the work you and the other women do," said Annie.

"Thank you for coming," said Martha. "It's rewarding to see our crowds getting bigger with each annual convention. We were a timid group when we started. Now we find supporters all across the country, and our voice grows louder. At first, the press ridiculed us, but we are now getting more reporting without commentary. I sense that Cincinnati is more conservative regarding women's rights than some east coast cities. The audience yesterday was more reserved overall but included some lively debate on both sides."

"I wasn't in attendance but read the newspaper reports," said Annie. I was sorry to have missed the lectures. The *Daily Gazette* was dismissive of the convention, saying that the speakers were short on facts or ideas about how to implement the proposed reforms."

"That is disappointing, but we are accustomed to criticism. We believe it is important to hear all voices. We want to hear any objections to our causes or platform. We'd rather hear them in the conventions than have silence and read dissension in the newspapers afterward, with no way to respond."

"Some critics are so vile and personal in their attacks. It must be difficult to hear," said Annie.

"I don't take any of it personally," said Martha. "We are glad for the attention—the more people who discuss the issues and become educated, the better for the cause. I'm sorry, but please excuse me. I must attend to the preparation. It was nice meeting you."

Annie took a chair near the back so that Max could join her when he arrived. She sat and watched people fill the room. She read the slate of speakers on the flyer. On the reverse side was a summary of the Declaration of Sentiments from the first Women's Rights Convention in 1848. She remembered cousin Lizzie talking about writing it with Lucretia Mott. Few people had heard of the women's movement yet, and they needed a way to articulate their platform. Having never written anything like it, they turned to the Declaration of Independence as a model.

Annie was familiar with the Women's Declaration, which started similarly to the revolutionary document with 'When, in the course of human events'. She skipped to the bottom of the flyer to the summary of injustices by men against women:

- *He has not given her the right to vote*
- *He has passed laws that impact her without her having any voice in them*
- *He has withheld rights from her that even the lowliest of men have*
- *He has removed all her individual rights once she marries*
- *He has withheld her right to own property*

- *He has allowed husbands to treat their wives as property, forcing them to agree to obey their demands*
- *He has made divorce laws that favor men and give guardianship of the children to them*
- *He has prevented her from most profitable employment and if she does work, pays her a fraction of what men are paid*
- *He has denied her opportunities for wealth and positions of distinction such as theology and medicine*
- *He has denied her equal education opportunities*
- *He has given her a subordinate place in churches and prevented her from participating in administration of the church*
- *He has instituted a moral double standard, shaming women, yet tolerating or ignoring similar behavior in men*
- *He has endeavored to lessen her self-confidence and self-respect*

As Annie read the document, she thought it was a brilliant summary of many of her feelings and experiences. She looked around at the other women who had started to fill the room and felt a sisterhood with them. She took a breath to keep from tearing up.

A middle-aged woman sat down in the row in front of her. She turned around. "Good morning. I'm Christina Kline."

"I'm Annie Bennett. Is this your first convention?"

"Yes, and you?"

"Yes. I'm a schoolteacher at the tenth district common school."

"I'm a clerk at the O'Donnell dry goods and grocery store in Covington. It was nice to see so many women here, like me, yesterday. Before this, I felt like I was the only woman in town who was frustrated enough to say my piece out loud."

Two women approached them. The first introduced herself, "I'm Carla O'Neill. I'm a seamstress for Jefferson Dressmakers. I've been working for better wages and hours for women for two years, now."

"I'm Mary Orchard. It was inspiring to hear the comments yesterday about Antoinette Brown Blackwell—the first woman Protestant minister in America, and the arguments against using the Bible to justify men's domination over women. My husband is a minister. He and I debated the topic last night, but I couldn't begin to articulate the arguments the way the women on the stage did. The ladies are brilliant."

"Good morning," said a young, neatly dressed woman who joined their circle. "I'm Sarah Thomas. I found yesterday to be life-changing. I heard so many ideas that I have been thinking about for years but never said them aloud. I wonder how many women there are like me?"

The room was almost full of women and a few men. The conversations going on throughout the hall created an energizing buzz. Annie looked around the room, watching the women interacting freely and openly, laughing and smiling. She felt transported to a different world that men didn't run.

"There you are." Max touched her shoulder, startling her back to the here and now. He leaned down and whispered in her ear over the din. "Good morning."

Annie's face brightened. "Good morning. I saved this chair for you."

"Everything all right?" he said.

"Yes, It's wonderful. I can't believe all the women here." Annie broke into a big smile. "Thank you for coming."

"It was no hardship for me—a room full of confident, intelligent women. They're all my type." Max raised his eyebrows. "Seriously, I'm looking forward to hearing it and learning today."

Mrs. Ernestine Rose, an active abolitionist and women's rights advocate, pounded the gavel on the podium, "Day two of the Sixth National Woman's Rights Convention will now come to order."

Martha Wright, the convention president, opened the meeting. The secretary read the proceedings from the first day.

The first speaker recognized was Mrs. Emerson from Cincinnati. She climbed the stage and spoke timidly "…. In looking across the United States, men have every advantage over women. Women will never obtain the rights we demand simply because men's brains are larger than women's. It is a reality of nature."

There was some hissing and mumbling in the audience as Mrs. Emerson returned to her seat. Lucy Stone looked at the other women on the stage, then stood and said, "Thank you for sharing that perspective. Most in the room disagree with you, and I believe my strong will, which I am extremely vocal with at times, is a personal demonstration that the size of a woman's brain is not a factor that will limit us from attaining our objectives.

"A further testament to the fact is this letter, which I will reference portions of, from a Canadian woman. Southern Canada has laws that consider marriage a contract between a man and a woman, and in Canada, women can own property. In Novia Scotia and New Brunswick, women vote in parliament elections. I don't believe Canadian women's brains are different from ours, are they? These are examples of what women can do if we have the will!" Lucy Stone shook the letter in front of her as the audience broke into applause.

A gentleman was recognized, "I am Mr. Joseph Barker, a resident of Ohio, but I originally lived in England. I must agree with Mrs. Stone. I offer the audience hope that over time, we men can learn. We may learn to grant rights to others. My experience has been that it is not always the case that the oppressed fail to gain their rights. I encourage all you women to persevere." The audience applauded.

Another woman in a skirt and pantaloons was recognized and took the stage. "I am Adeline Swift of Elyria, Ohio. I apologize that the existing laws cause me to become a fault-finder, but there is one code of laws for men and another for women and Colored persons. As such, there are two classes of nobility in this country—one: the slaveholders of the south who oversee their slaves and two: the nominally free men of the north, who rule their wives."

She paused as the crowd whooped and clapped. "Men's objection to women having the elective franchise is that women are not competent enough to vote. I ask the men if they believe that their wives are no better than the most ignorant and immoral men? Do they think the women they marry are truly less qualified than them?" More applause.

Mrs. Frances Gage, a temperance, anti-slavery and women's rights activist who had chaired the Cleveland convention the prior year, took the podium and delivered an eloquent address on the differences in the morality of the sexes. Ladies in the audience stood to make comments. The committee on stage read several letters from prominent supporters of the cause who could not attend.

They recessed for lunch.

As the audience slowly exited the auditorium, Annie spoke with the women around her and introduced Max.

"I commend you for accompanying your fiancé today," said one of the women.

Max said, "I deserve no merit. I am part of the half of humanity with full rights and privileges. You ladies are the brave champions who are stepping forward to lead. I am here to understand your position better and how my actions can support your cause."

Max and Annie made their way out onto the sidewalk. "Let's walk to the market and get something to eat. I am famished," said Annie.

They ate their lunch on a bench at the market.

Annie said, "That first speaker, Mrs. Emerson, was a surprise. I didn't expect to hear a woman stand against the convention's purpose. I don't know why she was there?"

Max said, "The other speakers flayed her. The poor woman was probably sorry she came by the end of the morning. I am impressed by most of the speakers' eloquence. They are excellent orators. You could do what they do."

"That's interesting that you say such a thing. I've been contemplating how I might contribute to the cause for women. It would be exciting to be one of these visible women, traveling the country and motivating audiences. But these ladies are well versed in the subject and provide thought-provoking ideas. I don't have the experience they do."

"You have daily first-hand knowledge of the topic of women. I have heard you speak as passionately and eloquently as they, and you are comfortable speaking to an audience," said Max.

"An audience of children, yes. These women speak in rooms full of adult women—and men."

"I think you could do it if you chose to."

When they finished eating, Max walked Annie back to the hall. "I have to go back to the shop this afternoon. I'll look forward to hearing all about it." He touched her hand and departed.

Annie returned to the convention hall and took a seat. She introduced herself to a young woman beside her, dressed in bloomers, with cropped, dark hair.

"I'm Mary Berry. I'm a school teacher at the school on Clinton Street."

"I'm a teacher, too," said Annie. "Tenth district school."

"It's a pleasure to meet you. These women are inspiring, aren't they?" said Mary Berry.

"Yes, I agree."

"I want to form a club here in Cincinnati—a women's club. Hold marches in the streets, in front of city hall. That sort of thing. Will you join?"

Annie hesitated, still assessing Mary. "I'll consider it."

"Great! Write your address here on this list. I'll include you in our organizational meeting." She handed a paper and pencil to Annie. "Cincinnati needs women like you and me. Women who are willing to make a statement. Let the polite women stay home with the babies."

Lucy Stone called the meeting to order, and the audience quieted. "I propose a resolution. Since one of the most effective means to secure equal political and legal rights is the circulation of petitions, it is, therefore, the duty of women in their respective states to petition their legislatures for the elective franchise and ask for it repeatedly until it is granted. I believe that we cannot wait for men to do this; thus, women must take action." The attendees broke into cheers and applause. Some stood.

Mrs. Rose waited for the crowd to quiet, then recognized a movement to pass the resolution, and it was voted on and passed.

Lucy said, "A printed petition is being drafted, and we ask that you secure a copy and submit it to the Ohio legislature before their next session. The petition should be available by early November."

Mr. Henry Blackwell, Lucy Stone's husband, stood. "First, I must say that the woman who stood this morning and suggested that women are limited by their relative brain size may suffer from such an affliction herself, but it is not a generalization I accept."

There was laughter in the audience. Blackwell continued. "I want to comment on women who choose to take up a profession. Why should they be robbed of respect? There are few professions women are allowed in, and in those, they are, paid so low a wage that many women, unable to support themselves, resort to prostitution, instead. It is a sad state of affairs across this country, and it exists here in Cincinnati, as well. For women to choose this course of life illustrates the dire position of many women."

Upon Mr. Blackwell returning to his seat, Mrs. Emerson couldn't help herself and stood again. "Mr. Blackwell, you joke about my brain, but given women's slight statures, I argue that if women's brains did somehow enlarge, it would be inconvenient, as our bodies could not accommodate them."

More laughter from the crowd. A voice in the back piped out, "Are you afraid we'd tip over?"

Mary Berry leaned over to Annie. "Is she for real? What a half-wit. She gives women a bad name."

Annie nodded silently, trying to stay focused on the messages from the stage.

Lucy Stone said, "The chair recognizes Mrs. Hibbard of Chicago."

Mrs. Hibbard took the stage. "I want to thank all of you for your work and ask that this movement be blessed by heaven. I pray for the day when women's state of taxation without their representation will be alleviated. We are taxed equally as men yet have no say in the levy of the taxes upon us."

"Thank you, Mrs. Hibbard. An important reason for us to gain the right to vote," commented Lucy.

The committee then discussed where the convention should be the following year. Chicago and New York were both proposed. They discussed the alternatives and agreed on New York City. Annie thought she would like to take Max to New York and attend.

The evening session continued with similar statements and discussions.

Lucy Stone retook the podium for her keynote speech. "I have been a disappointed woman from the time I was young, and my brothers denied me from participating in activities because I was a girl. I was again disappointed when I sought a profession but only found seamstress, teaching and housekeeper available to women. I have also been disappointed in education, marriage, and most other things.

"The reasons for women's place are often expressed as the natural order, but I point to the variation of women's place in different countries as proof that the position and treatment of women is a man-made creation of society and can be altered. Women are not paid the same as men, yet we are charged the same when purchasing goods. I encourage women to work to widen our lot. The first female physician had many difficulties, but it will now be easier for the next woman to pursue medicine. Antoinette Brown completed divinity school courses but was denied ordination; she finally achieved it, yet she is hissed at by men when she preaches. I encourage women to forge into new areas. We will face obstacles and face uncertainty of the results, but over time, we will change women's lives for the better." The audience applauded enthusiastically and stood.

"Amen, Sister," shouted Mary Berry. She grabbed Annie's hand and raised it with her own. "We will not be disappointed forever!"

The committee then took up a collection to defray the convention's expenses to cover the shortfall in what they had collected in tickets. Mary Berry passed the basket to Annie, "Cough it up, girl. We working girls need to subsidize the women whose brute husbands control their purses."

Annie dropped several coins in the basket.

"That's it? That's all your freedom is worth? You're worth more than that, and don't you let any man tell you otherwise," said Mary Berry.

Annie added a dollar to the basket and passed it on.

Mrs. Mott took a moment to reflect on the progress made for women over the last six years since the first convention.

Mrs. Rose took the stand and spoke to women's need to dedicate their time and money to the cause. She reiterated the need to push for women's right to vote until it is granted. She concluded the convention with announcements about upcoming lectures. Then she adjourned the meeting.

Mary Berry stood and shook Annie's hand. "A pleasure to meet you, girl. I hope to see you around the schoolyard, but you'll be hearing from me. Women for Women!" Annie heard her approach a group of women gathered in the aisle. "Greetings ladies, I'm Mary Berry. I'm starting a Cincinnati Women's Club. Who's in?"

Annie was energized and encouraged, yet a little saddened to be leaving the company of the room full of like-minded people. She wished she could stay in this room, surrounded by those who accepted women that wanted to be more than wives or teachers. These women were brave enough to stand up to society's ideas of what women should be. She felt validated and determined not to be suppressed in her efforts, yet she feared the ugliness she knew outside the room; people who ridiculed and derided women that dared to be different.

The conference inspired her with many ideas about what she might do to promote the causes they had discussed. She thought about what it might be like to travel with Lucy Stone and the other women's movement leaders, speaking in front of crowds of women and inspiring them. She wasn't sure if she could do that. What would she say? Had she lived enough to give testimony that would be compelling? Traveling across the country, seeing new places and meeting, so many new people seemed exciting. She knew she could write speeches that moved others. These women were already doing that— did the country need more? Would she be willing to put herself in front of an audience and take the scrutiny and criticism? She also felt that her contribution to the cause should be more active than speaking engagements.

Maybe she could organize Cincinnati women to lobby their politicians. Write and circulate petitions, organize letter writing to newspapers and invite others to lecture. The prospect of facing so many men who would be against her and navigating the political parties was daunting.

She thought of Antoinette Blackwell—the first ordained woman preacher. No, she didn't want to be a preacher. What about pioneering in other professions? She knew that there were women becoming doctors. No, medicine didn't suit her, either. However, she felt that doing work that proved women could be just as capable as men was as important as organizing speeches and writing letters and petitions. Women had to prove that they could do many things that men did, and they needed to do it in numbers, not just exceptions. She felt being part of the army of women doers was her role in the movement. But what did she want to do? How would she know what profession or occupation would suit her? She had no idea. How did men decide?

She didn't know what her role should be, but she was more convinced now that she had to play an active part in making America a fairer country for women.

#

The following evening, Max sat in his office reading the newspaper, including the convention reports. Below the article was a cartoon depicting a group of women orating on stage. A man in the audience speaks to the woman next to him, "They're speaking rational thoughts. Why haven't I heard this before?" The woman responds, "You never asked them."

CHAPTER 23

Annie knocked on principal Nye's office door at the end of the school day.

"Come in, Miss Bennett," said the slight man in his late twenties. He scrutinized her up and down from his chair as she entered.

"You wanted to see me?" said Annie.

"Yes, I have received a complaint from one of the parents regarding your conduct in the classroom."

"What is the nature of the complaint?" said Annie.

"You have been filling girls' heads with ideas that are disrespectful to their father's positions and not in alignment with the words of God as spelled out in the Bible."

"I don't know to what you refer. What is the specific complaint?"

"Did you tell Martha Owens that she was just as bright as the boys, and she shouldn't let any boy tell her otherwise?"

"Yes, I did," said Annie.

"Why do you put such thoughts and troublesome words in the minds of a young girl?"

Annie spoke with empathy as if she were Martha herself. "Martha is such a bright young girl. She has so much potential. The boys, they were crushing her self-confidence."

He cut her off. "Did you also say that if she works hard in school, she could someday be a doctor, preacher, or lawyer?"

"I did, yes."

"Is this a radical teaching philosophy you picked up at that Women's meeting? I knew we shouldn't have allowed you to attend."

"Mr. Nye, my comments to Martha were in the spirit of encouragement and support of her education."

"You're putting false ideas in the minds of our youth. Those ideas are counter to a productive and orderly society. Women taking men's jobs outside the home will lead to the moral decay of our community. Her father is angry and has called for your removal from the classroom."

"Mr. Nye, women are becoming doctors and preachers, and someday they will also be lawyers. You don't give enough credit to women, suggesting they can't have a profession as men do and parent their children. The moral decay of society is a gross exaggeration of the outcome. I am doing my duty to support the development of our students and encourage the development of good citizens."

"That is your opinion. Martha's father believes that his daughter should aspire to be a proper, good wife and mother, achieving the epitome of true womanhood. He doesn't want you promoting anarchy and the demise of families to his daughter. That is not your place."

"I merely suggested that Martha not limit herself if she wants more."

"More what?" he said.

"More from life," said Annie.

"The child is eleven years old. What does she know of what she wants from life? What does that even mean? Your judgment regarding what is appropriate for children astounds me. You are to teach the approved curriculum and not express radical progressive ideas to your students. Is that understood?"

Annie took measured breaths to remain calm. "Yes, sir."

"I will note this transgression in your file. If we have another incident or complaint, your employment will be terminated. Is that clear?"

"Yes, sir."

"That is all. You are dismissed."

Annie retrieved her things from her classroom and walked home. As she walked, she became angrier about the reprimand from Mr. Nye. He passed judgment on her without giving her an opportunity for discussion, just summarily dismissed her and her perspective. She understood that was his privilege as the principal but felt it was another case where a man had the power and forced his way.

Her mind raced. She didn't want to go on teaching. Not under these circumstances. She was trying to teach by being a role model and encouraging young girls, but she was chastised rather than appreciated. It was too hard. Maybe she should become a lecturer and travel like Lucy Stone or Martha Wright. She imagined that would be easier—the audiences were full of women who wanted to change. She could inspire other women—and let them slog it out with men. Or maybe she should go to college. Lucy Stone had gone to Oberlin College right here in Ohio. They accepted women in the same classes as men. Perhaps she could become a doctor. She didn't know what she wanted to do, but she hated her life, right now.

When she walked in the door, her mother greeted her. "Helen has supper ready. Join us in the dining room. After dinner, Stephen and I want to talk with you."

#

After they ate, Annie sat in Mr. Nelson's study and picked up the *Enquirer* newspaper from the top of a pile of papers on his bookshelf. She noted a circled article with the headline "Lucy Stone and Women's Rights." It was a scathing rebuttal to Lucy Stone and the entire women's movement. The reporter painted a gloomy picture of Lucy as a maniac blindly focused on women's issues, ignoring the natural order of men and women's roles since Creation. He suggested that most women are happy to assume their roles as the guardians of the home and all things domestic and have been the stabilizing force in the world. The women's movement threatens to cause a revolution in society, leading to its demise. He expressed gratitude that relatively few women were like Lucy, willing to unwoman themselves, cast off their modesty and propriety and reject their sphere in the world. He said the women's movement would not last and closed by saying that the men who support it are ridiculed as laughing stocks. Annie put the paper down and closed her eyes. All the positive energy she felt leaving the convention the prior week dissipated as she realized the odds were decidedly against her and the movement.

Her mother and Mr. Neltner entered the study and closed the door.

Her mother began, "Annie, you hardly said two words during supper, and you didn't eat much. You look like you're in one of your moods?"

"I'm tired. It was a long day at school," she said.

"We want to talk to you about Max and his proposal."

Annie looked at her mother. Her head ached.

"Dear, we know you feel like you're in love with Max. He is a fine young man, but we don't think you should marry him. We can't give you our blessing. It isn't in your best interest."

Annie said nothing. She took slow, deep breaths as a pounding started in her head. Feelings of hatred toward her mother rushed uncontrollably into her mind.

"We know you haven't had many suitors, and this is your first proposal, so you are inexperienced at judging the merits and navigating them. It's my duty as your mother and Stephen's, in place of your father, to guide you and look out for your well-being.

"You may think that you don't have a choice—that you have to say yes to him, but you don't. I know you're afraid that no one else will ever come along with a proposal, given your temperament, but plenty of eligible men would be delighted to have a girl such as you from a family such as ours.

"If he's not here in Cincinnati, I'll help you with a campaign to find one, even if we need to look back in New York. I realize the move disrupted your social standing. It will take some effort to reestablish one, but I'll help you. If your job as a teacher is too much to handle in addition to a social calendar, then you can resign from it. Your sister has already established a regular calendar of social calls, and several young men are potential prospects for her. We'll make it a project—you like that sort of thing. I know it's painful, but you'll be over him in no time."

Annie felt as if every beat of her heart was pushing thick blood into her forehead. She closed her eyes to shut out the light.

"Annie, are you listening?"

"Why don't you want me to marry him?" Annie asked.

"Well, dear, as I said, he's a fine young man. It's admirable that he now owns his own business, but he's not from a family of acceptable social standing and heritage."

Annie felt a stab of pain course from her forehead to the back of her head. She opened her eyes and squinted to minimize the light. "Not acceptable to whom?"

"To you, dear, and to your family. Do you not see it? Your brothers and sister do."

Annie closed her eyes again, trying to listen through the pain.

"First and foremost, he's a Catholic," her mother continued.

Annie took deep, slow breaths. She focused on understanding her mother's words.

"He's an immigrant," she said as if it were something dirty. "Annie, his family is of a different class than we are. It would be an embarrassment. The two of you are not compatible. With his background and upbringing, he couldn't begin to understand you or provide what you need to make you happy."

Annie expelled a laugh. She began chuckling as she shook her head.

"Why are you laughing?" said her mother. "Stop it. Stop laughing."

"Oh, that's rich. Mother, you have never understood me or what I need to be happy. You have no idea." Annie stood up and left the room, closing the door gently behind her. She ascended the stairs and quietly closed her bedroom door.

#

"Anthony," Annie whispered to her brother as she shook his shoulder, waking him.

He opened his eyes, squinting in the dark. "Annie, what time is it?"

"It's about 5:00."

"What's wrong?" said Anthony.

"I need you to take me to the train station," she said.

"Now? Where are you going?"

"Just get dressed and meet me downstairs in my room. Quietly, please."

She heard him coming down the stairs from the third floor and opened her door. She pointed to the trunk that she had packed and motioned down the steps.

"Annie, please don't go," said Caroline. "You can't travel unescorted without a man. Something awful will happen to you. I just know it will."

"Of course, I can. I'll be fine. Keep your voice down; I don't want to wake them. Tell Mother I've gone to stay with cousin Lizzie."

Anthony picked up the trunk and awkwardly carried it down the steps.

Stephen opened the bedroom door and peeked his head out into the dark hallway as Annie started down the steps. "What's going on?" he said.

"I have to leave early this morning. Sorry to wake you." Annie said.

He shut his door.

Annie and Anthony stood on the front porch with the trunk.

"What is this about?" Anthony whispered.

"I'll tell you, but first, you need to go fetch Mr. Neltner's horse and carriage at the stables and bring them to the end of the street. Don't bring them round front, or you'll wake up the whole house."

He shook his head as he headed down the block toward the stables.

A few minutes later, Anthony reappeared. He picked up the trunk and carried it down the porch stairs, with Annie following behind. She pulled closed behind her the wrought iron gate that Max had installed and held on to it for a moment. Then she followed her brother down the street.

Anthony drove the buggy, Annie by his side.

"Where are you going?" Anthony said.

"I have to get away for a while, to think. I'm going to Seneca Falls," said Annie.

"Why?"

"My mind is too full. I don't know what to do."

"Is this because Mother won't let you marry Max?" said Anthony.

"No. I don't know. That's part of it. I don't know what I want. I love Max, and he makes me happy, but I don't know if I can marry him. I don't know if marriage is for me."

"So why do you have to go to New York? Leave in the middle of the night?"

"I need to be around people who understand me to help me sort myself out. Cousin Lizzie is the only person who can help me, right now. She understands me. If Mother knew, she would forbid me to go."

"Annie, this is a bad idea for you to travel all across the country by yourself. How do you even know how to get there?"

"I checked the newspaper. There's a train leaving for Buffalo at 8:00 this morning. From Buffalo, I can take an eastbound train that stops in Seneca Falls. If you take me to the ticket office, I can get someone to take my trunk from there."

"How long are you going to be away?" he said.

"That depends on what I decide to do."

"What do you mean?"

"I might go back to New York City. There's more opportunity for me there," said Annie.

"But I thought you loved Max."

"I do."

"And you're just going to leave him?"

"I know, I feel horrible leaving without telling him, but I'm afraid he would talk me out of going. I need to decide for myself."

"You're acting irrationally, Annie."

"Maybe."

"I want you to be happy, whatever you decide."

"Thank you, Anthony. I think you're the only one in the family who understands."

They pulled up to the railroad ticket office. Annie went inside while Anthony stayed with the carriage. Eventually, she came out with a man to carry her trunk.

"They'll take me to the station in an omnibus from here." She handed him two envelopes. "Will you deliver this letter to Max at his office and take this one to the school for me? Thank you, Anthony," she said, hugging him.

CHAPTER 24

Max stood in the foundry, looking over a drawing with his chief engineer. "The Chicago Valve Company manager is coming to town, tomorrow. He'll want to know how long it will take to build it."

"Probably three to four weeks. This one is trickier than any we've done before, so I'd quote four weeks," said the engineer.

"Which machines can we demonstrate for him as examples?" asked Max.

"We don't have anything in the shop close to it."

"Have we built one similar for anyone in town? Could we take him to another customer's shop?"

"Closest is probably M&G," said his engineer.

"Can you ask them if we could bring a prospective customer over tomorrow?" said Max.

"I'll go see them this afternoon and clear it."

"Max, there's a boy here to see you," shouted a worker over the noise of the shop.

"Where is he?" shouted Max.

"Downstairs by the front door."

Max walked through the ironworks shop and saw Anthony watching a man heating and bending iron rods.

"Anthony."

"Good afternoon, Max. Annie asked me to bring you this," he said, handing him the letter.

"Everything all right?" said Max.

"She left this morning," said Anthony.

"Left for where?"

"New York."

"What? Why?"

"She went to our cousin's house in Seneca Falls. She said she had to figure some things out. I'm sure the letter will explain."

Max looked at the letter. "Thank you." He tore it open.

Dear Max,

I'm sorry I didn't have the opportunity to see you before I departed. I left in haste so as not to allow anyone to influence a change of heart. I'm traveling to see my cousin in Seneca Falls. After my father died, I spent the summer at Lizzie's house. While I was there, she helped me begin to cope with the loss of my father and know my life without him.

Lizzie knows women's plight. She has previously shown a degree of empathy that I am in dire need of today. I pray she will provide much-needed counsel to me as I feel lost.

I love you and want to be with you, but I am afraid of what I will give up if I enter into marriage. I already face a world that I feel is against me. I fear that if I marry, I will give up what little rights and freedoms I have. I want to pursue work that stimulates my mind and challenges me. I want to advance rights for all women. I don't know if this combination of my personal objectives and a family would be fair to you, me or any of our future children. Before I enter into marriage, I must come to my own decision about what I must do.

I love you as I have never loved another, and my heart aches thinking about a life without you. We are kindred souls who have come to know each other's natures, dreams, and disappointments. I thank you for your kindness, patience, and undying support. My dilemma is not one of your character or worthiness; it is my search to know my own heart.

Please understand and afford me this pilgrimage. I ask for forgiveness for any pain my quandary causes you.

I love you,
Annie

CHAPTER 25

Annie stepped down from the carriage in front of a large white clapboard-sided farmhouse surrounded by fields and bare trees. She was exhausted from the thirty-hour trip but felt a sense of peace now that she was here. The cab driver carried her trunk up the drive and set it on the front porch. Annie paid him and knocked on the door.

A simply dressed woman opened the door, a three-year-old girl at her side.

"Good afternoon, may I help you?" said the housekeeper.

"Amelia. I'm Annie Bennett. I don't know if you remember me? I'm Elizabeth's second cousin. I spent the summer with you several years back."

"Yes, Annie. Oh my. How are you?" said Amelia.

"I'm sorry to arrive unannounced, but I've come on the train from Cincinnati, hoping to see Elizabeth."

"Come in, please. You must be exhausted."

"Hi there," Annie said to the young girl, hugging Amelia's legs.

"This is Margaret."

"Hi, Margaret. I'm Annie."

"Mrs. Stanton is in the kitchen. Come on back."

"Well, my Lord," said Elizabeth, wearing an apron, dark hair pulled back into a bun. "What a surprise! Little Annie has grown into a beautiful young lady."

"Cousin Lizzie. It's so wonderful to see you," Annie burst into tears; the flood of the memory of her last visit after her father's death, combined with her current anguish and the lack of sleep, caused a total loss of Annie's self-control.

Elizabeth pulled Annie into her arms and let her cry against her ample bosom. "My Goodness. There, there. Shh. It's all right." She let Annie cry it out.

"I'm sorry. I'm so exhausted from the train, and I'm in such a way. Please excuse me."

Elizabeth handed her a clean dish towel. "Don't worry. Sit down here and tell me about it. I'm making pies, but I'm all ears."

"I'm sorry I didn't write first, but I left Cincinnati suddenly yesterday. I'm going through some emotional times, and I was hoping to talk to you. You were so kind and helpful to me after Father died. I look up to you and respect you, and I need your advice."

"Don't you worry about that. We've extra bedrooms, and I'm used to guests. Henry says our house is like a women's movement hotel. You aren't the first woman to show up unannounced. We've plenty of room for you to stay as long as you need."

"Thank you. You're very kind."

"Are you hungry? Thirsty?"

"Just some water, please."

"This is Carla. She helps me with the cooking."

"Please to meet you, Miss," said Carla.

"How are your mother and sister and brothers?" asked Elizabeth.

"Mother's happy with her new husband, Mr. Neltner. He's been very kind to us all. He bought a grand house for us. Caleb is off to West Point. The boys are in school. Caroline is meeting the eligible young men of Cincinnati."

"And you? In your last letter, you mentioned a young man."

"Max, yes. He's wonderful. He's asked me to marry him."

"Well, congratulations."

"It's just. I don't know where to begin."

"What's the matter, dear? Are you with child?"

"Oh, no," said Annie, blushing. "We haven't."

"I'm sorry. I didn't mean to imply that I thought you would have improper relations."

"I don't know if I can marry him," said Annie. "Marriage will just further restrict what liberties I do have. I love him with all my heart, but I don't know if I can do it. That's why I'm here. You understand these things. I don't know what to do."

"Yes. The life of a woman is not easy, is it?"

Annie cried into the towel again. She tried to speak, but only gibberish came out between her sobs.

"I am happy to talk with you about this and anything else you want to, but right now, I think you need to get some rest. You're in no mind to think clearly. Why don't you have a bath and get some rest? Sleep as long as you like. We'll fix you a plate when you wake up, don't worry about coming down for supper. Does that sound right?"

"Yes, thank you," said Annie.

"Amelia!" called Elizabeth.

The housekeeper appeared in the hallway. "Yes, ma'am?"

"Please show Annie to the green room and help her get settled. Help her draw a bath. She's going to sleep after her long train trip."

Elizabeth walked to the back door and yelled out, "Daniel!"

The boy came inside. "Yes, Mother."

"This is my cousin's daughter, Annie, from Cincinnati. Do you remember her? She stayed with us one summer?"

"Hi, Annie. Yes. you played the piano."

"Daniel, carry Annie's luggage upstairs to the green room for her."

"My trunk is on the front porch. Thank you, Daniel," said Annie. "Thank you, Lizzie. I'm so grateful to be here with you."

\#

Annie woke to Elizabeth's boys' voices and their quick feet bounding down the stairs. She smelled bacon and realized she hadn't eaten since she left Cincinnati. She looked out the window. Most of the trees were bare, and the grasses in the fields were brown. The garden was the remnants of the summer's harvest, with only yellow and brown leafed plants and dried sunflower stalks remaining.

She remembered the yard in full green, a lush garden and playing in the barn with the boys as Elizabeth worked. The boys' nonjudgmental acceptance of her, free spirits, and unending energy had been a solace to her that summer. In the evenings, she sat and listened as Elizabeth talked with her friends about women's injustices and possibilities. She met the timid, the bold, the articulate and the brash and was inspired by their frank discussions and ideas of what might be. Over the summer, she gradually replaced her father's reassuring presence with an inner self-voice that allowed her to go back home and face her life without him.

She dressed and joined the family in the dining room.

"Good morning, dear. Did you sleep well?" said Elizabeth.

"Very well, thank you," said Annie.

"You saw Daniel and Margaret yesterday. This is Henry Junior, Gerrit and Theodore. Say good morning to your cousin Annie."

Annie greeted them and asked, "How old are you, Theodore?"

"Four."

"Such a big boy. You and Margaret weren't even born last time I visited. Henry and Gerrit, you're both so grown up."

"Finish your breakfast, boys. Don't be late for school," directed Elizabeth.

Annie watched the three older boys devour the food on their plates, rise, kiss their mother, and dash for the hallway. She heard shuffling and shouts, then the door slammed.

"That was quite a squall," said Annie. "Are they always so lively in the morning?"

"You have no idea," said Elizabeth. "We have relative quiet until they return this afternoon. Help yourself to what's left of the eggs, bacon and pancakes. Would you like some coffee?"

"Yes, please."

"Carla, could you please pour a cup of coffee for Annie?"

"Where is Mr. Stanton?" asked Annie.

"He is in Albany this week. He's helping to establish a new Republican Party organization for the state. He'll return on Friday."

Annie said, "The town is growing. I don't recall so many factories and enterprises along the river."

"Yes, it's changing," said Elizabeth. "The railroad has opened up new markets. And the factories have brought many new residents to work them. It's not all good change. Did you notice the old grain mill across the street? It's now a distillery. The air reeks at times. Not the fresh country air we used to enjoy. And the factories' jobs can be taxing. Men work twelve-hour days in them, leaving their wives to fend for themselves with the children. I wish there were a kinder way to help the masses earn a living."

"I see it in Cincinnati, too," said Annie. "I teach in a district of primarily German immigrant families. Many live in tenement apartments crowded with three or even four families. Some of the children come to school hungry. They have so little."

"God bless them. And you for your work. Tell me, what were your impressions of the convention?"

Annie shared her observations from the conference and the motivation it inspired in her. Elizabeth spoke of the women who organized it and the work she was continuing to do on behalf of women, temperance and the abolition of slavery. "Since the children, I let the other women do most of the lecturing and traveling. Susan B. Anthony comes to stay with me, and we work on platforms, speeches and petitions together. I do the writing, and she goes out into the world and speaks. She's become a part of the family. We make a good team."

"How do you do it all? A marriage with a household and children and pursue your work? I wonder if it wouldn't be easier to stay unmarried."

Elizabeth said, "Yes, I think it would be easier in many ways, but lonelier. I don't envy the spinster who spends her nights alone with no one to confide in or share her joys and sorrows. I was fortunate to meet Henry. He was an abolitionist, fighting against slavery before I came along. We found that our shared passion for human rights allowed us to understand each other. We have our shared interests, but we each allow the other to pursue the things that fulfill us."

"I look at the life of a wife and see it as a huge sacrifice. Must I give up my own identity to have love?" said Annie.

"Companionship and passion are part of what makes us whole as humans. These are two good reasons to get married. A woman's passion is as alive as a man's. We can't suppress it. So, if you find passion, embrace it. It doesn't require you to abandon your identity."

"But a woman's role in a marriage is subservient. I've read the law. Men have all the rights over women," said Annie.

"The position of women in society today is a product of history. It will take time to change. We, women, find ourselves at this time needing to make the best of our situation while we change it. Whether you marry or not, you face the same injustices. If you choose to marry, marry wisely. Listen to the passion, but marry a man who has an open mind and a commitment to you as an equal partner. The important thing is that he be committed and receptive to understanding you and working with you against the powers of history."

"I don't see how that makes it possible to be a wife and an individual," said Annie.

"In my marriage, Henry respects me and allows me my freedoms, but I'm responsible for our children and home. He has no interest in caring for children, cooking or running a household. At times, I get frustrated, seeing him off with his associates for an evening or taking a trip to Albany, leaving me to care for our children, but someone has to do it. I pray that someday, men might accept that role, but I haven't seen a man yet who takes it on. And for now, women can't earn the wages themselves to provide for a family, so I accept the responsibility. I love my children and want to shape them to be good men and women."

"How do you see to your children and your work?"

"Henry and I agree that taking care of the children is only part of my role. I am free to pursue a vocation that enriches and satisfies me. I can do this because we have the means to pay for help. Amelia has been with me for years and is like a second mother to our children. I could not do what I do without help. It would be physically impossible. With her help, though, I make it work. I have also employed cooks, laundresses and maids. I spend most of my days working in my study and leave the daily drudgery of the household to them. Most of the women I hire only stay for a period and then move on for higher-paying wages or other reasons. Housework is not glamorous. I pity poor mothers bound to their homes with no support, and I thank God that I have been blessed with my position in life. Unless we inherit wealth, we as women are subject to the standard of living of our husbands. Does Max have the means to hire domestic help for you?"

"Yes, he does. Even so, I have been searching my heart to determine if I want marriage and children or if I am better suited as a spinster with a profession."

Elizabeth poured more coffee for herself, then refilled Annie's cup. "Over time, I've learned to accept that I can't have it all," said Elizabeth. "One must make compromises. Life is a series of choices. There's no absolute way to do things. I've learned not to worry about the less important things. If my house is a mess because I don't have time to tidy up every day, no harm will come to my children. I don't let others' judgments of what they think I should do cause me angst. I've learned not to insist on having everything I want. It's not possible and will only cause grief. Choose the things to fight for that are most important in your life and stand firm for your rights.

"You're so pragmatic. I don't know if I can do it," said Annie.

"Does Max know your heart and desire to be an independent woman?"

"Yes, he does."

"Does he respect that and you as a person?"

"Yes."

"Do you think he can accept the compromises he will need to make to live in a non-traditional marriage with you?"

"I think so, but how does one truly know?" said Annie.

"Yes, does one ever truly know another person?" said Elizabeth. "All you can do is judge based on his actions, beyond his words. Look past the attraction of early romance and into the soul. Does he have the grace to love, to admit fault and the commit to a life with you as you are?"

"He has a good heart that comes from his Christian education and empathy for others," said Annie. "I think he understands me as well as any man could. I love him deeply, but my mother has forbidden me to marry him. His family is from the German community, Catholic and of little means. She fears my loss of position in society. I do not care about such things. She does not know him and is judgmental of him based on his family's history."

"Your mother is a product of her own circumstances," said Elizabeth. "She was raised to regard one's position in society as very important. Your father was less concerned with such things. I imagine his passing and her loss of income and standing, and then having to leave New York, was devastating to her personally. She wants to protect her children and will do so in the best way she can."

"I hadn't considered her perspective that way," said Annie.

"Position does afford a person freedoms and opportunities that those without do not have. One must make a living to feed a family, and wealth can give you the means to aid others."

"Max was born of little means but now owns his own business," said Annie. "He has accumulated some wealth as a self-made man. But our families will never love each other the way Max and I love each other. The prejudices of class keep the two divided. Max and I have accepted this, but my mother cannot."

"You must decide then if you can marry without her blessing and potentially no longer have her in your life."

"You grew up with my father. What do you think he would say?"

"I believe your father would want you to be happy. He wouldn't want any harm to come to you. He would worry that you would marry and be disappointed when your life fell short of your dreams. He would want to protect you but would trust you to make your own decision."

"I miss him. If my mother doesn't agree to my marriage, the church won't marry me. What do I do?"

"If it's not important to you, you can have a ceremony outside of your church or a civil ceremony. Not being married in a church is probably more of a problem for Max as a Catholic. Have you and he discussed this?"

"Yes, he understands and accepts it. His only request is that our children be baptized as Catholics. My dilemma is, what if I don't want to have children, or at least not right away? I don't know if there's a way to prevent children."

"Did you also discuss this with him?" asked Elizabeth. "Catholics don't believe in preventing pregnancy."

"No, but I don't even know how to prevent it. I don't know anything about it," said Annie.

"It's a delicate subject, but I understand its importance to a woman who wants to pursue a vocation beyond child-rearing. There are several ways to prevent pregnancy. The first is to abstain from relations with your husband. Do you know what I mean by relations?"

"I think so, but I'm not sure exactly."

Elizabeth explained the general mechanics and science of sex to Annie, then explained abstinence, condoms, new experimental spermicidal lotions, abortion, and the withdrawal method of birth control. "All of this will make more sense to you once you've had relations with your husband, but you are wise to consider it and discuss it with him."

"I don't know. It's all so embarrassing," said Annie.

"These topics are not spoken of in polite conversation, but it will be tremendously helpful if you can discuss them openly with your husband. I understand you will be uncomfortable at first, but you must try."

Annie sat thinking and began controlled breaths to calm herself.

"Is there anything else you want to talk about?" said Elizabeth.

"No, not right now. Thank you. You've given me plenty to ponder. You've been so helpful and kind."

"I need to attend to some matters in my office," said Elizabeth. "We can talk more later. Make yourself at home, play the piano. There are books on the shelves. Take a walk or a nap. Let Amelia know if you need anything."

"Do you have any of your speeches? I'd love to read them," said Annie.

Elizabeth gave her a stack of papers to read, suggesting the ones she might find of most interest. "The savages will return around 4:00, and we'll have supper at 5:30."

#

Annie spent the afternoon reading some of Elizabeth's writings. She enjoyed dinner with the family, and she and Elizabeth talked further into the evening. She went to bed but couldn't sleep. She tossed and turned, wanting answers to come but not finding them. She felt a calling to lead in the women's movement but was afraid to venture down that path alone, without Max. He made her feel secure in the world and capable.

CHAPTER 26

The next morning, she took a long walk into town and back and then sat on a bench in the garden amongst the fruit trees. She reflected on all she and Elizabeth had discussed. She wanted it all. She loved Max and wanted him by her side. She wanted the freedom to pursue a career beyond teaching. She wanted to be judged on her abilities and merits, not dismissed as a lesser person because she was a woman. She envisioned children and a family with Max someday, too. Why couldn't she have it all as men do? She felt like she could do it. She wouldn't be told she couldn't.

Max came into her life by chance and was a source of joy and support that surpassed even her father. She didn't think anyone could replace him, ever. If she let go of Max, she might become lost on her own. She had to trust what her heart was telling her. She needed his love. The rest of her life would evolve.

A strong breeze blew a swirl of leaves into the air. She watched a squirrel make several round trips from the ground to a nest in a tree with peach pits in its mouth.

"Annie."

Startled, she stood and turned to see Max standing, hands in his overcoat pockets.

She broke into a smile. They moved to each other, embraced and kissed. When she saw his blue eyes glisten with tears, she shed tears of her own. He wiped her cheeks.

"What are you doing here?" she asked.

"I couldn't let you run away and choose your life alone. I want to be a part of it, and I wanted to be here to remind you that I'm here. I'll always be by your side. It's unfair that you have to choose one path over another because you're a woman. I can't imagine what that must be like. Let's find a way to make a path together."

She bit her lip to suppress more tears and nodded.

They sat on the bench and talked for several hours. She poured out her thoughts and feelings.

"Let's get married. Now, here in Seneca Falls," Annie said.

"Are you serious?"

"Yes. Mother won't approve of our marriage, so Pastor Fee won't allow us to be married in his church, anyway."

"Annie, is that really what you want?"

"I want to be with you. I don't need an elaborate wedding. I don't need my mother's blessing. I know I would have my father's. Does it surprise you?"

"Yes, but I'm growing accustomed to your surprises. You're certain this is what you want—to be married? Now?" said Max.

"Nothing is certain in my life, but I'm as certain about marrying you as I am about anything. I don't want to face the future alone. I love you."

"I love you, too."

#

After supper, Annie and Max sat talking with Elizabeth. They told Elizabeth of their desire to get married, and she offered to see her minister the next day.

"I don't have a ring for you, Annie. I'll buy you one when we return home," said Max.

Elizabeth excused herself and returned. She presented a gold wedding band to them. "It was your father and my grandmother's, your great grandmother's. You should have it. It's too dainty for my pudgy fingers."

"Oh, Lizzie." She took it and tried it on. "It's perfect. Thank you."

#

Max and Annie stood before the minister in front of the Stanton's fireplace, with Elizabeth's family standing witness to their marriage. Annie wore the most formal dress she had packed in her trunk. Max wore the only trousers, waistcoat, and the finer of the two jackets he had in his bag. Elizabeth invited a friend to stand as best man, and she served as Annie's matron of honor.

The preacher began reading from his prayer book, "Dearly beloved, we are gathered together here in the sight of God, and in the face of this company, to join together this man and this woman in holy matrimony."

He continued, then prompted them, "Max Mueller, wilt thou have this woman to thy wedded wife to live together after God's ordinance in the holy estate of matrimony? Wilt thou love her, comfort her, honor, and keep her in sickness and in health; and, forsaking all others, keep thee only unto her, so long as ye both shall live?"

"I will," said Max.

"Annie Bennett, wilt thou have this man to thy wedded husband to live together after God's ordinance in the holy estate of matrimony? Wilt thou love him, comfort him, honor, and keep him in sickness and in health; and, forsaking all others, keep thee only unto him, so long as ye both shall live?"

"I will," said Annie.

"Take Annie's right hand," the preacher said to Max, "and repeat after me. I, Max, take thee, Annie, to my wedded wife to have and to hold from this day forward, for better for worse, for richer for poorer, in sickness and in health, to love and to cherish, till death us do part, according to God's holy ordinance; and thereto I plight thee my troth."

When Max had finished, the preacher continued with Annie's vows, then the giving of the ring, followed by The Lord's Prayer and the pronouncement of their marriage. He gave a final blessing.

Elizabeth turned to Max and Annie, both beaming, "May God bless and keep you both."

"Thank you for your kindness," said Max.

"I will be forever grateful for your counsel, inspiration and charity," said Annie.

"Let us celebrate. Amelia has prepared a meal for us," Elizabeth announced.

Annie and Max dined with Elizabeth and her children and guests.

"Congratulations on joining the club of Lucy Stoners," said Elizabeth to Annie.

"What does that mean?" asked Max.

Elizabeth explained, "Lucy Stone is one of the national women's movement leaders. She was the first woman in the movement to refuse to take her husband's name in marriage. Other women have followed, and they are referred to as Lucy Stoners."

"Lucy was the woman who gave the speech about being a disappointed woman at the Women's convention. Do you remember," said Annie?

Max asked, "Is she also the one with the idea to remove the bride's promise to obey her husband from the wedding vows?"

Elizabeth said, "No, that is one that many of the movement's women have convinced their preachers to remove. I took it out of my wedding vows, as well. We see that one-sided promise as a symbol of women's subservient place in marriage and society. Including it in the vows sets the wrong tone of the marriage from the start."

"I'm not sure Annie has obeyed anyone in her life, so I would stand little chance in asking for that as a promise," Max laughed.

\#

"Thank you again for the beautiful wedding day," Annie said to Elizabeth.

"My pleasure, dear," she said. "Good night."

Max and Annie climbed the stairs. When they reached the door of Annie's bedroom, Annie said, "Let me prepare myself for bed, then I will come to your room."

Max nodded and continued down the hall. A half an hour later, Annie knocked on his door. When he opened it, Annie stood in her nightclothes, hair down, curls framing her face.

He smiled, still dressed in his trousers and shirt. He took her hand and pulled her into his arms, pushing the door closed behind him. They kissed gently at first, then more passionately. Max felt the unrestrained softness of her curves for the first time in her loose nightclothes. His passion was enflamed. He guided her toward the bed and onto it. He kissed her and moved to her neck, kissing and reveling in the softness and wonder of her body. He explored her bosom with kisses and gentle touches. She responded with her own awakened passion and felt him through his clothes. She reached down to untuck his shirt. He pulled it over his head and then began removing her nightgown, asking for permission with a nod of his head. She nodded in assent. They pressed together, feeling the charge of skin against skin, both pressing their bodies and lips closer to bury themselves deeper in each other for the first time.

He caressed her, slowly and gently exploring her body. She relished the sensation and swam in the euphoria of his adoration. They made love.

Afterward, he fell asleep in her embrace. She untangled herself from him and sat up. She pulled back the covers and studied him, seeing a man naked for the first time. She gently brushed her fingertips along his collar bone, down the center of his chest and along the light hair that led below his navel. He stirred, and she drew her hand back.

He opened his eyes, smiling. "What are you doing?"

"I'm sorry."

"It's all right. I'm yours, now."

"It's just that I've never seen a man undressed other than my brothers when they were boys. A man's body is very different."

He sat up and kissed her, lightly brushing her bosom. "And I am in awe of the beauty and wonder of yours."

They made love again.

When Max slept, Annie stood, slipped on her nightgown and quietly returned to her room.

#

On the long train ride home, the newlyweds sat closer than was respectable but ignored the passengers' stares. They enjoyed their window into the beauty of the American landscape of hills, trees, meadows, lakes, rivers and growing towns. They put off talk of life's realities, enjoying their honeymoon as long as possible.

When they passed Columbus, Ohio, Max's pragmatism broke the spell. "I'll need to ask the Carsons if you can stay in my room until we find a place of our own. Unless you want to stay with your family?"

"No, that isn't possible. I fear Mother will want nothing to do with me when we tell her what we've done. I have accepted the fact."

"We'll go together to tell them in a day or so. We'll also need to tell my family. That will be easier. What will happen with your position at school?"

"Anthony delivered a letter to Mr. Nye for me, asking for a personal leave, but I suspect he is already in the process of hiring my replacement. No matter. I have decided that I can do more to advance women by doing work that stimulates my intellect rather than teaching or lecturing about the women's movement. I will promote women's position by doing rather than talking about it. I may go to college to do that or find an employer who will hire me. I'll start exploring a plan, soon."

Max said, "In the meantime, will you assist me at Miller Industries? I need the help. You've proven you have many of the intellectual and organizational skills to help with growing the business. It's our family business, now, so you have a vested interest in making it successful."

"What do you want me to do?"

"There's so much you can do. Put together sales proposals, meet with clients, organize the files, and manage the accounts. Once you learn how things work, I'm sure you'll have suggestions on how you can make it better."

"Managing a manufacturing business. It's a traditional role for a new bride, don't you think?" she considered.

"Little about our marriage will be traditional, beginning with our wedding," he said.

CHAPTER 27

Upon their return to Cincinnati, Max arranged for his new bride to share his rented room. He quickly found a house to rent near the city's center and began to shop for the essentials to fill it. Annie put off going to visit her family, afraid of their reaction. She finally decided it was time, more to claim some of her needed clothing than to confront her mother. She felt it best if she went alone to break the news.

The next morning, Annie let herself into her family's house and found Caroline playing the piano in the parlor.

Caroline stopped and ran to Annie, embracing her. "Annie, you're safe! Oh, thank the Lord."

"Of course, I'm safe. What did you think happened to me?" said Annie.

"We were worried—you traveling alone. You've been gone nearly two weeks. Mother wrote to Aunt Lizzie, but we haven't heard back from her."

"Well, as you can see, I'm unharmed and healthy," said Annie.

Sarah came into the room, "Annie, thank heavens you've returned. I was fraught for your safety. Why did you run off like that?"

"I'm sorry, Mother, it was something I had to do. I needed to get away and think."

"Annie, you must learn to control your impulses. That was so irresponsible of you. I'm very disappointed."

"Mother, try to understand, please."

"Annie, your behavior was unacceptable and dangerous. What possessed you?"

"Mother, please, listen. I'll tell you. Can we sit?"

"Very well," Mother said. They all sat.

"Mother. I had to get away to think. I felt trapped as if I had nowhere to turn."

"Trapped by what?"

"I don't know if you can understand, but trapped by my situation. Working at the school under a man, Mr. Nye, who didn't respect me. I was doing my best to advocate for the girls in my class, but he disregarded my efforts and treated me like a madwoman. I couldn't continue working in a position where I was suppressed daily."

"Have you resigned from the school?" said mother. "Or were you terminated due to your sudden absence?"

"That doesn't matter," said Annie. "Please listen."

Her mother sighed.

"On top of lack of support at school, I also received none from you or anyone else in the family, save Anthony."

"Dear, we are only looking out for your best interests. You are still young and need our guidance. You can be difficult at times."

"I know you believe you're acting in my best interests, but ever since Father died, I have felt alone."

"I'm sorry you feel that way, dear. Honestly, we…"

"Please stop talking, Mother. Listen. I am not like you. I can't accept the place in this world that you and polite society expect me to fill. I want to do work that challenges me. I will never be content to be only a wife and a mother. I want those things, but not at the cost of giving up on my dreams. I will work to be accepted for who I am, and if that means changing the accepted norms for women, that's my cross to bear. You haven't supported me, but Max does. He's the only one since father that does. That's why I married him."

"What do you mean?" said her mother in astonishment.

"Max and I were married in Seneca Falls last week."

"Oh, Annie, what have you done?" said her mother.

"Annie," gasped Caroline.

"I decided that I wanted a life with the freedom to pursue my vocation and the love of a supportive husband. I can have that with Max."

"No, Annie. You're making a mistake. Look at what you're giving up."

"What am I giving up? A life of frustration, surrounded by people who judge me by criteria that I disagree with. Do you have any idea how hard it is to be me? You and most of society tell me that what I think and do is wrong at every turn. Every day. It makes me feel as if my very essence is somehow flawed. But I am not broken. I don't need to be fixed."

"Annie, your unconventional ways only make your life more difficult than it needs to be. You need to temper your behavior within acceptable limits of polite society."

"Mother, I can't. I'll face the difficulties that come with who I am. I can accept that more than attempting to live as a person I am not. Please try to understand that."

"I don't want you to be unhappy, but you risk more than just your own reputation. What about Stephen's and mine? Your sister's? Your brothers?"

"If you can't accept me for who I am and the decisions I make, then I'll leave. You won't have to worry about me damaging your reputation."

"No, I don't think we need to do that. You just need to temper yourself."

"No, I won't. I'm sorry. It pains me to walk away from my family, but Max is my family, now."

"Oh, Annie," said her mother. "You went directly against my word and married him. What kind of a life will you have?"

"One filled with love and support."

"Love? Child, love fades. You have succumbed to youthful passion. You don't know. Stephen can fix this. We'll ask him to annul the marriage in court. No one here knows about it. It's not too late."

"I love Max. He is my world, now."

"Annie, be reasonable."

"I hoped that I could make you understand or at least accept my decision. Accept him. But that's not possible, is it?"

"No, dear, I can't accept what you've done."

"I'm sorry, then. I'll go."

"No," said Caroline. "Mother, don't make her."

"Caroline, Annie has made her bed," said Mother. "Now, she must live in it."

"It's all right, Caroline. I'm happy with Max. I truly am," said Annie.

"What am I going tell your brothers?" said Mother.

"Tell them I love them and that I'm doing what father encouraged me to do."

"Don't project the ghost of your father on this. This is you, not him."

"Father impressed upon us to stand behind what we believed was right. That's what I'm doing."

"No, he wouldn't have wanted this for you," said mother.

"He does. He stands with me," said Annie. "I know he does."

"Daughter." She shook her head. "You're as stubborn as he was," she said as she left the room.

"Oh, Annie, please don't go do this. I don't understand. You're going to pick Max over your family?" said Caroline.

"I wish I didn't have to choose, but I must," said Annie tearfully. She hugged her sister.

"Don't go," said Caroline.

"I must."

"I'm afraid for you," said Caroline.

"Be happy for me," said Annie. "I hope you can be happy, too."

Annie broke their embrace. "I need to gather a few things from my room. I'll come later to pack the rest and have it taken to our new house."

"Where are you living?" asked Caroline.

"We've rented a house on Eighth Street."

"I can't believe you're married. What's it like?"

"It's wonderful. I feel like I belong with him."

"I'm happy for you, then. I feel like I don't know you, anymore," said Caroline.

"We're both growing up."

"Are you afraid?" asked Caroline.

"A little, yes, but I'm more excited for what the future holds for me."

CHAPTER 28

"Good morning," Max said, smiling at Annie, lying next to him on the bedroom floor of their newly rented home.

"How long have you been staring at me?" she said.

"I don't know." He stroked her face with a fingertip. "I still can't believe we're married." He kissed her. "How did you sleep?"

"I slept fine."

"This floor is hard. I can't wait to sleep in a bed tonight," said Max.

"I am not complaining. The two weeks we spent in the Carsons' house were awkward. It's so nice to have a house of our own."

"I know the house is far from perfect, but it was available to rent, now. It will give us time to decide where we want to buy a house. Maybe the suburbs? Mount Auburn? Clifton?" said Max.

"We have time for that. We have our privacy here."

"I've decided I'm going to do it," he said.

"What?"

"I'm going to run for city council. Now that you're helping me manage things at the shop, I can afford the time it will take to campaign."

"Good. I'm glad. We need men like you in office. Men with a heart," she said.

"You'll help me with the campaign, won't you?"

"Your speech editor awaits your first draft."

"Patrick's men will deliver the bed and other furniture this morning," said Max. "This afternoon, will you come to the shop to tabulate the wages and pay the men?"

"Yes." She pulled him to her and kissed him, reaching under the blanket.

"Don't do that, now. I have to get to the shop. I'm late already." He jumped up and began dressing. "We can christen the new bed tonight."

She watched him, admiring him. Although much of her future was unknown, she felt secure and confident in facing it.

#

After calling on his hardware supplier, Max returned to his office mid-morning. Coleman approached his desk. "Max, there was a message for you. One of your parents' neighbors. It's bad news. There's been a fire at the Eichen Garten."

"Oh no. How bad?" said Max.

"I'm afraid it was tragic. He said it took your father and your sister. I'm so sorry."

"Oh, Jesus. Which sister?"

"I don't know. He didn't say."

Max lowered his head for a moment. "I'm going up there. Can you mind things?"

"Yes, you go. I'll manage fine."

"When Annie comes in this afternoon, will you tell her? She needs to do payroll, but then, she knows where to find me."

Max sprinted north toward the canal. He became winded and walked for a while, then ran again. As he approached the bridge, he smelled the smoke in the air. He saw two fire engines and a crowd of people standing in the street in front of the saloon. The second-floor windows were broken out, and black soot covered the brick around the openings. The firemen were packing up their hoses and gear.

Max approached one of the firemen, "Where is my family?" he asked.

A neighbor approached, "Max, your mother is up in Mrs. Becker's apartment across the street."

Max walked between the two buildings and up the outdoor stairs in the rear. There was a crowd of neighbors on the back porch. As he walked by them, they offered words of comfort or sympathy, but he was oblivious to them and went inside. His mother sat in a chair in a daze, Peter and Helene at her sides. Albert stood nearby. He hugged Helene and began to cry, "Oh God. Father and Marie."

"No, it was Elli," Helene said.

He buried his head in her shoulder and sobbed. Once he stopped crying, he went to his mother, "Mother, Oh, Mother." He squatted down to her level and took her hand. "I'm sorry."

She nodded her head. "He's gone."

He held her hand for another minute, then stood up. He motioned to Peter to join him outside. The neighbors stood respectfully as the two passed.

"Let us know if we can do anything," said one of the women.

"We pray for their souls." Some crossed themselves.

They met Saint Mary's priest, Father Hammer, on the street. "Father."

"Peter, Max, what a tragedy. How is your mother?"

"She's upstairs," Max said.

"I came as soon as I heard. I sent for the undertaker. The parish will help your mother in this time of deep sorrow."

"Thank you, father. We'll come by the parish office to make arrangements for the funeral," said Max."

"Tomorrow. Come tomorrow. Comfort your mother, today. I'm going to go up and see her, now."

"Thank you, father," they said.

"Where are the others. Do they know?" Max asked Peter.

He shook his head, "Oskar and Albert had already left for school this morning when the fire started. Marie had gone to work."

"Do you know what happened?"

Peter said, "I was with Mother at the market, buying groceries. Helene had gone to get her sewing for the day. When Mother and I came home, we smelled the smoke. I tried to get upstairs, but the fire was too strong. I could hear Elli crying. I shouted for Papa, but he didn't wake up."

"Oh, God, how awful for Elli," said Max.

"I told Mother to go for help. I yelled for Elli to go to a window, but she didn't. Then I couldn't hear her anymore. The fire crew from the Union Fire Company up on Race Street came first, after about twenty-five minutes. Then the big steam-powered fire engine got here a few minutes later, and they ran in there with their hoses. When the ladder company arrived, they broke out a window, but the fire was too consuming for them to go in. I told them Elli and Papa were in there. They said they couldn't go in. It took them over an hour to extinguish the fire. After it was out, they went in through the windows and brought them down. Mother stood across the street and watched it all. She hasn't said much since."

Max started crying again. Peter put his hand on his shoulder and squeezed it, his eyes tearing.

The undertakers arrived with their carriage. Max and Peter greeted the two men and were joined by Constable Kuhn and Officer Lichtendahl from the police. They conferenced for a minute, then went inside the Eichen Garten. The smell of smoke was heavy, and the room was damp, water running down the walls and dripping from the ceiling. Max looked around the room, which was hardly recognizable. He feared for his family; their livelihood was now destroyed.

"I need one of you to identify the bodies," said the constable.

The brothers looked at each other in horror. "I'll do it," said Max.

Max splashed through puddles as he made his way to the tarp-covered bodies. The undertaker pulled back the tarp on the smaller mound. Max immediately smelled the charred flesh and held his breath. He recognized Elli's face, blackened all over but identifiable from her round cheeks. He stepped back and exhaled. "It's Elli."

"Full name?" said the Constable.

"Ellen Mueller," said Max.

"Age?"

"Twelve."

"Christ, that's a shame," said the officer. "Address?"

"407 Vine Street."

"You ready for this one?'

"Uh-huh," mumbled Max.

The undertaker pulled the other tarp back. Again, the smell of charred flesh. It was a discernable body but burned beyond recognition. Max stared.

The cop, looking at his notebook, said impatiently, "Well?"

"I don't know. I can't tell." Max began to cry. "I don't know."

The cop looked at him and motioned to the undertaker to replace the tarp. "It's all right. Do you know if the deceased had any identifying features, body marks or jewelry that we might use to confirm identification?"

"I don't know," said Max.

Peter said from behind them, "He wore a wedding ring."

The cop pushed Max back with his arm and motioned to the coroner.

Max stood next to Peter with his head down. He sniffled and tried to regain his composure.

The cop approached them and held out his palm, holding the blackened wedding band.

Peter said, "That's his wedding ring."

He handed it to Peter.

"What was his name?"

"Karl Mueller." Peter was answering this time.

"Age?"

"53?" Peter said hesitantly.

Max nodded in agreement.

"Address?"

"407 Vine Street."

"Thank you, boys," said the cop and left with the precinct officer.

The undertaker came over to them. "I'm sorry for your loss. We'll take the deceased, now. We'll be in touch with Father Hammer regarding the funeral and burial. Who's the next of kin?"

"Our mother, his wife. Katharina Mueller."

"Same address?"

"Yes."

"Thank you."

Max walked around the bar and took a bottle of whiskey from the shelf. He opened it and took a drink. He handed it to Peter, who did the same and handed it back. Max took another pull and set it on the bar. He let out a big sigh. "What a mess." He walked to the stairwell and looked up. The top of the stairs had burned completely. "We'll have to get someone in here tomorrow to assess the damage and board up the windows. Do you know if she was paying the fire insurance premiums?"

"I don't know," said Peter.

"I hope so. I'll go to the insurance office, tomorrow."

"Max, you in there?" called a man's voice in German.

"Yes, back here."

Willy Jackson walked in. "Max, Peter, I'm so sorry. This is terrible. Your poor mother. How is she?"

"She's still in shock," said Max.

"The Eichen Garten is a fixture in our community. I just left Turner Hall. Your friend Gustav is already rounding up a group of men to help with the cleanup. They'll be here, tomorrow."

"God bless him," said Max. I'll check on whether the insurance premiums were paid up, tomorrow. If not, I'll get the money. We appreciate the Turners mobilizing with the manpower."

Willy said, "Peter, does your family need a place to sleep tonight? We can let you sleep at the hall if you need it."

"Mother and the girls will probably stay at the Beckers'. Albert, Oskar and I could use a bed, yes."

"I'll let them know to expect you."

"Thank you, Willy," said Peter.

Max picked up the bottle from the counter. They took another drink, and he put it in his coat pocket. They crossed the street and climbed the Beckers' stairs. Thankfully, the gallery of spectators and sympathizers had thinned. They found Mother and Helene in the same chairs where they left them. Neighbors had left food on the table.

Out of nowhere, Mother spoke, "Peter, we need to open up. People will want to come to ask about Papa and Elli."

Peter said, "Mother, we can't open up. The fire burned up the saloon. We have to repair it first. We're going to stay closed, today. The Turners are bringing some men to help clean up tomorrow."

"No, No, they'll want to come to say goodbye to Papa and Elli at the Eichen Garten."

Max said, "Mother, I spoke with Father Hammer. We'll have a funeral at Saint Mary's in a few days. They'll say goodbye there."

Max waved Helene over. "Mrs. Becker, can we talk with you?" Peter, Helene and Max gathered with her in a corner. "Thank you so much for taking Mother in."

"Of course, she would do the same for anyone on this street," said Mrs. Becker.

"Can Mother and the girls stay here for a few days?"

"Yes, of course. We'll make room."

"Thank you. Peter, Oskar and Albert will stay at the Turner Hall for tonight, anyway. It looks like neighbors have already started bringing food."

"Father Hammer said to let the church know what clothes or anything else you need," said Mrs. Becker.

"Helene, can you take care of that?" She nodded.

"I'll take care of the funeral mass and burial arrangements," said Max.

"Peter, I need you to be in charge of the Eichen Garten cleanup and restoration. I can't be here to supervise every day, so you'll need to do it. If the Turners don't have the men, I'll find a construction crew. Let's see what they say after they look tomorrow. If we can get the water and smoke out and get the saloon back in operation first, we can worry about the house upstairs later. Also, go around and let the brewery and the baker and anyone else know we won't be buying supplies this week.

"Keep a watch out for Albert and Marie. When they come home, they will go through the same shock we did. I'll retrieve Oskar from Saint Xavier at the end of the school day. I want to talk to him and prepare him before he comes home and sees all this. I'll bring him by to see Mother and the girls. Do you think I should have Oskar stay with Annie and me downtown?"

Helene said, "No, he needs to be around a familiar neighborhood until he gets through this."

"All right. I'll bring him to you after he sees Mother."

"What can we do to help Mother through this?" asked Helene.

"Mrs. Becker, any suggestions?" said Max.

"We'll keep her comfortable and warm. Someone will stay by her side. I'll see if she'll eat something. She'll go through waves of emotions, but it could take a while. Everyone grieves differently."

Max pulled the bottle of whiskey out of his pocket. "This might help her relax. Can you give her a cup?" Max took another big swig before surrendering the bottle to her.

CHAPTER 29

Max and Annie sat quietly with Oskar in the wooden pew with Max's family. Annie took in the surroundings of the ornate Catholic church, the first she had ever visited. A large painting of Jesus floating in the clouds was poised above the altar, framed by golden arches and intricate, cast gilded leaves and vines. Gold columns flanked the altar, and six life-sized statues of Mary, Joseph and other saints rested atop bases on both sides. The altar was elevated several steps above the church; its focal point was a large gilded tabernacle below the painting of Jesus. Candles lit the altar. The church's tall ceiling was covered with a fresco painting of rectangles and circles, creating a three-dimensional symmetrical pattern.

The congregation stood as the procession moved up the center aisle. An altar boy led, carrying a tall crucifix, followed by the pallbearers with the caskets, two more altar boys, and Father Hammer, holding a gold incense burner suspended from a chain. When the priest reached the coffins, he waved the incense over them, then moved across the altar, waving it at the painting of Jesus, the altar table beneath it and the statues on both sides of the altar. He handed the incense to an altar boy, stood in the center facing the back wall, and began speaking rapidly in Latin.

Annie could barely hear him, but everyone else in the church seemed to understand what he was saying. The congregation knelt as the priest continued to pray rhythmically, almost a chant, and at points, the mourners would respond in unison in Latin. Even young Oskar had memorized the prayers they recited as they alternated between standing and kneeling. Max's mother sat with closed eyes, lips moving as if speaking to her husband or God.

The priest approached the altar and took a chalice from the ornate tabernacle, and began praying before it. The altar boy rang hand-held bells in between some of the prayers. Then the priest and altar boy moved down to the communion rail. In an orderly fashion, the congregation moved in two lines to the front of the church. Each knelt at the rail, stuck out their tongue and let the priest place the communion bread on it. They crossed themselves, stood and returned to their pew. Max leaned to Annie and whispered to her to stay seated since she wasn't Catholic. Annie watched the lines move along. There were hundreds there to show their support for the family. Many stopped and put their hands on the caskets as if saying goodbye to Elli and Karl before proceeding to the rail. Some mourners shed tears as they approached the caskets. Max's mother remained stoic, throughout.

After communion, Father Hammer stood in the pulpit on the side of the altar and spoke in German. "Today, we mourn the loss of two of God's children. Young Ellen was born and lived with a kind heart but a slow mind. At the mercy of others, but always greeting you with a smile. She was taken in her youth and is now perfect in mind and body in heaven for eternity with her father nearby."

He moved on to "Karl Mueller left the Fatherland as a young man, left his homeland after persecution for standing and fighting for better conditions for the working man. He was released from captivity on the condition that he leave his homeland and never return. He came to Cincinnati and joined our community, where he met his wife, Katharina."

Max turned momentarily to Annie with a concerned look on his face, but she couldn't understand the German eulogy.

The priest continued, "The American blacksmiths rejected him as an immigrant, so he opened the Eichen Garten to support his growing family. He and Katharina created a haven where we all feel welcome. Many of us gather there on Sunday afternoons to revel in the blessings of each other and all of God's gifts. The memory of his incarceration and the disappointment of losing his trade haunted him until his death. His soul now joins Ellen's in heaven, and he is at peace. We will all miss him."

The priest and altar boy approached the caskets with a vessel of holy water. The priest dunked a rod into the cup and shook it at the caskets, sprinkling them with the water. He then approached one side of the church and sprinkled the people. The worshipers crossed themselves as he did this. He repeated the blessing on the other side of the church. As somber organ music filled the church, the priest, altar boys and pallbearers took their places and proceeded out of the church with the caskets. Max's sisters cried softly, and his mother finally broke down and cried silently as she said goodbye to her husband and daughter.

The family filed out of the church and down into the church basement for a meal prepared by the parish women. The family stood near the entrance to the room to receive the mourners. Max's mother nodded at the guests, but she said little. Max and his brothers spoke to the mourners on behalf of the family. Annie stood at Max's side and nodded politely as he introduced her to them, most speaking in German. As she met them, she sensed weariness on their faces. She thought it was deeper than grief or the solemnity of the occasion. Their countenances reflected years of toiling at work layered with cycles of hope and disappointments. She felt a flush of embarrassment in her new dress and hat.

#

Afterward, Annie, Max and his siblings went to a saloon further up Vine Street. Friends and neighbors greeted them in the more light-hearted setting. They sat drinking beer.

Albert said, "What did Father Hammer mean when he said persecution and incarceration?"

Max said, "I don't know. I was as surprised as you were when he said it. I only remember the story that he left Germany for political reasons and came to America for greater opportunities. They never talked about any of the specifics or dangers he encountered."

Peter said, "Papa told me the story. After Napoleon was defeated, the leaders of Europe held the Congress of Vienna to try to restore the order that the French revolution and other uprisings caused across Europe. The small Germanic nations were organized into the German Confederation. The new government censored the press and education, and suppressed any political or economic developments impacting their power. There were different factions within Germany disagreeing about what form of government should lead a unified Germany—democracy, republic or other. Papa was a political activist against the aristocrats and fought for reforms to aid the common man. He was arrested and imprisoned. They released Papa on the condition he leave the country, so he left Germany and fled to America. He met Mother here."

"No wonder he was so adamantly supportive of freedom of expression," said Albert.

"And nervous that the government could put down any attempt for the working class to gain power," said Peter.

"What did Father Hammer mean when he said that Papa was rejected and lost his trade as a blacksmith?"

Max said, "Mother once told me that he had been an apprentice in Germany and tried to find work as a blacksmith when he came to America, but he couldn't get anyone to take him on. She said he became disillusioned with America and gave up."

They sat silently, taking in this new information.

"Thankfully, after they married, he was able to build the Eichen Garten to make a living. Mother had been a maid for a wealthy family before they married," said Peter.

"I didn't know that," said Max.

"Yes, she left them when she and Papa married."

"And then we all came along," said Albert.

"All of us, plus little Agnes, taken by cholera, and now, Elli is gone, too," said Marie.

"Sweet Elli. She always had a smile for you. She was an example for us that no matter what happens, your attitude can make things better," said Max. "A toast to Elli."

"Prost!"

"And a toast to Papa!" said Peter.

"To Papa!"

"Peter, what are the Turners saying about the Eichen Garten renovation?" said Max.

"They have a man who does construction, Matt Wesselhoeft," said Peter.

"Yes, I know, Matt."

"He's going to put together a bid for us. He has a crew of men. The Turners cleaned out much of the debris over the past couple of days. They told me to leave the windows open to air it out. They brought some boards to put over the windows on the insides if it rains. They also brought a ladder for the stairwell. I went upstairs. The whole second floor is ruined. The third floor is unburned but smoky. He said we might have to replace the plaster on the walls if we can't wash the smell of the smoke away. Girls, if you want anything from your bedroom, I can go up the ladder to get it. Your clothes will need washing on account of the smoke."

"I went to the insurance company. The policy is paid up, so we will get money for the repairs," said Max.

"Thank God," said Peter.

"It may not be enough to cover it all, depending on how much. I'll make sure you have the money you need," said Max.

"Max, what happens now, I mean with Father and Elli, at the cemetery," asked Marie.

"The undertakers will bury them, and after a few weeks, they'll lay the headstones."

#

Over the next few months, Max periodically checked in on the restoration of the Eichen Garten. They were making good progress. He looked in on his mother, who was slowly emerging from her grief. He sat with her in Mrs. Becker's parlor one evening after work. She kept a blanket over her legs as they sat in front of the fire.

"The snow was beautiful today," she said. "I used to love to play in the snow as a child in Germany. We would have grand ice-skating parties."

"You don't talk much about your life. Did you have a happy childhood?" asked Max.

"I have fond memories of youth. As I got older, things became difficult for my family. My father died, and my mother had no way to support us. My uncle paid for my passage to come to America to live with friends who had settled in Cincinnati. It was a long journey, but I quickly found work keeping house for a family downtown."

"I'm glad Father Hammer talked about Papa's persecution in Germany. Papa had told Peter, but he never told me that."

"He didn't like to talk about it. It pained him to remember," said Mother.

"Papa and I never talked or got along as he and my brothers did."

"Boys need to respect their fathers; they don't have to be their friends. He took care of you."

"I understand what you're saying, but he never encouraged me or even took an interest in me," said Max.

"He had four sons to divide his attention."

"No, it wasn't that. It was only me. I want to understand. Why didn't he love me like the rest?"

She shook her head. "Your father had a troubled mind."

"I just wish I knew. Please tell me, Mother. What did I do to warrant his rebuke?"

"I'm sorry you felt that way." She sighed. "It wasn't your fault."

"Why, then?"

"There are reasons he treated you differently that you don't know. They happened long ago and cannot be undone, so there is no point in discussing them."

"What reasons?" Max pleaded.

"It's too painful for me to reveal."

"Mother, please. What?"

"Your father is gone, now, so I will tell you this. When I came to Cincinnati and went to work for a family downtown, the man of the house was often the only one in the house. The rest of his family lived on an estate in Kentucky. He would ask me to sit with him, dine with him. I was lonely in the house all day. He flattered me and helped me with my English. Papa and I were only acquaintances at the time. One evening, the man and I drank wine. I was an innocent girl, and he had his way with me. I was afraid to resist him because I needed the job."

"Oh, Mother, I'm so sorry. That must have been so difficult for you."

"Yes. I became with child and didn't know what to do. When I told the man, he dismissed me. I confided in Papa, and he agreed to marry me so I could avoid disgrace."

"That man raped you, and that child is me?"

"Yes, Maxwell," she said, touching his forearm.

"That man is my father, then. Not Papa."

"Yes. He did the best he could to raise you as his own, but he resented the privileged man, and I think he resented you, also."

"Why did you keep this from me? How could you?"

"I'm sorry, Max. I wish it weren't true. I tell you because I don't want you to hold anything against Papa. He saved me."

"He wasn't my father. Some American man is. I am a bastard. Am I even German?"

"Of course, you're German. You're my son."

"No wonder he didn't love me."

"He was just a man. He endured so much," Tears ran down her cheeks as she reached for Max's hands.

He pulled them away and stood. "I'm sorry. I have to go, now," said Max.

"He did the best he could," his mother called after him as Max left the apartment.

#

Max shook the snow from his coat and hung it on a hook inside the front door.

"How was your mother?" asked Annie.

"She's getting better," said Max.

"How much longer until they can move back into the Eichen Garten?"

"I think the saloon can open in a couple of weeks. The house will be a month or so after that."

"I haven't seen this much snow since I left New York. It's cold out there. A warm bath would feel nice, don't you think?" said Annie.

He walked to her and kissed her. "That's a wonderful suggestion."

They sat in the bath together, Annie leaning back against him.

"You're quiet tonight. You've had so much on your mind lately," she said.

"Yes, it's been trying. I learned something else today. From my mother. It's terrible."

"What is it?"

Max ran his finger up and down her arm, not saying anything. Finally, he took a deep breath and spoke slowly. "It's so awful…," he started and stopped. "My mother told me that when she came to America and worked for a wealthy family, the man of the house raped her."

"Oh, that's terrible. The poor woman. Of course, there was no consequence for him."

Max continued over the top of her in monotone speech, "She bore a child…me."

Annie froze.

His voice changed to anguish, "I'm a bastard," he dropped his forehead down on her shoulders and pulled his arms around her. "Oh my God. Who am I?" He began sobbing.

She tried to turn around. He held her in place.

"Don't look at me," he said.

"Max, darling. You're still you. It doesn't matter who your father was. You're Max Mueller, my husband. I love you. I love you."

"I couldn't understand why he showed such disdain for me. Now I understand. I wasn't his son. He had to raise the bastard son of another man. A wealthy man who defiled his wife and left her to live across the canal. Papa must have choked down his distaste every time he looked at me."

Annie started crying, "I'm so sorry, I'm sorry. She kissed him several times, then embraced him as they cried together."

After a few minutes of quiet, she said, "Let's get out. You're getting chilled." She stepped out of the tub, dried and placed a towel around herself. She took another towel. "Stand up."

He stood, shivering.

"Step out." She dried him and led him to the bedroom. "Lay down under the covers." He complied, and she climbed in with him and wrapped her arms around him. They slept.

CHAPTER 30

Max sat on the stage with several others in the Mason's Hall. The room was filled with men who had come to hear speeches from the two candidates running for the fifth ward city councilman. A few of Max's supporters and friends also attended. Annie wanted to attend, but after a protracted discussion, Max convinced her that attempting entrance would jeopardize his candidacy.

The incumbent councilman, Benjamin Eggleston, delivered his speech first. Ben was a well-respected businessman on the board of the Washington Insurance Company and a partner in Wilson, Eggleston & Company, a commission merchant enterprise that invested in other businesses. He was a member of the American Party, the successor to the Know-Nothings that had contributed to the riots in the previous year's mayoral election. The party was progressive, standing for labor rights, working people and anti-slavery, anti-immigrant and anti-Catholic. As Max watched Eggleston speak, he wondered if the councilman's confidence came from his two years in the job and his profession or if it was something more fundamental—because of his birth. Did he feel the world was his to command without giving it a second thought? He longed to know what that felt like.

In recent weeks, the *Daily Gazette* newspaper had presented the merits of the American party slate of candidates and painted the Democrats as men of questionable character. Similarly, the *Enquirer* newspaper presented the Democrat candidates in the best light. Max knew Eggleston would be tough to beat, but more Germans would vote Democrat than in the previous year as the American party's strong anti-nativist sentiment was now common knowledge. Eggleston's speech highlighted his accomplishments in his first term and why he should be re-elected. He had strong backing in the crowd, who applauded and cheered enthusiastically.

After he was introduced, Max stood before the podium and began, "Cincinnati has been dubbed the Queen of the West. Like most of you, I am a lifelong citizen who is proud of what the men of this city have built. We are the sixth-largest city in America, with a population of 115,000. We are leaders in industries from pork production to furniture building to ironworks. We're a commerce center not just for our citizens but for the entire west and beyond. We supply the goods that are helping build a free America that provides opportunity for all. We also claim the finest in cultural exhibits and performances west of the Alleghenies.

"As I stand before you as a candidate for city councilman for the fifth ward, I know that we must continue investing in and improving our city to ensure that the Queen's crown remains proudly atop Cincinnati. As we grow, we encounter new challenges with a larger, more diverse population. We face competition from rival cities emerging in the west. We are presented with new modern inventions. I vow to you that I will do all I can to help Cincinnati adapt and remain strong.

"If elected, I will serve you, the people of Cincinnati, in accordance with my Christian beliefs. In addition to meeting the requirements of the office, I will work with my fellow councilmen to suggest improvements focused on three areas: Education, Transportation and Modernization. To meet the challenges of the second half of the 19th century, we must take specific actions. I propose the following.

"Education. We must build upon the tremendous foundation that our leaders in government and the school board have built with our common schools to establish a city college to provide access to the young men and women who are the future of our city. I will call upon the city's business leaders and philanthropists to partner in such an endeavor.

"Transportation. Cincinnati was founded on transportation due to its strategic location on the Ohio River. Our forefather's built upon that and invested in the Miami and Erie Canal to make Cincinnati the focal point of the west. We cannot rest on our laurels. The railroad and land transportation now threaten our dominance as a commercial hub. We must invest in better connections to the rapidly forming national railroad system. We must also consider the natural expansion to the suburbs and connect those places to the city by roads, rail or canals.

"Modernization. Being one of the west's first major cities means we must renew and improve what's already here. I suggest two areas. First, I envision a city with more parks and public spaces where all classes of people can gather and recreate. Second, we need to accelerate the plans set forth by the city's chief civil engineer, Mr. Gilbert, and begin building a system of publicly-funded underground sewers to protect our citizens' health and improve the aroma for us all.

"These are ambitious goals. I can't promise that we will achieve all of them. But we need leaders in city council who are willing to think creatively and boldly, put forth the ideas, and then work with others to accomplish what we collectively decide is most important.

"I love this country and this city. As a resident and a business owner, I want to make sure that all of our children and our children's children will be as thankful to God as I am that they live and work in Cincinnati. If elected, I promise to work diligently to bring the community's different peoples together to ensure that our Queen's crown remains proudly affixed on our great city. I ask for your vote. Leave your party affiliations for national elections. Party platforms won't impact your city as much as the character and contributions of the man you elect to city council. Thank you."

The assembly applauded, and several cheered in support.

A voice shouted, "He still holds allegiance to Germany."

Max looked for the source of the voice and recognized Aaron Johnson, the bully who tormented him at Saint Xavier as a boy.

Aaron continued, "His family runs a saloon that flaunts our city's temperance laws. His morality is reproachable."

Max's friend Patrick stood, "I object to this outburst by a man of the opposing party. I have known Mr. Mueller for years in both a personal and professional capacity and attest that there is not a man among us with a stronger Christian ethic that guides his every action and intercourse with men."

"Says one Catholic immigrant about another," Aaron heckled.

Patrick continued, "Recently, I presented a commercial topic with Mr. Mueller at the Ohio Mechanics Institute in which he demonstrated his intellect, creativity and vision for the future. His personal and professional ethics are of the highest moral character."

Aaron went on, "His wife was dismissed from her schoolteacher position for teaching young girls counter to the virtues of true womanhood."

A murmur spread through the crowd.

The host for the evening took the podium. "Thank you, Misters Eggleston and Mueller, and thank you for coming tonight, gentlemen. We are adjourned."

Max stepped down off the stage, greeted and shook hands with several supporters. A man approached him, "Mr. Mueller, I'm Tom Arnett from the *Daily Gazette*. Would you care to respond to the gentlemen's comment that your wife was dismissed as a teacher for instructing young girls in indecency?"

"My wife's employment is not a public matter nor relevant to my candidacy for city council," said Max.

"The common school's teachers are taxpayer-funded positions listed in the city's annual report. Was your wife a teacher in the common schools?" said the reporter.

"Yes, she was."

"Was she terminated for instructing indecent topics?"

"No, she was not. She was terminated for being absent from her position for an extended period due to a personal situation."

"Anything else you'd like the readers to know?"

"No," said Max.

"Thank you, sir," said the reporter.

"Excuse me, please," Max said, breaking away from the small group remaining around him. He followed Aaron into the stairwell, "Aaron, wait."

Aaron stopped and turned from his companion to Max. He stood smirking.

"Could I have a word with you in private?" Max and Aaron stepped into a small meeting room.

"Why did you do that to me?" asked Max.

"The voters of the fifth ward need to know what kind of man they're voting for," said Aaron.

"You may tell lies about me, but why did you make a comment about my wife that is untrue?"

"That's not what I heard. I heard she's one of those women fanatics. You try to pass yourself off as a respectable leader by marrying a native. The only woman who would have you is deranged herself." he sneered.

"How can you call yourself a man for others? You're a Catholic yourself. Why make that comment about Patrick and me?" said Max.

He shrugged. "This is politics. We can't have dirty Dutch running the Queen City." He turned and walked from the room.

#

"How did it go? I'll bet you charmed them," said Annie.

"I thought the speech itself went very well," said Max. "I hope I inspired or had a few men considering voting for me. Ben Eggleston's speech elaborated on what he accomplished for the voters last year. I don't think either of us changed anyone's minds. So many men's minds are set, or they will vote the party ticket regardless of what we say."

"You sound less confident tonight. Where's that positive young man who stood on the deck of the steamboat excited to make his fortune in Cincinnati?"

"At the end of the speech, a man in the audience heckled me."

"What did he say?" said Annie.

"He said I had allegiance to Germany. He pointed out that my family runs a saloon that breaks the temperance laws. I couldn't deny it. Patrick stood in my defense. Then the heckler attacked your character."

"My character?"

"He said my wife was dismissed from her schoolteacher position for teaching young girls to break the norms of common decency."

"That's not true. That's not what I did, and that's not why I was dismissed. How did he know about that?"

"I don't know. The American party has plenty of connected people," said Max. "I confronted him after the meeting."

"The heckler?" said Annie.

"Yes, I know the man. Aaron Johnson. I went to school with him at Saint Xavier. He and I didn't get along very well."

"Max, you get along with almost everyone."

"He hated me because I was an immigrant's son. We were young. At that school, we were all made to accept and get along with one another, no matter our backgrounds. There were Irish, German, Mexican, Italian and even Jewish boys in my class. We didn't care, except he did. At that age, how does a child learn bigotry? It had to come from his parents.

"When I saw him tonight, it brought back those feelings of inferiority—that I'll never be good enough, I know it's not rational, but it's still there inside me. When I confronted him, he said the voters deserved to know what kind of man they would be voting for, and he couldn't allow a dirty Dutch to be elected to run the city."

"I'm sorry. He sounds awful."

"When I confronted him about bringing you into the election discussion, he further attacked you by calling you names."

"What names?"

"It doesn't matter."

"I have heard plenty of disparaging comments about my attitudes. I have less sensitivity to it, now," said Annie.

"There was more. A reporter from the *Daily Gazette* was at the meeting. He approached me afterward and asked me if it was true you were dismissed for improper teaching. I admitted that you had been dismissed, but it had been for a prolonged absence."

"Hmm," she said.

"I'm sorry that this man brought your name into this, and I hope he doesn't publish anything embarrassing in the paper, tomorrow."

"Well, I hope not, also. Max, I'm sorry if my positions create negative press for your campaign. I see now how connected you and I are. I never dreamed my behavior would negatively impact your public image." said Annie.

"Unfortunately, men with political ambition will stoop to tactics such as lying, bending the truth or painting their opposition in a negative light to excite the electorate," said Max.

"I see that, but I hadn't realized that what I say and do will now impact me, you and our entire family. You were worried about your background affecting my standing in society and what we never contemplated was my affecting yours—the status and respect you've spent your whole life earning. I'm sorry."

"Annie, I contemplated it. I knew before we married that your unconventional ideas could impact how we'll be received. I knew that was a risk, and I still wanted to marry you."

"Thank you, Max. You're a dear for saying it. I don't know if I would have agreed to marry if I truly understood the impact on you. I would be freer to push if the only reputation I was ruining was my own. We would have both been better off."

"No. How can you say that? We're better off together." He embraced her. "We have each other to lean on. Don't say that. We just need to pick our battles, right? Be smart about it. We'll be all right."

Annie hugged him, unconvinced.

Max lost the election to Ben Eggleston, who received 390 votes to his 162.

CHAPTER 31

Six months later – Fall 1856

Mary Berry, dressed in bloomers, and Annie sat in Annie's parlor. Annie was showing her the latest cartoon she had published in the paper.

"You're amazing, Annie," said Mary. "How do you get them to publish these?"

"I deliver them anonymously to a reporter I know to be sympathetic to women's rights. About half of them end up in the paper. I think they like the controversy they spawn. It sells newspapers."

"We need more of them. Keep it up!"

"If you have ideas for the cartoons, let me know. I can draw them; I just need more ideas. I have to find the right balance of subtlety and getting the message across. If it's too subtle, most men won't get my point," said Annie.

"I hate to ask again, but I need to know. Can I count on you to join in the march around the market next month? At our last Women for Women meeting, you said that you were undecided."

"I don't think I can, Mary. I'm sorry."

"Why not? You're one of our most ambitious career women. The other ladies look up to you."

"Well, things have changed. Max and I agreed I would curtail any of my more radical activities for a while."

"It's sad. Ever since you married, you're not in charge of yourself, anymore. The brutes can't help themselves—even gentlemanly ones like Max."

"No, it's not just him. I'm pregnant," said Annie.

"Well, I didn't expect that from you. How do you feel about it?" said Mary.

Annie lowered her voice so Marie wouldn't overhear from the kitchen. "Honestly, I have mixed emotions. I had hoped children wouldn't come so soon. I know I will lose some of my freedom."

"Some of your freedom? Ha! You might as well create a nest of twigs and grass there in the corner and settle in."

"I'm becoming a mother, not an invalid."

"Oh, poor Annie. And you were so much fun to have around."

"I'll still be a force for women."

"I know you want to, Annie, and I think you believe that, but you've already started caving in to the pressures of your husband's and society's expectations of wives and mothers."

"I'm not caving in. I'm being reasonable. This child will need a mother to care for it. I am the mother. I'll have Marie to help so I can still work at Miller Industries and do my women's charity work and such."

"You sound like you're trying to convince yourself. Do you want to be a mother?" asked Mary.

"Yes, I do. It's just inconvenient that it's happening, now."

"Have you considered maybe seeing a doctor to postpone becoming a mother?"

"No, it's my child, a part of Max and me. I couldn't do that," said Annie.

"Your cross to bear, then."

"It won't be that bad," said Annie.

"Have you ever cared for a baby? I had a little sister. They're parasites."

"Mary, that's awful."

"Babies are eerie. They have big bald heads. They're always drooling and spitting and messing themselves. Not to mention what they do to a woman's body while inside you. I shudder just thinking about babies."

"You paint a one-sided dreary picture of them," said Annie. "I'm trying to think of the positive aspects. I have the opportunity to raise a son or daughter that will not see the world through the eyes of men only. This is another way I can help make the world better for women."

"Agreed, the little one will be lucky to have you. Better you than me. It sounds like your priorities are shifting already, though."

"I can't help it. I don't know what it will be like. It seems I just got used to being married and working, and now everything is up in the air, again. Some days I'm excited about the future, and other days I just want to stay in bed with the covers over my head." Annie started to cry.

Mary put her arms around Annie and pulled her head to her chest. "I'm sorry, Annie. I imagine this is all very challenging for you. I know I'm not helping. It is women's lot that we are mothers rather than fathers. The movement will never change biology—we'll always have to bear the children. Is Max sympathetic at all?"

"I think he tries, but he can never understand what it feels to be a woman. He said all the right things before we married, but the realities overrule the good intentions. It must be nice to be a man, where fatherhood means you get to choose how and when you interact with your children."

"Have you told him how you feel?"

"Some of it, yes, but I don't want to come off as complaining or ungrateful for what we have."

"Annie, do not apologize for wanting the same things as men. We'll never rise to be equal if we don't assert that right."

"I know, but I think it will just be easier to accept the role of mother. I don't know what our family looks like, otherwise."

"Do not settle for that!"

"I don't expect you to understand. You're a single woman with no responsibilities and no family reputation to protect. No pending child's health and destiny to manage. No husband to compromise with. It's not that simple."

"I realize it's not easy. But women are counting on you to push past what's easy. We're charting new paths for women. Yours is taking a detour from what you thought it would be. That's what life does to us. It's an opportunity. Create a new path for the many women who will find themselves in similar situations."

Annie sat in silence, contemplating her situation like she had done so many times since learning of her pregnancy. She finally spoke, "Thank you for the encouragement. You're a gem. I may need more in the coming months."

"Of course. We have to support each other. But I'm going to miss you at the marches."

"After the baby comes, I can bring her. Push her in a baby carriage."

"Who knows, maybe I'll grow to like the little one. Your baby won't be eerie; she'll be beautiful. She can call me Auntie Mary Berry."

Annie hugged Mary. "Thank you."

#

Max and Annie sat in their parlor with their guests, David and Allison Smith, who had called on them.

"Your home is lovely," said Allison.

"Thank you. We were fortunate to find it shortly after our wedding. It has all the modern conveniences," said Annie.

"I've become accustomed to the luxuries. I would miss the bath and the steam heater if I had to go back to a house without them," said Max.

"Annie, you have exquisite taste. I love the wallpaper in this room."

"Thank you. Max selected all the furniture. His friend Patrick Sweeney builds it in his factory."

"Max, I didn't know you were interested in such things," said David.

"It's a matter of practicality. With Annie working at Miller Industries, we have to share some household responsibilities."

"What do you do at Max's business?" asked David.

"I am the bookkeeper," said Annie. "I created a new ledger system that will allow us to better monitor the profitability of our different lines of business. I have also written patent applications for several of the company's innovations. My favorite part of the job is payday. I've grown fond of some of the men as I've learned about them and their families. To some, I'm like a sister."

"To others, she's like a strict mother. Some are afraid of her," laughed Max. "It took some a while to get used to a woman telling them their wages for the week and handing over their pay. Most of them are used to it, now."

"It's been gratifying work, but I will take a break for a time after the baby arrives," said Annie.

"You intend to work with a baby?" asked Allison.

"Yes, after I recover. I don't anticipate that motherhood will degrade my abilities."

"No, but who will care for your baby when you are not at home?"

"Max's sister Marie has moved in with us. She keeps house, now, and will take on helping with the baby. She's quite capable."

"That just seems like so much for one woman to do. In addition to caring for your baby, your social calls and your charity work," said Allison.

"I intend to find a way to balance all of those things. I know women who have done it. I understand it's not for everyone, but it is my choice."

"We will take things easy at first, right, Annie?" said Max. "Annie is transferring most of her duties to one of the men in the office. We don't want to jeopardize her health or the baby's."

"That is only temporary," said Annie sternly. "I will fully resume my duties after a few months. We've discussed this, and it's settled."

"Let's just be open to making course adjustments, if necessary," said Max, nodding at Annie, who remained tight-lipped.

Sensing the disagreement and the chill between the couple, Allison changed the subject. "What charities have you devoted yourself to? I haven't seen you at the Daughters of Temperance society meetings of late?"

"I have focused my efforts on a new charity that Max and I are starting."

"What is that?"

"It's a program for girls Over-the-Rhine. Women volunteers will meet with an assigned girl once a week. We will train the volunteers to support the girls in a way that encourages but doesn't demean them. Give them someone else to talk to besides their families and expose them to women who obtained an education. I saw the need for it when I taught school. The girls are often discouraged from completing their schooling. We feel it's so important to their futures. The overall goal is to help more girls stay in school and go on to high school."

"What an ambitious endeavor. You're quite progressive in your thinking about women's position," said Allison.

Annie replied, "I'm doing what I can. I've also started hosting a monthly ladies' discussion at my home. I've invited those with an interest in furthering women's causes. Would you like to join us next month on the third Wednesday afternoon?"

"No, thank you. I have a standing appointment on Wednesdays, I'm afraid."

"That is a shame," said Annie. "Maybe if we change our regular time?"

"Hmm. I suppose it would depend on when you change it to."

David said, "Max, are you considering another run at public office?"

"Yes, I'm contemplating a run for city council, again. We learned some things this year that I'll do differently next time. I need to use the newspapers and town meetings to make myself better known and establish my reputation. I think I have a better chance of winning against James Walker, whose term is up this year. I still believe there is so much to do. I know I can contribute much if people will let me."

"You're a good man Max, and maybe you're too nice to win at politics. Don't wait for people to let you contribute. We need you. You should run," said David.

#

Max climbed into bed next to Annie and pulled the covers over them. "That was a lovely evening, don't you think? "

"Yes," she said quietly with her eyes closed, laying on her side and trying to get comfortable with the growing baby inside her.

"I like having a home where I am proud to bring friends. I've never had that." He snuggled up behind her and spooned his body around hers. He reached around and felt her baby bump, kissing her neck softly. Annie placed her hand on top of his and lay still, exhausted. Max continued kissing and rubbed his fingers lightly up and down her belly. She felt him pushing against her backside.

"Max, please," she said.

"Annie, it's been weeks. Don't you love me, anymore?"

"Of course, I love you. I'm tired."

"Please."

"I'm exhausted. I can't. Working and then preparing the house and the food for tonight. The baby makes me tire easily. Not tonight."

"Is this how you'll feel from now until the baby comes? We can't lie together until after the baby is born?"

"I don't know. I just know that the thought of being with you that way isn't the same, right now," said Annie.

"Am I to be replaced in your heart by the baby? You're losing feelings for me?"

"No, I'm just so tired."

"Maybe you should stop working at the shop, then. Stop now, instead of waiting until the baby arrives. If it's too much for you?"

"It's not too much for me. I need the work to keep my mind occupied. I can't just sit at home and wait for a baby."

"It seems to me if you don't have the strength to love your husband, anymore, you should stop doing something. What am I supposed to do?"

"I don't know. Do whatever you did before we were married. Somehow you survived."

"But I have a wife, now. You should want to."

"Says who?"

"It's what wives do."

"According to men. Max, I love you, and there are moments when I want nothing more than to lie with you, but I ask you to respect my feelings and wishes."

He moved away from her and lay on his back. He let out a theatrical sigh. "Is this what our marriage is going to be like?"

"Like what?"

"You doing whatever you please," said Max.

"What? Well, isn't that what you do? What all men do? It doesn't feel good, does it?"

"No, it doesn't, but I don't think that's what I do. I'm very accommodating of your pursuits."

"Isn't that good of you to allow me to pursue my interests? You say that, but you're pushing yourself on me, right now, not even aware that you're doing it."

"How am I doing it, now?" said Max.

"Trying to force me to let you have your way with me when I have no interest."

"I'm trying not to, Annie, but there are certain things that are just so. Men are supposed to be the providers. We're supposed to take care of our families. You and I have agreed to do things differently, but I still need to earn a living to support us and now a baby and create a respectable family reputation. I don't know when to let you in. I don't know how to do what I'm supposed to do with you trying to do that, too."

"What are you talking about?" Annie sat up.

"I know we need to compromise, but I'm afraid we'll fall short of what's expected if I let you do too much and I become less manly."

"Is that what this is about? Your manhood?"

"I don't know. I'm confused. Can you keep your voice down? I don't want Marie to hear us. I worry people will look at me like I'm not strong and capable if I'm not in charge."

"You've cared little what others think about you in the past. Why is this an issue, now?"

"I do care what people think of me. If I'm to be a business leader and run for city council, I can't be seen as a hen-pecked husband. No one will respect me or vote for me. And in the end, I have to be the one to provide for our family. You can't do it."

"I recognize that society won't afford me a path to provide for a family financially. I'm dependent upon you for that. But we agreed that I could continue to pursue my dreams next to you, and you would be supportive of that."

"We did. I want you to; I do."

"It sounds like you're now saying I can do that as long as I don't infringe upon any of your man-given rights and privileges, including your assumed right to bed me whenever you want!"

"Would you forget that? That's not what this is about."

"You say that's not what this is about until you want it, and I don't. Then it is about that."

"Oh, my God. You're so difficult!"

"I'm difficult because I am making points that aren't aligned with your manly order of the world."

"Jesus, woman!"

"Shush. Now who's going to wake Marie?" said Annie. "Should we get her in here and see what she thinks of the rationality of your arguments? I think as a woman, she would see things as I do."

"Let's leave her out of this. This is between you and me," he said.

"It is between you and me. I wish it to be like it was before. Disagree calmly and come to a place where our love and respect for each other overcome our differences? I don't like not being on the same side as you. You're my solace. When I'm not sure what to do, you're who I go to." Her voice faltered, "I'm afraid, Max. I feel like you're changing our agreement."

"I'm concerned, too. Look at how difficult our marriage is now. Imagine what it will be like when the baby comes. I'm afraid for the baby. What kind of parents will we be? What if it doesn't feel loved? I don't want him to feel that way—unwanted."

"Why wouldn't he feel loved?" she asked.

"If we're so busy doing other things, he might feel alone."

"You mean if I'm so busy doing other things, don't you? Go ahead, say it. It's what you're thinking."

He hesitated, then said, "Someone has to. I have to provide for us."

"Max, I know that." She softened her voice, "And I accept it. I wish the world were different, but right now, it's not. I will be the child's mother and love it and care for it. I'm just asking that you let me also have the liberty to do my work. That's why we asked Marie to live with us. The child will have her and me and you. It won't be conventional, but it will be full of excitement and wonder. I'm afraid, but also, I'm excited. I need you to be excited with me. I love you, and I need you to be my true partner in our family."

Max put his arms around her. "I love you, too. I will. It's so hard to know what to do."

"I know the unknown is unsettling for you. We have each other." She kissed him and let him put his arm around her again.

"I'm sorry for some of the things I said," said Max.

"I know you can't help it. You're a man. I love you, anyway."

He kissed her neck, then softly rubbed his fingertips across her belly until he fell asleep.

Annie slipped out of bed, put on her dressing gown and went downstairs to the parlor. She lit the table lamp and sat in a chair. As she looked around the room at the things she and Max had acquired, she felt disdain for them. The room was starting to look like her mother's parlor, full of attractive but useless items; the glass bowl, the silver tray, the two birds carved from wood. Max had insisted they purchase much of it. He, like her, was changing, slowly, day by day, in response to the world around them, their relationship, the realities of having a child. Their dreams were slowly adjusting to fit into what was possible instead of what could be imagined. How had she arrived here? This isn't what she wanted her life to be.

"Daddy, why is this so hard?" she whispered. She thought her father would be proud of her now for not exploding with emotion and ranting at the world. She had learned that doesn't help. She wondered how her life might have been different if he hadn't died? If she had stayed in New York? She wouldn't have met Max, and she wouldn't be married, and she wouldn't be pregnant. What would she have been? Who would she have been? She imagined sitting in a salon, talking with other women. She imagined herself attending a college with men and women and studying literature. Could that have been her life? What would it have led to? She would never know. Her father did die, and she came here and married Max. This was her life, now.

She loved him, and he made her feel loved and respected, but she sometimes felt suffocated and didn't even have children, yet. Was this her fate?

She felt her baby move inside her. Her life was no longer hers alone. There was no chance of turning back to what might have been. Life was choices, and she had made hers. Her dreams of other lives would remain dreams kept inside her. The world wouldn't let them be more than that, not for her, not now.

Annie let herself cry for a minute, then wiped her tears. She took deep breaths and resolved to pick up where her new life left off earlier in the day. She had a supportive husband and opportunities beyond most women. She had friends and his family to surround her. She was going to be a mother, and although it terrified her, she also felt a significance that she hadn't expected. Women bore the children and shaped the lives of the next generation. She would continue to make a better place for women through her work and through her child. She would hold on to that purpose to sustain her.

She decided further ruminating would only make her more tired in the morning, so she went to bed.

CHAPTER 32

The following day, Annie and Max sat holding hands in the Eichen Garten courtyard at a table with the family. The Sunday crowds had returned, and business was booming.

Annie pulled her latest cartoon drawing from her bag. "What do you think?" she said quietly, handing it to Max.

He looked at it. A woman, dressed in bloomers holding a ledger book in one hand and a fistful of money in her other, smiles face-to-face with a man holding a ledger book in one hand and a baby tucked under his other arm. The title read '*New* ~~True~~ womanhood meets *New* Manhood.' Max shook his head and tossed it on the table. "They won't publish this one."

"Why not?" she said.

"You make the man look like a..."

"A what?"

"Well, a woman, almost."

Annie scowled at the drawing.

The barmaid brought a round of beers and set them down on the table. Beer sloshed on the drawing as she set a mug on top of it. Annie watched the paper absorb the liquid and spread across her work. She tuned out the conversation, considering Max's reaction. He was right. The world wasn't ready for her, for women who wanted to be equal to men. Men weren't ready to sit as equals with women, take on their tasks. Beer foam ran down the side of the mug and onto her drawing, fading the pencil drawing to a blur.

"The bar looks better than before the fire. The gas lights make the bar room more inviting," said Max.

"And having hot and cold water behind the bar now will make things easier," said Albert.

"Have you heard from Peter?" asked Max.

"Mother received a letter from him this week. He loves his studies at Ohio University and says he'll come home to visit at Christmas," said Albert.

"It's so nice to have you sitting with us and relaxing on a Sunday, Mother," said Max.

"With the new girl we hired to work full-time, I don't feel the need to be in the bar every minute," said Mother. "I want to have time to spend with the baby." She smiled at Annie.

Annie smiled in return, unsure what she said, but recognized the word baby, the same in English and German.

"Annie, do you hope for a boy or a girl?" Helene asked. "Annie?"

"What?" said Annie, snapping out of her thoughts.

"The baby. Are you hoping for a girl or a boy?"

Annie said, "The world can be full of joy or hardship, depending on the chance of one's birth—man or woman, Black or white, rich or poor. I see so much more opportunity for a boy. For a girl, I see a lifetime of frustration and disappointment. I pray that it is a boy."

Max's mother said something in German to Helene, who translated for Annie. "Mother says she agrees with you, but she hopes you have a girl. A girl needs a mother like you."

AUTHOR'S NOTE

I've lived in Cincinnati for over forty years and grown to love the vitality of its not too big, yet big enough city life. Cincinnatians are staunchly proud of their city and heritage, many of German descent. After our children left home, my wife and I moved to the historic Over-the-Rhine neighborhood. We love walking its streets, appreciating the architecture, the small shops and the diversity. One weekend, we joined a walking tour of Over-the-Rhine given by the Over-the-Rhine museum. Hearing the stories of the German immigrants and their lives sparked my interest in learning more about its history and eventually led to my writing the Queen of the West series.

I spent hundreds of hours reading materials from the Cincinnati History Museum, the Cincinnati Public Library and the Library of Congress. The more I learned, the more I could envision myself transported to the Queen City of the nineteenth century. It must have been an exciting, dynamic place, full of opportunities for young people chasing early versions of the American dream. As I walked the streets of Cincinnati or ran along the Ohio River, I could almost hear the voices of the people who came before me.

I wrote the book to tell their story and Cincinnati's place in American history. Situated between North and South, the population's attitudes reflected the country's diversity. Like all times and places, the story looks very different, depending on who you are. I tell the story from Annie and Max's perspective, and in Book Two, add John, an emancipated enslaved man. As I researched and wrote their stories, I was struck by how much is the same today. As my young characters came of age, they had similar inner conflicts, faced challenges of acceptance by others and society and were influenced by the norms of the day and the politics and power of the leaders and media of the times.

The story is set in Cincinnati against the backdrop of America's national politics and growth story. Westward expansion was in full steam when the story opens, and Cincinnati, the Queen City of the West, was at the heart of it. I placed Max and Annie at the center, amongst real people, places and events. Max and Annie's stories are fiction, but their experiences are true to life.

I took a few liberties for the story.

Niles & Company was an actual foundry and machine shop owned by the Niles brothers, and Coleman Sellers was a talented engineer who worked for them. They did sell their business and move back to New England in 1856 but to other parties—not Max.

Elizabeth Cady Stanton was a pioneering feminist who was instrumental in the first Women's Rights Convention in Seneca Falls, New York and annual conventions for years afterward, including the one in Cincinnati. She had an egalitarian marriage with abolitionist Henry Stanton and hosted and influenced many of the national feminist leaders at her home in Seneca Falls. Her relationship with Annie's family is fiction.

Many of the speakers and comments at the Cincinnati Women's Rights Convention are abstracted from news reports and transcripts from the Cleveland and Cincinnati Conventions. Annie's interactions with fellow attendees are imagined.

Nicholas Longworth was an eccentric wealthy man in Cincinnati who made his fortune in real estate and owned the Belmont mansion on Pike Street and the vineyard in Mount Adams. He supported countless causes, including funding young artists such as Hiram Powers. His sponsoring a young boy to attend St. Xavier is a fabrication but in the spirit of his philanthropy.

As depicted in the story, St. Xavier College was run by the Jesuits and prepared young men for life. A Father Horstmann taught German. I imagined his personality and philosophies in the spirit of the Jesuits.

The events surrounding the 1855 mayoral election, alleged stuffing of ballot boxes, raiding of the ballots, rioting and barricading of the canal bridges to Over-the-Rhine all happened. I inserted my characters into these events.

To discover what happens to Annie and Max, please read Book Two, *Queen of the Union*, which begins on the eve of the Civil War.

ACKNOWLEDGEMENTS

I want to thank the following for their help in completing this book. Jill Beitz at the Cincinnati History Library for her ongoing assistance with my research. My friends and neighbors who read early drafts and provided feedback and encouragement. William Zink and John Williams who generously shared their writing and publishing experience. And my wife, Peggy, for her unwavering support always, but most recently in my journey as an author.

ABOUT THE AUTHOR

JR Zink enjoyed a successful career as a consultant and corporate leader before stepping away from the business world to develop his right-brain talents as an author. In addition to writing, he coaches high school swimming and enjoys running, backpacking, bicycling and travel. JR and his wife raised a family and now live in the historic Over-the-Rhine neighborhood in Cincinnati.